ZitrO Publications

Presents

Lady Scarface 3.4

By

Divine Ortiz

ZitrO Publications
PO Box 25594
Fayetteville, NC 28314

This is a work of fiction. Any character references or likenesses to persons living or dead are completely coincidental. Actual people and places have been added to give the story a sense of reality.

ISBN-13: 978-1495228254
ISBN-10: 1495228258

For information about special discounts for bulk purchases, please contact ZitrO Publications at:
910-475-7919
zitropublications@yahoo.com

Cover Design by Nikki Ortiz/ZitrO Graphics

Here are what some people are saying about the Amazon best selling novels, Lady Scarface and Lady Scarface 2:

5.0 out of 5 stars **OMG!!!**, December 10, 2013
Gapeach314 "cjoseph21" (Atlanta, GA)
I just loved this book!!! Kept my attention and looking forward to Part II!! Street fiction at it's finest...encore for more of Lady Scarface!!

5.0 out of 5 stars **Lady Scarface**, November 19, 2013
Naturally12
OMG!! This book was so good! The characters were so believable and it was like I was watching a movie! I can't wait to read what will happen next with lady Scarface.

Awesome Read! !!!, November 5, 2013
Debronda Jones (Charlotte,NC)
This young lady had a hard childhood but made life work for her. People didn't know who they were dealing when they came up against her. I really recommend this book for all to read if you want to read a great book.

5.0 out of 5 stars **Good Read!!!**, November 1, 2013
Theresa T. Foggie "BookHead"
Lady Scarface is not the one to play with!!! I loved this book. I can't wait to read Part II. Job well done.

5.0 out of 5 stars **good**, October 28, 2013
trina
Really good book I could not put it down. Read it in one day. Can't wait to read pt. 2.

Awesome, October 21, 2013
kelra "G.A.W BookClub" (Baytown,Texas USA)
This book was picked for my book club GrownAssWomen~BOOK~Club   BKA   G.A.W.BookClub... This book was off the hook. I cannot wait to start reading book

2.. If you haven't read this book please don't wait. You will not be sorry. The story line kept me wanting more. I was so deep into the story that I felt that I connected with each and every one of the characters. I give it five stars hands down. Great Job KDS. GAWBookClub.

5.0 out of 5 stars **I Want More!!!**, December 15, 2013
lynlyn - See all my reviews
Amazon Verified Purchase(What's this?)
This review is from: Lady Scarface 2 (Kindle Edition)
This was a great read, so much so that I read it non stop from beginning to end. A true love story with a gangsters twist. I shed a tear when she lost her God. Please hurry with the next installment. Peace

5.0 out of 5 stars **Being an Attorney has it's privileges**, December 12, 2013
O. Moss "Reading is My Life" (Tennessee)
I LOVE the fact that part 2 picks up right where part 1 left off. The story intertwines the past and present lives of the characters. I am really enjoying Divine Ortiz stories and look forward to reading more on Tiana "Lady Scarface" Brantz and future works by Divine. I am glad to have this author's stories as a part of my reading library.

5.0 out of 5 stars **hidden surprise**, October 18, 2013
Mlle. Butterfly (Brooklyn, New York)
This blew me away and I loved it because it wasn't all about women with <u>fat</u> asses and having sex. It was good to read a book that was well written, has a story line, and the characters were relate-able. I read this story in a day and half and I read part 2 in 24 hrs. This is a must have and I will be expecting more from the author in the future.

5.0 out of 5 stars **From beginning to the end**, October 16, 2013
lizyounger
This book is awesome I read it four times. I cannot wait until part 2 comes out!!! Love it....

Omg!!!, October 2, 2013
Brenae706

This is the best money I've spent in a while!! Tiana was the truth. She didn't let money change her, and Shabazz remained loyal!! Divine played the background but he's about to come up. Can't wait for part2!!

****

LADY SCARFACE 2

5.0 out of 5 stars **Couldn't put it down**, October 18, 2013
Cvrgrl
I read this in one day ~ I was surprised when Victor revealed that he took care of Tiana's case problems but there are still some more hidden situations. I wonder if Tiana is still going to retire now or what is she going to about and in Divine's absence. She has lost the two people she loved the most. *Tragic*

addicted, October 18, 2013
Mlle. Butterfly (Brooklyn, New York)
I loved everything about this storyline. I love the fact that this book doesn't have a bunch of sex scenes and has an actual plot. I feel for Tania because it seems like right when everything is perfect something happens to turn her world upside down again. I can't wait until Part. 3 hopefully i don't have to wait too long.

5.0 out of 5 stars **Omg**, October 17, 2013
Courtney Lawson "Mz SIRR" (columbus oh)
OMG I loved this book where is part 3 I need it like today after all that T goes through why is all I can say? I will not give the book away but it is a 5 star and must read.

5.0 out of 5 stars **Lady Scarface 2**, October 17, 2013
antoinette
This was an awesome read. I can't wait for book 3 to come out. Just keep up the good work Mr. Divine.

Lady Scarface 2, November 29, 2013
Rietta R. Branch
This book was off the chain for me. But it ended so sadly for me because someone killed Divine on his wedding day. But who is this mysterious man looking into her life? Please do not make us wait too long for Part 3.

5.0 out of 5 stars **wow**, November 27, 2013
Vanessa
Lady Scarface 2 is on point. A must read. I couldn't put it down. Tiana, Divine and the crew are like the family you wish you had. Can't wait for part 3.

5.0 out of 5 stars **FIRE**, November 13, 2013
Crystal Daniel (Milwaukee, Wiscosin ,USA)
This book is so good. I loved the main character. She fell in love and still took out her enemy in the end.

5.0 out of 5 stars **A must read**, November 13, 2013
The Reader
I give it 5 stars. I read both books in 1 day. I am waiting on book 3. I loaned the books and she has to read them in 1 day.

5.0 out of 5 stars **Addictive**, November 1, 2013

Corey L. Conard
I feel like Tiana and the crew are my family!!! I love them all especially Tiana & Divine. Why can't she catch a break though? I cried at the ending and can't wait until the next one is out. Please keep up the good work Mr Divine Ortiz!!! Another fan for life!

5.0 out of 5 stars **ON POINT!** October 8, 2013
Marina Chestnut-Jefferson
For a minute I thought you were going to do the unthinkable but I was wrong! I can't believe what happened but I know you have more in store for your readers. I'm anxiously awaiting part three. I would definitely recommend this book to everyone.

Well, you asked for it, and here it is! I hope that Lady Scarface 3.4 was worth the wait for you and I hope you will leave your reviews as soon as you are done.

ZitrO Publications
Presents

Lady Scarface 3.4

By

Divine Ortiz

PART ONE

LS3

1

"It's on you God." Shameek said to Seven across the table.

The Gods were engrossed in an intense game of spades in the living room as Annie was twisting Meesha's hair in the kitchen. Lil Lexus was at the table rolling blunts for everyone.

Seven played a jack of hearts. To his left, Divine plays the king of hearts and Shameek puts the ace on top of it. Shabazz cuts it with the four of spades.

"I ain't got none o' them God!" he exclaims as he scoops the book up and places it in front of him. "Y'all niggas might be set for real!" he exclaims as he plays the ace of spades. After a few more plays, Shabazz slams an eight of spades on the table.

"Set that shit!" he yells as he reaches over to give Divine some dap. Just then, the front door opens, and in walks Tiana.

"Hey baby," greets Divine as Tiana walks towards him.

"What's good sis?" adds Shabazz.

Tiana greets everyone at the table and throws a salutation in the direction of the kitchen where the 3 women were engaged in a world all their own.

"Hi love," she says as she bends her head to kiss Divine on his lips. After a long and sensuous kiss she pulled her lips from Divine's.

"You two should get a room," Seven joked.

"Maybe we will," Tiana responded as she pulls one of her Desert Eagles from the small of her back and puts a hole the size of a quarter between Seven's eyes. His head fell back and half of his brain oozed out of the softball-sized hole in the back of his head. Tiana then turned the gun on Shameek and stroked the trigger twice, putting two bullets into his forehead. Shameek fell over in his chair and was dead a half second before he hit the ground. Shabazz looked up at Tiana in shock as she pulls another Desert Eagle from her waistband.

Thpt...thpt...thpt...thpt...the gun coughed as she put four bullets into Divine's chest.

Thpt...thpt...thpt...

She caressed the trigger three more times sending its silent death into her brother's head. Then she walked towards the kitchen table.

"You wanna hit this T?" Lil Lexus asks nonchalantly as she holds up the blunt that she just lit.

Tiana doesn't respond. Instead she shoots Lexus in her heart. Twice.

As Lexus is about to fall out of her chair, Meesha grabs the blunt out of her hand.

"Let me get that from you girl," she says as she takes a hit. It proves to be her last hit when Tiana shots her in the face three times. Annie never even looks up, still trying to finish the last twist she was on as Meesha slowly slides off of the chair. Tiana blew the top of Annie's head off.

Tiana puts one of her Desert Eagles into the small of her back, then tucks the other into the front of her waist. She walks to the front door.

The door opens before she gets there, and standing before her was Beverly Roman.

"You aren't through yet," Beverly says to Tiana.

In silence, Tiana sighs, then she slowly pulls both of her Desert Eagles and empties what is left of both clips into Beverly Roman's face and chest...

Tiana woke drenched in sweat. Sweat and tears.

She buried her husband, Divine, 2 weeks ago, and since that time she had been secluded in her home. She refused to take visitors or even phone calls. When she was awake she was crying, and when she was able to cry herself to sleep she was woken up with nightmares. Her nightmares were all different, but the message was clear in all of them. The message was always the same. At least it was to her.

Everything that Tiana touched dies.

With that thought Tiana pulled herself out of bed. She sat on the edge of her bed with a million thoughts running through her head. She had entirely too much going on in her life, and locking herself in her home was not going to make any of her issues resolve themselves. Victor was becoming increasingly impatient, and she had to figure out how to iron out that wrinkle. She had a meeting with the Georgia Bar Association's Ethics Committee next week. Big Head and Click Clack have been missing since the day after Divine was killed. But the most important thing on Tiana's mind, understandably, was the same thing on everyone else's mind...

Who killed Divine...and why?

Tiana intended to find out.

And God have mercy on whoever was responsible...because Tiana wasn't planning on having any.

****

Divine was the first man that Tiana had ever allowed herself to love other than her brother, Shabazz. Her and Divine had unmanifested feelings for each other for years. Those emotions were awakened like a sleeping giant during the war with Cashmere Adebisi in New York.

The war that killed Shabazz.

After Tiana killed Cashmere, she convinced Divine to leave New York and move to Atlanta to resume business. Along with Divine came Mecca, Divinity, Scientific and a crew of about 15 men and women ready to reign terror on the streets of Atlanta in their quest to take over the drug trade and the streets there.

And terror they did reign. But during their rise to the top, lives were lost and lives were taken. And just when everyone thought that the storms were over, and seas were calm, Tiana was arrested for murder.

As always, Divine was by her side. So much so, that he decided to take their love to the next level. He wanted to marry Tiana. And while Tiana was fighting for her life in the Atlanta City Detention Center, she made a decision.

She wanted out of the life she had been involved in for over 20 years. She wanted out of the drug game. She had one other motivation for making that decision.

Tiana announced that she was carrying Divine's child.

Once the charges against her were dropped and Tiana was released from custody, they announced their engagement and planned a quick wedding.

Then tragedy struck once more.

After Tiana and Divine exchanged vows and spoke the words "I do," Divine was struck down by two bullets from a sniper's rifle.

He was pronounced dead at the scene.

2

"What are you gonna do about them Tiana?" Vikki asked.

"There's really nothing to do. Fuck them. What can they really do to me anyway? Take my license? That's the least of my worries or concerns right now. I've got people missing, I've got to sit down with your father, and I need to find out who killed my husband. The Ethics Committee can kiss my light skinned ass."

Tiana had finally gotten herself together enough to take a shower and eat something. The first person she called was Vikki. Vikki rushed right over.

"Can I ask you a question Tiana?"

"Of course Vikki. Anything."

"Well, we've been friends a long time haven't we?"

"About 20 years I guess."

"And in all that time, I've seen you go through a lot, and I don't ask you a lot of questions about your business. I just stand by your side and show you unconditional love."

"That you do Vikki. What's up? What's on your mind?"

"Why did you kill Trey Clark?"

Tiana didn't expect that question. She took a deep breath.

"You know what Vikki, I really didn't have any reason to at all. I just got tired of his shit. Every fuckin' time I went to go see him at the jail he was so damn smug. So arrogant. He acted like he was on top of the world and like he didn't realize that his life was entirely in my hands. He was such a filthy piece of shit. One day he asked me to bring him a pair of my panties. So, the night I got him acquitted, I agreed to meet him at one of his homes. I seduced him, then I killed him. And since he was kind enough to give me access to his safe before he died, I helped myself to all the money he had stashed there, along with all the drugs in the house. I stashed the money away, and I gave the drugs to Shabazz to take to New York. That's it."

Vikki took in all that Tiana had just told her.

"Can I ask you another question T?"

"Go ahead."

"What's this business with you and my father? I mean, I'm not stupid and I'm not blind. For years I've watched you and my father and there is a lot more than either of you let on. So, what's really going on Tiana?"

"Vikki, you're asking me to betray a trust that is years old."

"What about our trust T? How old is that? If you don't feel you can trust me then how I am supposed to feel about that?"

"I love you Vikki. You are the sister to me that I never had. I trust you with my life. But I need you to understand something. Something that Shabazz taught me. He told me that my word should never be less than my bond. That is something that I have lived by my entire life. It is also something that I gave to your father many years ago—my word. My word that certain aspects of our relationship would always remain between us. I never spoke of it with Shabazz and Divine never really knew the full scope of our relationship. If you truly must know Vikki, then I'll have no choice but to tell you. But I hope you'll respect my loyalty to your father as much as you respect and value the love and loyalty I have for you." Tiana had tears in her eyes now as she spoke to Vikki. Vikki looked into Tiana's eyes and spoke softly to her.

"You're right T. Your word has always been your bond and I have no right to ask you for any less. I love you too Tiana." Vikki took Tiana into her arms and hugged her tightly.

"Thank you Vikki."

3

It seemed like forever, but it had actually only been a little over a week since Big Head and Click Clack had been taken hostage. They were given water and food once a day, and at least 10 times a day they were each given a shot of heroin. They both were strung out. They tried to be strong, even though secretly they both couldn't wait for their next fix. None had come today and they were getting restless. They were being held in a dungeon-like cell in total darkness. The only time the lights were turned on was when they were fed and given water, and also when they were given their "fix". They both still had on the same clothes that they had on the day they were caught by surprise coming out of their apartment and stun gunned. They were standing back to back with a cross between them, and they were duct-taped firmly together so that they looked like one crucified body with two heads. The stench in the air was unbearable as the feces and urine ran down their legs and pooled on the floor at their feet.

The door to the cell opened and the light was turned on. Up to this point, the only person the twins had seen was a tall gothic looking oriental woman. She would spoon feed each of the twins, give them water, and plunge a needle into each of their arms. No matter what the twins said to her or cursed at her, she never spoke a word. She did what she did, then she turned the light off and left.

This day, she was followed into the cell by two more people. One was a scrawny, edgy oriental and the other was a very large, bald oriental man.

"Who the fuck are you?" Big Head asked. Click Clack couldn't see who had entered the room at first.

"First eat," the large man responded. "Then we will talk."

The woman fed the two brothers, gave them both a full bottle of water each, then she stepped aside.

No fix.

"Who are you?" Big Head asked again. He kept his eyes on the large man the entire time him and his brother were being fed and watered.

"My name is Chen. My associate's name is Benny and the lovely lady who has been tending to all of your needs is Sue. And may I ask who you are?"

"Ain't this bout a bitch!" said Big Head. "You snatched us up, but you don't even know who we are. What are you, fuckin' retarded?"

"I did not say I do not know who you are. I simply do not know your names. What I do know is that you are associated with someone of whom I am very interested in. I only asked your names as a cordiality."

"And who are you interested in fat boy?!" yelled Click Clack from behind his brother.

"Fat boy?" Chen asks as he walked around to face Click Clack. "Have I been disrespectful to you?" he asks.

"Fuck you fat motha fucka! What do you want?"

"Sue, can you teach this one some manners please," he said as he looked down at the woman. She was dressed in tight black leather pants and a leather bra with a spiked dog collar around her neck. She smiled and walked over to Click Clack. Then she turned around and walked out of the room, only to return 30 seconds later with a bottle of water and a washcloth. She placed the bottle of water at her feet and the washcloth over her shoulder. She took a straight razor out of her back pocket and carefully cut the duct tape in the front of Click Clack's pants. She pulled the tape away, then she cut a slit in the front of his pants and pulled his manhood free.

"What the fuck!" he yelled as she poured some water on his dick and began to wash it with the washcloth. She poured a little more water on it and repeated the process two more times as he began to harden.

Then she squatted in front of him and took him into her mouth. He didn't know what to think as she began to give him one of the best blowjobs he had ever had. Then his dick began to sting. Then it got very painful. It felt like he was on fire.

"Aaggh shit! What the fuck! Aaaagghh!" he screamed.

After another minute, she stood up and looked into his eyes. From her mouth, blood was dripping and running down her chin. Click Clack's dick was cut into shreds. She opened her mouth and let two razor blades drop out as she smiled. Then she reached down with one hand and grabbed hold of his balls, and with the other hand she took the straight razor back out of her pocket and cut off his balls in one smooth motion. She walked around to face Big Head. He looked into her crazed eyes and bloody mouth and was silent. She leaned forward and kissed him in the mouth, reached around him with the straight razor and drug the straight razor across his brother's neck.

"Oh shit! Noooo!" he yelled when she pulled away and he realized what she had just done. He felt his brother's head fall forward as he died.

"What is your name?" asked Chen again.

"They call me Big Head. What do you want?"

"Tiana Brantz."

"I don't know any Tiana."

"Maybe I should allow Sue to ask you. She seems to have a way with words. Now, you were at Miss Brantz's wedding. Who is she to you?"

"She's nobody. Just a friend. She was my brother's lawyer once, that's all."

"I think you are lying. Sue…"

"Ok! Ok! What do you want to know?"

"That's more like it."

After about two hours, Chen was satisfied with the information that the twin had provided him with.

"Benny, give the man what he really needs."

"Ok boss," Benny said as he took a hypodermic needle from inside his jacket pocket. He handed the needle to Sue who walked over to Big Head.

As she plunged the needle into his vein, feelings of shame and disgrace swept over him. Not only was he ashamed that he had been anxiously awaiting that needle, but he had also betrayed his friends.

"What are we gonna do with him boss?" Benny asked as the twin began to nod, high off of the heroin flowing in his blood.

"Here, give him this and let's get out of here. We've got work to do." He gave Benny a larger needle. In it was a mixture of pure heroin and pure cocaine. Enough to kill a herd of elephants. Benny pushed the deadly mix into Big Head's vein and the three of them walked out of the cell, locking the door behind them.

4

"Ok, who did we have a beef with?" Tiana asked Mecca, Divinity and Scientific. "And more specifically, who might have had a personal beef with Divine himself?....... And where the fuck are the twins?!"

"As for the twins," Scientific began. "Ain't nobody heard shit from them. It's like them two niggas just vaporized into thin air. Their ride is parked at the crib in Lithonia. The crib ain't fucked with or anything. The shit is weird. But me and Young God bout to check on that nigga Riff that they had pushin' work on that end for 'em."

"That's a good idea, when are you going to see him?" Tiana asked.

"Tonight."

"Ok, good. What about the Ward? Anybody there have what it takes to pull this off?"

"I really wouldn't think so T, but we're gonna check everybody out. If a nigga even act like he had a problem wit us, he does now" Scientific declared confidently.

"Mecca. Divinity. Please tell me something good."

"First of all, how are you really holding up T?" asked Divinity. This was the first time that they had seen Tiana since Divine's funeral.

"I'm better Princess. Thank you."

"You know T," Mecca interrupted, "I've been doing a lot of thinking. And really, shit been running real smooth for a while. I mean, I know niggas could be tryna rock us to sleep. I know the Atl wasn't ready for how we just rolled up and took over this bitch a couple years ago, and we had our share of beefs and bullshit here. But for real T, motha fuckas can't complain right now. The work is the best it's been in years around here and the prices are official. Everybody is eatin' good. I really can't see anyone trippin'. I just don't see it."

"That all sounds good Mecca," Scientific retorted. "But somebody around this motha fucka got to be trippin because my nigga is lying in the ground right now and that sure as fuck wasn't no stray bullet!"

"I know that Sci! I'm just saying."

"Sayin' what?!"

"I'm just saying that maybe we need to think outside the box on this. Motha fuckas we deal with roll up deep and start blastin'. They don't pick a nigga off from a distance. Who the fuck shoots like that? We don't even know where those shots came from."

"You two calm down." Tiana stood up. "I can see where the both of you make sense. I want this city shook down. I want it done quietly, but effectively. If they are suspect, find out what you can, then eliminate them. Scientific, question who you think you need to, but anyone you question, you kill. I don't want anyone in this town talking. You question them, you kill them, then you dispose of them. Simple as that. No bodies. It's open season and it will be until I look into the eyes of the person who killed my husband." She looked into Mecca's eyes. "You say we should think outside the box. Then that's what I want you to concentrate on. Think outside the box and figure out who pulled the trigger, but I also need to know who ordered it. Until this matter is resolved, nothing moves. No product exchanges hands. Not even a gram. No exceptions. None of us are broke, so we are in no danger of starving to death. Shop is officially closed. Effective immediately."

"Ok T. If that's the way you want it, then that's the way it is. We out," said Scientific as he stood up to leave. As Mecca and Divinity stood up, Mecca spoke to Tiana.

"Any change with Victor?" she asked.

"I haven't spoken with him. I called him just before you three showed up and I'm supposed to go see him today."

"Ok, well let us know what happens with that. In the meantime, we'll handle our business. You just deal with yours, ok."

"I will. You all be careful."

5

The ride to Victor's was long, and Tiana definitely was not looking forward to it. Victor had made it perfectly clear that he did not want to let her go. And he also made it clear that he would not let her go if it was going to cost him even one dollar. Tiana had no idea how he would receive the news that she was about to give him as she pulled up to his home.

Manuel, Victor's brother, was standing at the front door with a solemn look on his face. He extended his arms to embrace Tiana.

"Como esta Tiana," he said as he took her in his arms and kissed her cheek.

"Bien Manuel, gracias. Donde esta Victor?"

"La officina," he answered as he stepped aside to allow her to enter the house. Victor and Manuel both treated Tiana like a second daughter, and had come to her aid on more than one occasion. But Tiana's troubles have caused tension between them. Tiana was here to try and ease that tension, but she had a feeling that it would get worse before it got better.

Tiana approached the door to Victor's office and took a deep breath before she finally knocked.

"Entra Tiana," he said from behind the door.

Victor stood and crossed the room to greet Tiana.

"Tiana, mi amor. How are you?"

"I'm good Victor. Thank you. We need to talk Victor," she said, getting right to business.

"Very good. Sit," he responded, leading her to the sofa.

Tiana took a seat and Victor sat next to her. She couldn't hesitate any longer.

"Victor, I'm gonna need additional time before I can make the necessary transition of power on my end."

"What sort of time frame are you speaking of?"

"That's the thing Victor. I'm putting a cease to all of my business transactions until I deal with some very pressing personal issues. It's just something that cannot be avoided at the present time."

"And what of your shipment due in four days. I have already postponed this shipment twice due to your little vacation at the City Detention Center. It will not be postponed any further. Please do not try my patience Tiana."

"Try your patience. I just buried my husband. Does that not count for anything?" Tiana was visibly agitated now.

"The man was your husband for no more than four seconds. And that has nothing to do with your obligations."

"I don't give a fuck how long he was my husband for! He was my husband goddammit!" Tiana was on her feet now, and no sooner than she stood up, Victor stood up with her, a snub nosed .38 caliber colt revolver suddenly in his hand. With his left hand he grabbed Tiana by her throat and he pushed the gun into her temple.

"You will watch your tone in my brother's home and mind your manners. You seem to have forgotten where you came from. You have lost respect for your maker. I made you Tiana. It was I who placed you in the position you are in. Have a bit of respect for your benefactor. Now, you will accept delivery in four days, as agreed, of 250 kilos. We will have no further discussions of your retirement. Are we understood Tiana?"

Tiana was shocked by the fact that Victor had pulled a weapon on her, but she tried not to show it. She remained calm.

"This is how you repay years of loyalty? Of friendship and love? By putting a gun to my head Victor?" She was staring into Victor's eyes and they showed no emotion at all. Not anger. Not contempt. Not fear. They were emotionless and cold.

Victor took the gun away from Tiana's head, turned around, and walked towards his desk. He sat down in his chair, placed the gun in the top drawer of his desk, then he looked at Tiana.

"Tiana. Please make no mistakes. You are indeed a valued friend of mine. I have loved you as my daughter since the very first day I had the pleasure to meet you, and we agreed that 'friends help friends'. But then you walked into this very office one day with over a million dollars in cash. You wished to purchase 100 kilos of cocaine. You did this of your own accord. At that moment, you wished to do business. Once that business was conducted, you added a new element to our relationship. We became business associates. I need for you to understand something very clearly because this is very important. I love you as my own daughter Tiana, but as a business associate of mine I will not hesitate to kill you if you ever betray me or intentionally cost me money. Is that understood?"

Tiana stood silent and still, looking at Victor and absorbing all that he was saying. She didn't respond.

"Please allow me to tell you a story Tiana. Has Victoria ever spoken of her mother?"

Tiana still didn't respond.

"No, of course she hasn't. She was too young to remember much about her mother. Victoria's mother was a very beautiful woman. She was young when we fell in love and she gave birth to Victoria. Catalina was her name. When we met, I worked the fields for a very powerful man. One day I chose to kill that man and take over his fields. Catalina was pregnant with Victoria. Once Victoria was born, and my power grew, Catalina grew restless. She was worried that the dangers associated with the lifestyle I had chosen and created would eventually touch our home. One night we argued and she expessed her concerns. It was our first major argument. She threatened to report me to the Policia de Bogata. I loved my wife very much Tiana. But that night I cut her throat from ear to ear. To cover her death I summoned one of the field workers to the house and killed him also. I made it look as if they had run off together. My brother, Manuel, disposed of the bodies for me. Soon after, I sent Manuel to the United Sates to conduct business. Then, when Victoria was 8 years old, I sent her to live here as well."

Victor paused for a moment to study Tiana's reaction. She was still silent. He continued. "I share this with you mi corazon so that you will not underestimate my resolve."

"Are we finished here Victor?" Tiana interrupted coldly.

"Yes. You may see yourself out. I will contact you in four days."

Without another word Tiana walked out of Victor's office and out of the house. Once in her car Tiana was furious. She was shaking.

"That man just made the biggest mistake of his life," she said to herself.

"He has evidently underestimated my fucking resolve," she said as she pulled away from the house.

6

At the same time that Tiana was leaving Victor Maldonado's house, Scientific and Young God were following behind Riff's dark green Chevy Impala. They followed him until he pulled into the Crest View Apartments off of Panola Rd in Lithonia. Scientific was driving an all-black Cadillac Alante. Young God sat in silence, cradling a .9mm Uzi on his lap with a 32 round clip. Scientific had a .45 caliber colt commander with a silencer in his right hand as he drove. They pulled the Cadillac about 5 cars away from where Riff parked in front of one of the buildings. They waited for him to get halfway up the stairs before they got out of the car. Just as Riff reached the top of the stairs Scientific and Young God came running up the stairs three at a time. Weapons drawn and pointing at Riff.

"Shhhh…" whispered Scientific as he got to the top of the stairs. "Keep it moving to your apartment nigga," he said, pushing the silenced gun into Riff's side.

"Aight, aight yo. Just don't trip," Riff said, leading the way to his apartment. Scientific gave him a quick pat down and pulled a .9mm out of the small of Riff's back.

"Who's in there?" Young God asked when Riff fumbled with his keys at the apartment door.

"My baby mama," he answered.

"That's too bad," said Scientific as Riff got the door unlocked and the pushed him inside.

"Oh shit! What the fuck," exclaimed Riff's baby mama when she saw the guns. Young God ran over to her and smacked her in the face with the butt of the Uzi.

"Shut up bitch!" snarled Young God. "Go sit at the table wit yo faggot ass nigga!"

Scientific pushed Riff into a chair at the kitchen table. Young God pushed the baby mama into the chair directly across from Riff. Scientific sat next to her. Young God put the Uzi to Riff's head and Scientific did the talking.

"Where are the twins?" he asked.

"The twins?!" responded Riff. "Man, I haven't seen 'em. I swear. I been tryna call 'em for a week now. They was supposed to hit me, but then them niggas ain't been around. I swear."

Scientific looked at Riff to see if he could tell if he was lying. He couldn't really tell either way. So he put the silenced .45 to his baby mama's head and pulled the trigger. She fell over the side of the chair she was sitting in.

"Oh fuck!" cried Riff. "Man, I'm serious, on my mama! I don't know where dem niggas is at," he begged.

"Too bad," Scientific said as he turned the gun on Riff and shot him four times in his heart. Then he stood over him and pumped 2 bullets into his head. He grabbed a napkin from the kitchen and used it to open the door and him and Young God made their way out of the apartment.

Smurf and Tyson were sent to the apartment to pick up and get rid of the bodies.

7

Tiana took delivery of the 250 kilos from Victor's people. Manuel was there to oversee the transaction and Tiana did not speak a word when the van she was driving was loaded by Manuel's men. She just opened the passenger side door of the van and motioned towards the black duffel bag that contained 2.5 million dollars. Manuel took hold of the bag's handle and hefted it out of the van. After the van was loaded, Tiana closed the passenger side door, walked around to the driver's side, climbed into the van, and drove away. The cocaine was delivered to two different stash houses.

****

The next day, Tiana dressed in a champagne colored Vera Wang business skirt suit, got into her Maserati's Gran Turismo and headed towards downtown Atlanta to meet with the Georgia Bar Association's Ethics Committee.

Tiana noticed that she was the last to arrive—even though she was almost 20 minutes early. Once she was settled into her chair the hearing began.

"Miss Brantz, the Ethics Committee has a few questions concerning your financial portfolio as well as questionable practices and alleged involvements with individuals who may be involved in continuing criminal enterprises."

Tiana laughed out loud, which shocked everyone in the room.

"Ha! Alleged involvement with individuals who may be involved in continuing criminal enterprise? Does it not say in your little file there who I am and what I do? I am Tiana Brantz and I am a Federal Defense Attorney. There is no alleged involvement. Absolutely everyone I represent has either robbed a bank, committed some sort of fraud, or is accused of being involved in some sort of continuing criminal enterprise. It's the nature of my job. As far as my financial portfolio. It is common knowledge that my parents were killed when I was young and that at the age of 18 I received a substantial amount of funds that I was entitled to as a result of their deaths. Funds that were in interest-bearing accounts for over 10 years. I have been an attorney for many years, and I have done very well for myself in certain investments. What is the real purpose of this inquiry if I may ask, because so far this seems to be a waste of time for all parties involved."

"May I ask your involvement with Trey Clark?" another committee member asked.

"There is no involvement between Trey Clark and myself. Mr. Clark was a client of mine and he is now dead."

"And your involvement in his death Miss Brantz?"

"I had no involvement in Mr. Clark's death."

"It says here that you were arrested and accused..." he read before Tiana interrupted him.

"Those charges were dropped and should not be a topic of these proceedings," Tiana said, irritated.

"Oh, but that's where you're wrong Miss Brantz. We are not a Judiciary Committee. We are an Ethics Committee and as such, we are interested in subjects of an ethical nature. The charges of first degree murder were only dropped as a result of some sort of evidence misplacement as well as the mysterious murder of the state's witness against you. How unbelievably convenient for you Miss Brantz."

"Actually, the events that resulted in the charges against me to be dropped were rather inconvenient, since I was innocent of the charge and intended to prove it in trial. Look, what are you really after? What is the real purpose of these proceedings? Because honestly, this line of questioning is not only irrelevant, but also fruitless. Tell me what it is that you're after and I may just make it easy for you."

"Ultimately Miss Brantz, if this committee finds you to be guilty of violating Ethics Codes of the Georgia Bar Association, your license to practice law in the state of Georgia could be suspended or revoked."

"My license! That's what you want?!" Tiana stood up. "I'll tell you what Mr. Chairman. Why don't I gift wrap it, Fed Ex it to you, and all of you can take turns shoving it up each other's asses! How about that?!" Tiana turned around and stormed out of the conference room, leaving everyone in the room bewildered.

In the hallway she ran right into the last person she wanted to see.

"Miss Brantz. I've been waiting for you," said Detective Santana as he grabbed Tiana's arm.

"Get your hands off me Detective!" Tiana snarled.

"Calm down counselor," Santana said as he let her go. "I just wanna talk."

"About what? Shouldn't you be trying to figure out who killed my husband?"

"Actually, that's one of the things I wanted to talk to you about. I've got some information that might interest you."

"Let's go somewhere and talk," said Tiana, looking at the door to the conference room she just came out of.

"Ok, where are you parked?" Santana asked.

"Downstairs garage, second level."

"I'll meet you there, then I'll follow you."

"Fine," answered Tiana. She walked away and headed towards the elevators, leaving Detective Edwin Santana standing there with a file in his hand. He watched Tiana get into one of the elevators and then made his way to one of the other waiting elevators. He had parked his black Crown Victoria on the first level of the parking garage. He got to his car, and drove to the second level to find Tiana.

She was leaning against a silver Maserati waiting for him.

"Have you had breakfast?" she asked him when he pulled up in front of her.

"You buying?" he asked.

"Follow me Detective," she said as she opened her car door. He pulled away and circled the parking deck before falling in behind Tiana's car. Tiana led the way to the Venus House, a small restaurant that only served breakfast. It was in Marietta. Santana pulled his state issued Crown Victoria into the parking lot and parked it right next to Tiana's 300 thousand dollar customized Gran Turismo.

"I've never been here," he said as he stepped out of his vehicle.

"I don't doubt that one bit Detective," Tiana responded, looking at the vehicle that Santana had the nerve to put next to hers. "I really hope this isn't a waste of my time Detective," she continued, leading the way into the Venus House. "Two please," she said to the hostess that greeted them.

"Right this way please."

As soon as they sat down, a waitress appeared and placed two menus on the table.

"Call me when you're ready to order," she said carefully.

"I'll just have coffee and a cheese Danish please," ordered Santana.

"Same here," added Tiana.

The waitress took the menus and walked away.

"Ok Detective Santana, you said you wanted to talk. So, what do you want to talk about? You said that you have some information for me. What do you have?"

Detective Santana placed the folder in front of him on the table.

"Look Miss Brantz, I haven't figured you out. Yet. You're young, beautiful, successful and extremely wealthy. But despite all of your good fortune, you, for whatever reasons killed Trey Clark." Tiana was about to protest, but Santana held up his hand. "I can't prove it anymore of course, but you and I know the truth. I just can't figure out why. But it doesn't matter to me. It didn't matter to me 2 years ago. Right now what matters to me is the murder of your husband." Santana opened the folder and began looking at some papers. "The ballistics reports are back on the bullets that killed your husband. One of the bullets was destroyed when it made contact with his spine. The second bullet was lodged in his heart. That was the bullet that killed him. According to our forensic firearms expert, those bullets were fired from a special made Belgian FLN Automatic sniper rifle. The rifle itself most likely costs more than I make in six months. Now, by the angle in which he was hit, we had our same experts go out and find out the possible locations that the shots could have originated from. They've determined that the shots originated from the window of an abandoned apartment—almost a mile away."

"A mile?" Tiana asked just as the waitress placed a pitcher of coffee, sugar and milk on the table.

"Yes. A mile. But the strange thing is that normally, that particular rifle is so powerful that, even at that distance, those bullets should have torn through not only your husband's body, but they should have continued through yours also. According to our experts, those shells were custom made to cease their velocity on impact. Basically, what that means is that they were made to kill him, but not to pass through him and on to you. Now, even with that particular rifle, there are still only a handful of people that could have made that shot. Much less twice in as many seconds."

"How do you know that they were fired from that particular window?" Tiana asked.

"Evidence left at the scene. Powder burns on the window sill, and signs that someone had been there when it was supposed to be a vacant apartment. The bottom line Miss Brantz is that it was a professional hit. Now what you need to ask yourself is who may have wanted to kill your husband?"

"My husband was a real estate investor."

"Oh come on Brantz! Can't you see I'm not your enemy here? I'm trying to help you."

"I don't know what you want from me Detective."

Santana took some black and white 8x10 photos out of the folder. He put one in front of Tiana before he spoke again.

"These pictures were taken at your two bail hearings. Can you tell me who the individuals are that have circles around them?"

Tiana looked at the first picture. It showed some of the people who were on the benches at her first bail hearing. All those who had circles around them were part of Tiana's crews.

"I have no idea who most of them are," lied Tiana.

"That's funny because they were all at your wedding too." He took that picture away and showed her another photo. Mostly the same people were in that one too. But in this picture, only two people were circled.

Passion and Shorty.

"I guess you're gonna tell me that you don't know these two right here, even though they were at both of your bail hearings, and at your wedding too. But these two interest me just a little bit more. You see, after they left your second hearing, in what appeared to be a random act of violence, they assaulted a woman directly outside of the courthouse. They coincidently both end up in the same unit as you at ACDC. That night, Tina Hutchinson ends up in the hospital with a fucked up spleen and some other shit. Now, being the investigative genius that I am, I think what happened is that your friends, Persia Syth and Lashawndra Benson saw that black eye you were sporting, got themselves locked up, and took care of Tina for you. I already asked around and found out it was Tina who gave you the black eye."

"You should write for Comedy Central Detective. Or maybe The Twilight Zone."

"Ok." He took another picture out. "Do you have any idea who this man is?" he said as he placed the picture in front of her.

Tiana looked at the picture then looked up at Detective Santana.

"I have never seen that man before either."

The man with the circle around him was Victor Maldonado. He was sitting in the back row. Tiana looked back at the picture though and her attention was drawn to another figure in the picture. He was sitting two spaces to the left of Victor.

He was a slender Asian man.

****

XO jumped into the driver's side of his 600 series Benz so fast that he didn't notice the woman crouched behind the driver's seat. That is until he felt the garrote wrap around his neck and tighten. His hands, out of reflex, grabbed at the wire. That's when the passenger side door opened and a large Asian man climbed into the car.

"Please do not struggle Mr. Ortiz," he said to XO as he reached into his waistband and relieved him of his Glock 17. "I simply want to send a message to your employer. Sue," he said, looking at the woman behind XO. "Could you be so kind as to send Mr. Ortiz's employer a message, as clearly and inhumanely possible."

Sue pulled on one side of the thin wire that was wrapped around XO's neck. She pulled back until her other hand was touching his neck. Then she pulled hard with that hand and the wire cut deeply into his neck. As the man got out of the passenger side he leaned back in and spoke to XO.

"Tell Miss Brantz that I'll be calling on her soon." He got out of the car with XO's Glock, using it to shut the door behind him. When the door slammed shut, XO's head fell from his shoulders and dropped between his legs. The woman named Sue grabbed his head and put it in a bag as she got out of the car.

8

"Hi Miss Brantz! What are you doing here?" asked Tiana's personal assistant, excited to see her boss up and around.

"Hello Kemya. Please follow me into my office," Tiana said as she walked straight to her office.

"Yes ma'am." Kemya grabbed a legal pad and a pen and followed behind Tiana. Tiana left the meeting with Detective Santana at the Venus House with the strangest feeling that she had to find out who that man was in the photo, and why was he at her bail hearings. She sat behind her desk and turned on her computer as Kemya walked in her office.

"Sit down Kemya. How are you doing?"

"I'm fine Miss Brantz. But how are you? I thought you were taking some time off."

"I am Kemya. I just need to take care of a few things and I may need your help."

"Anything Miss Brantz. Name it."

"This is gonna have to remain strictly confidential Kemya. Are you ok with that?"

"Miss Brantz. You've done a lot for me over the years, so if you need my help, I'm here for you. Just tell me what you need me to do."

Kemya Bennet had been working as Tiana's personal assistant for over 12 years. Tiana paid her extremely well, gave her a very generous Christmas bonus every year, paid her rent, and even provided her with a car to use as her own along with a gas card. But none of those things mattered to Kemya. Her true loyalty to Tiana stemmed from a situation in Kemya's life when Tiana was prepared to come to her aid, and Kemya believed that she did.

Kemya's husband was a very abusive man towards her as well as towards her son. When she first started working for Tiana she was late often, and missed days on a regular basis. Tiana liked her a lot though and valued her as an employee so she spoke to Kemya one day and asked her what the problem was. Kemya told Tiana about her husband.

"Why don't you leave him Kemya?" Tiana asked her.

"Because he won't let me Miss Brantz. He says that if I try to leave him he'll find me and kill me. I wanna leave him Miss Brantz, but I'm scared of him," Kemya cried.

"Do you really want to leave him Kemya?" Tiana questioned.

"Oh yes ma'am. I'm just scared for me and my son."

The next day, Tiana gave Kemya a raise and offered her a contract to work for her, with a progressive salary, until Tiana retired. Kemya accepted Tiana's offer.

The day after that, Kemya's husband left and she never heard from him again. She felt deep in her heart that Tiana had something to do with his leaving. Her husband actually just disappeared. He never said a word. He was there one day, and then he just wasn't. She secretly thanked Tiana for her intervention, even though they never talked about it. So yes, if Tiana needed her, she would help her in any way she could.

"Do you remember the Clarkston case? I think it was Charles Clarkston? Embezzlement and computer fraud case?"

"I think so Miss Brantz. It's been a few years. About five or six right?"

"Something like that. Can you get him on the phone for me? I don't care what he's doing or where he is. Tell him it's very important that I speak to him. Do that for me please. I'll be here for a few hours going over some files."

"Ok Miss Brantz. I'll get on that right now." Kemya finished writing on her pad and left Tiana's office.

Ten minutes later the intercom buzzed.

"Mr. Clarkston on line one Miss Brantz."

"Thank you Kemya," she said as she picked up the receiver and pushed the button for line one.

"Mr. Clarkston. How are you?"

"I'm doing great Miss Brantz. How about yourself? I was keeping up with your case on the news. I'm glad to hear you got out from under that mess. What can I do for you?"

"I need to see you Mr. Clarkston. Today. As soon as possible."

"Today's no good Miss Brantz. If I could, you know I would, but there's no way I could get away today."

"Mr. Clarkston, it's very important that I see you today. So important that if you could be in my office in the next hour, I will pay you ten thousand dollars cash for your time. If after we meet it is determined that you can help me, I'll pay you an additional fifty thousand dollars. Also in Cash."

"I'll see you in thirty minutes Miss Brantz," he said and hung the phone up.

Twenty-seven minutes later the intercom on her desk buzzed.

"Miss Brantz?"

"Yes Kemya."

"Mr. Clarkston is here to see you."

"Send him right in Kemya. No calls please."

"Ok Miss Brantz."

Tiana stood up to greet her guest as the door to her office opened and in walked a tall clean-cut white man that very much resembled Michael Douglas.

Years ago Tiana represented Charles Clarkston in court. He was charged with embezzling hundreds of thousands of dollars from the company that he worked for by creating a program that cloned company accounts as they were opened and he syphoned funds gradually and almost unnoticeably. He hacked into the files and records of many of the top executives of his company and accessed their personal information. DMV records were changed. Credit scores were lowered. Criminal files were even created for some of them. Clarkston once bragged to Tiana that there wasn't a system or computer he couldn't hack into. Tiana was able to get him acquitted of all charges when it was realized that the Secret Service had confiscated the wrong computer and set of files from his office. By the time the mistake had been revealed Clarkston had erased all of his files and completely destoyed his hard drive.

"It's good to see you Mr. Clarkston," Tiana said, extending her hand to him.

"The feeling is mutual Miss Brantz. How can I be of service to you?" he responded, eyeing the stack of money on Tiana's desk. Before he arrived, Tiana took ten thousand dollars out of her office safe and sat it on her desk. When she saw him looking at the stack of bills she picked it up and handed it to him.

"This is for you Mr. Clarkston. As agreed. Ten thousand dollars cash. For you time today."

He took the bills from Tiana, thumbed through them, then took a seat. "Just for my time huh?" he asked, still looking at the money in his hands.

"Yes. That is for your time today. But I may require your special skills. If you decide to help me, I will pay you fifty thousand dollars on top of that at the completion of the job."

"My special skills huh."

"Indeed."

"In cash?"

"Of course," she responded.

He put the stack of bills into his inside pocket.

"I'm listening."

"Ok. Do you still know how to hack into systems, or have times changed and advanced, leaving you behind?

"You are very funny, Miss Brantz. Times, as you say, are doing all it can to keep up with me. I'm a maverick Miss Brantz. What do you need?"

"I need copies of all the files in a certain law enforcement officer's files. Home and office. I also need all of the digital photos taken from the courtroom cameras at all of my recent court appearances."

"Is that all?"

"No, once I have those files and photos, then I'll need you to identify a particular person in the photos using all domestic and international identification databases. Can you handle that?"

"Miss Brantz, I don't like to toot my own horn but I could probably do all of that using just my smart phone."

"How long will it take?" Tiana asked him.

"Give me the officer's name and I'll have all his files for you in a day or so. Once you let me know who you want identified, that should take another couple of days."

Tiana wrote Santana's name on the back of one of her cards.

"Call me on my cell phone," she said as she handed him the card.

"It's been a pleasure as always Miss Brantz." He put the card into his pocket and left her office.

9

Tiana lay in her garden size tub, soaking in the bubbles, listening to the soothing sounds of Sade, and thinking about all that had happened in the past two weeks. It seemed like her world was falling apart all around her.

"Oh Shabazz," she sighed. "Where are you when I need you?"

Shabazz had always been Tiana's rock. After Shabazz's death Tiana fell in love with Divine and though she was able to lean on him and turn to him at times, he could never be what Shabazz was to her. After Shabazz was killed Tiana vowed to become her own rock. She grew stronger, drawing strength from her pain as a result of her losses. The loss of Divine was a devastating blow to Tiana because Divine was the first man the she had ever given her heart to. But he was gone. She couldn't change that, and right now she had to get herself together, take back control of her life and her affairs and move on.

Right after she left her office she found out that XO was found dead in his car, decapitated. The twins still haven't been found—dead or alive. She was in the middle of a war it seemed. A very quiet war. A war with an unknown enemy. She was on the verge of losing her license to practice law. But the heaviest thought weighing on Tiana's mind was Victor's complete disrespect. He had been like a father to Tiana since she met him. That is, until he put a gun to her head.

With all these thoughts dancing through her head, her cell phone rang. She wasn't going to answer it, but when she picked it up and saw that it was Vikki she knew she had to.

"Hi Vikki," she said as she put the Bluetooth into her ear and stood up in the tub to grab a towel.

"Hi Vikki my ass! Bitch, why haven't you called me?" her best friend yelled into the phone.

"I'm sorry Vikki. I got so busy today that my mind was everywhere else."

"Fuck that. What happened this morning with the Ethics Committee?"

"The hell with them Vikki."

"That sounds great, but what did they say?"

"They want my license."

"Oh shit! Are they crazy?! You're the best lawyer in Atlanta. Probably the state. Did they actually say that?"

"Yes they did."

"What did you say? What are you gonna do?"

"I'm not gonna do shit. I basically told them that they could have it."

"No you didn't!" Vikki gasped.

"Yes I did. I told them they could shove it up their asses."

"Are you fuckin' crazy?! Tiana, they will take your shit. It's what they do! What are you gonna do if you lose your license? What's gonna happen to your office?"

"I own the firm Vikki. It doesn't matter to me if I never set foot in another courtroom. I have some of Atlanta's top defense attorneys working for me. Life goes on Vikki."

"If you say so. Let me know what happens."

"I will Vikki." Tiana's phone went dead. She picked up her phone and dialed Mecca's number.

"Hi Mecca," she said when Mecca picked up on the second ring.

"Hi Tiana. What's good?"

"Can you make it over here?"

"I'm on the way."

While Tiana was talking to Mecca, her best friend was making a call of her own.

"Bendicion poppy."

****

When Mecca arrived 35 minutes later, Tiana was dressed in a pair of light blue sweatpants and a matching Baby Phat tee. She was barefoot.

"Hey Mecca," she said, opening the door wide allowing Mecca to enter.

"Hi T. What's up?"

"Shit, what's not up? What's going on in the streets?" Tiana asked, leading the way into her home office.

"Well, right now we're just cleaning up old garbage. Nipping shit in the bud so to speak. Like you said, if we even think someone was a problem, or might be a problem, we're solving it. Quick and quiet. Later tonight, Bitty Bit and me and gonna go slump Big Julio and his main man Parrish. Bitty don't like those two too much anyway. She says they remind her of a couple of old ass perverts."

"Ok, that's good. Now, I want you to listen to this and let me know what you might think."

Tiana detailed for Mecca the encounter she had with Detective Santana and everything he told her about how Divine was killed. Mecca listened intently as Tiana spoke. She also told Mecca about the Asian man who was at her bail hearings.

"I've hired an ex client of mine to do some computer hacking to get me a copy of all of Santana's files, then he's gonna identify the mystery man for me. When he does, I intend to find out what he was doing in court on those days. What are your thoughts?"

"I'll say this T. You definitely might be on something with that Chinese motha fucka. As for that sniper shit. I don't know. I've only ran across one person in my life that could shoot like that. And that's that ugly black ass nigga Smurf."

"You know what Mecca. I thought of that too, and as my word is my bond, if Smurf wasn't standing six feet away from Divine at the time, he'd be lying next to him right now."

"You might need to holla at him though. He might know of someone who can shoot like that."

"Oh I do plan on asking him," Tiana responded.

"Have you talked to Victor?"

"Oh yes. I've talked to him alright."

"What's on his mind?"

"He doesn't want me out and won't allow the changes. And just to make himself perfectly clear, he put a gun to my head."

"What the fuck! Are you serious T?" asked Mecca in shock.

"Do I do much joking Mecca?"

"Well, what are you gonna do about that shit?"

"Same thing we always do when someone disrespects or threatens us. We eliminate them. Victor Maldonado is no exception."

"That's what I'm talkin' about," Mecca said in excitement.

"For right now though I just want to chill. Rock him to sleep while we deal with all this other shit ok."

"You just give the word T."

"Ok love. You and Bit go handle your business, and be careful ok."

"We will."

****

"What's good with my two favorite ladies?" Big Julio asked as he pulled up and Mecca and Bitty Bit walked towards them. Mecca called Julio and told him that they needed to see him. That was good with him, he said, because he needed 20 kilos anyway, so the timing couldn't be better. As the two women approached, Parrish pushed the button to open the trunk. Without a word, Bitty bit reached inside the trunk and grabbed the bag which contained the three hundred thousand dollars for 20 kilos. She threw the bag into the back seat of the Lexus they were driving. Then she turned around and faced Julio's car.

"Here's the thing Big Julio, we're gonna need to shut down for a little bit. We got some shit we need to deal with right now."

"For how long you talking about?" asked Parrish, noticing that Bitty Bit had made no attempt to put what they had just paid for into their trunk.

"Forever nigga," Bitty Bit answered pulling out her .9mm Daewoo DP-51 and shooting him in the side of his head. Mecca pulled out her .45 caliber Trapper and the both of them unloaded their clips into Parrish and Big Julio. Bitty Bit then reached into the front seat of the Lexus and grabbed a three liter bottle that was on the floor. It was full of gasoline. She poured the gas all over the two dead men. She took a twenty dollar bill out of her pocket, lit it on fire, and threw it into the car onto Parrish's lap.

Whoosh!

The car ignited into flames as she jumped into the Lexus and Mecca pulled away, with a three hundred thousand dollar bonus.

They were too far away to hear the explosion.

****

Tyson stepped out of the shower and dried himself off. He put on his boxers then stepped out of the bathroom and into his bedroom. He grabbed a half smoked blunt out of the ashtray on the nightstand next to his bed. He sat on the edge of his bed and lit the blunt. He didn't hear Sue creep out of the closet behind him, and by the time he caught a glimpse of her out of the corner of his eye it was too late. She was already too close and swinging the razor sharp sword at his neck.

Chino, downstairs playing Need For Speed: Most Wanted on the PlayStation 3 didn't hear a thing. He was so engrossed in the high speed pursuit on the big screen that another thing he didn't hear was Sue coming down the stairs. He saw the movement on the screen but he thought it was part of the action.

He felt her sword before he realized she was there.

Game over.

With both of their head in a black trash bag, Sue left the house and got into a waiting car a half a block away.

10

"Meet me at your office in two hours. I've got what you need."

"I'll be there."

Charles Clarkston called and wanted to see Tiana. He evidently had the files she asked for.

It had been two days since she hired Clarkston. The bodies of Tyson and Chino were discovered. They were decapitated just like XO. She was sure that the oriental man in the pictures was a key to what was going on, and also to Divine's murder.

Tiana stopped by a local computer repair shop on the way to her office. She bought a used Sony Viao laptop so she could view the files Clarkston had. When he arrived he had a briefcase with him. After they exchanged brief pleasantries, Clarkston opened his briefcase and took out a small box, about the size of a large paperback novel with a card attached to it. He sat the box on her desk.

"That right there is a 100 gig external hard drive. It contains all the files on Detective Edwin Santana's computer at his desk as well as everything on his home computer. It also contains the video and audio archives for both of the surveillance cameras in courtroom 212 on both of the dates you requested, from docket call to adjournment for the day." He smiled.

"That's what I want to see first," she said, taking the cord and pushing it into one of the USB ports on the laptop.

"Take me right to the surveillance cameras. The first court date. The very beginning," she said as she spun the laptop around to face him. She walked from behind her desk and stood next to him as he accessed the right file. The screen spilt and filled with images from both of the courtroom cameras simultaneously.

"That's it! That's him!" she said pointing to the slim Asian man. "I want to know who that man is right there. Find out who he is and get me all of the information you can about him. Can you do that?"

"Miss Brantz. Your lack of confidence in me hurts my feelings."

Clarkston was punching keys on the laptop and manipulating the mouse board. He had isolated several still photos of his target, zooming in for close up shots from every angle. He created a separate folder for all his work. Made a copy of that folder and transferred the file onto the laptop's hard drive.

"I'll leave you with the external and take the laptop, just in case you wanted to look at more. I'll bring the laptop back to you in a few days." He disconnected the external drive and closed the laptop, securing it in his briefcase.

"Call me when you're ready," Tiana said, walking him to the door.

"I sure will Miss Brantz." As he was about to step out of her office he turned around and whispered at Tiana.

"All hundred dollar bills please."

Tiana just smiled as she closed her office door.

****

Tiana bought another laptop and headed home to look over all of Detective Santana's files. She locked the door behind her when she entered her home and quickly made her way to her office. She hit the light switch just inside the door and almost dropped her briefcase.

Victor Maldonado was sitting behind her desk.

****

Scientific was driving his new Dodge Charger through the Ward listening to The Game on his CD player. He pulled up to a stop sign and felt a sudden stinging sensation on his neck like he'd been stung by a hornet.

"What the fuck!" he exclaimed as he grabbed his beck. He felt a dart-like object sticking out of his neck. He began losing consciousness. Benny and Sue walked up to his Dodge Charger as it started to roll through the stop sign. Benny reached into the car, put it in park, then grabbed Scientific's head and pulled it out of the window. Sue raised the sword high and brought it down hard on Scientific's neck. Benny put the head into the trash bag he took out of his pocket.

****

"Victor!" Tiana was startled.

"Tiana. How are you? You have a lovely home."

After she got over the initial shock of seeing Victor, she was furious. Victor had violated her home. He had gone too far this time. But Tiana concealed her true emotions.

"I'm fine Victor," Tiana answered, walking across the room and putting her briefcase on her desk. "And how did you get into my house?"

"If you must ask then surely you underestimate my resources."

"Evidently I underestimate my alarm service."

"We must talk Tiana."

"About what Victor? It's business as usual with us. Just like you ordered."

"I did not order anything. I merely required that you fulfill your obligations."

"And I'm doing that."

"I understand that you're having problems and that your license to practice law is in jeopardy."

"It might be," Tiana responded.

"And so why do you antagonize them."

"What do you mean?"

"Did you curse them and suggest that they put your license in their asses?"

"I may have said something to that effect."

"You shouldn't have."

"Well, it's too late for regrets now Victor."

Victor stood up and looked out of the window.

"You have much to learn still Tiana," he said, then turned around to face her again. "I am going to have those problems or yours taken care of for you so that you may get back into focus. It seems that you have been losing sight of what is important lately."

"Hold on one minute Victor." Tiana was losing control. "I am a grown ass woman and I can deal with my own problems. If I felt that

I needed or wanted your assistance with something, I know how to ask. Please do not overstep your boundaries Victor."

"Boundaries? And what boundaries would those be? May I remind you that you are an attorney who deals drugs. But to me, you are an attorney first and foremost. That is what is important to me. It was I who gave you Brantz and Brantz. Half of your clients were referred to you by me. But make no mistake. If you are no longer an attorney, you are nothing but a drug dealer to me. Drug dealers are easily found, but a good Federal defense attorney is a rare and priceless thing to have on one's side. If you are no longer an attorney you are virtually insignificant to me."

It was another threat, and Tiana knew it. A little more subtle than a gun to her head, but a threat nonetheless.

"Are we done Victor? I would like to eat, shower and get some sleep."

"Yes, of course. Excuse me. So, I will tend to your little problem, and our business will go on as usual."

"If you say so Victor."

"I sense distaste in your words. Tiana, this is the life that you have chosen for yourself. When you first came to me you simply wished to purchase for your brother. But after your brother's death you chose to become a drug dealer. You wanted to be a boss. Well, you must accept all that comes with the position. Is that clear?"

"Yes."

"Good. I'll be in contact Tiana," he said as he left her office.

When Tiana heard the front door of her house close she was fuming.

"I'm going to kill you myself Victor. Word is bond!"

11

"Brantz and Brantz. How may I direct your call?"

"Miss Brantz please."

"I'll see if she's available. Who may I say is calling?"

"Santana."

"Please hold." Kemya put Detective Santana on hold and buzzed Tiana.

"Miss Brantz. There's a Santana on line three for you."

"Tell him I'll be with him in a few minutes Kemya."

Tiana was looking at all of Detective Santana's files. She continued for another 6 or 7 minutes before she finally picked up the phone.

"Detective Santana. What do you want?"

"Who is Xavier Ortiz?" Santana asked.

"I don't know. Why? Should I?"

"Well, you should. His body was found dead behind the wheel of a very expensive Mercedes Benz. And when I say body, I mean that literally, you see, the head was not found."

"So, and all that concerns me beeecauuse..." she said sarcastically.

"Because his prints came back along with a photo. A N.Y. Department of Corrections photo. And he looks a lot like one of the men who were at your bail hearings. And if that isn't enough, he was at your wedding too."

"Have you ever asked yourself this question Detective...that just maybe, all of these people you keep asking me about could have been acquaintances of my late husband? I didn't know every one of his friends."

"Look Miss Brantz. I'm not accusing you of anything, because I don't know what's going on yet. But if you are involved in anything at all, you may want to talk to me because it may be a little more than you can handle."

"I'm fine Detective, and have nothing to talk about."

"You have my number Miss Brantz."

"Yes I do Detective."

"Look, I'm not after you Miss Brantz. I'm not your enemy in this. I just think that you're in way over your head, and I'm trying to help you. I know you killed my partner. But he was a racist asshole so he had it coming."

"I was in jail when your partner died."

"Anyway. People around you are getting hurt and killed. How long before I see you in a body bag?"

"When it's my time, it just is."

"I'll be in touch Miss Brantz."

"I'm sure you will Detective."

****

"Will you please step away from the car Shorty."

Shorty had just pulled up to the back of her apartment complex and got out of her car when she was faced by a large Asian man pointing a gun at her. Standing on either side of him were a smaller man and a tall, sinister looking Asian woman.

"Fuck you!" was Shorty's reply as she reached for the Glock 40 tucked into her waist.

She never got to it, because Benny quickly pulled a taser and shot Shorty in her side, sending 50,000 volts of electricity through her body. She crumpled to the floor.

****

When Shorty regained consciousness her arms were raised high in the air and her hands were tied to an overhead ceiling fan. Nothing covered her mouth, but she couldn't open her mouth. She couldn't part her lips for some reason.

They were glued together.

"So, I've been told that you have a rather nasty sadistic streak to you." It was Chen speaking. He was sitting directly in front of her. It was evident that Big Head left nothing out when he provided Chen with information about Tiana's organization, because he was clearly referring to Shorty's revenge on Malachi and her chosen methods of retribution.

"Well, Sue here also has a rather sadistic nature as well."

Chen noticed that Shorty was trying to open her mouth.

"You're wasting your time. Your lips were glued with three different types of industrial strength adhesives. It serves its purpose since you have nothing to say I want to hear."

Benny was standing in the corner with a handheld camcorder. "But I will," he continued, "as a courtesy, tell you why you are here and why you are about to die. A very painful death I might add." He stood and lit a cigar. "You see, just as those before you, you are to send a message to your employer. And that message is that Chen Ayngen is not to be stolen from." Chen then stepped aside to allow Sue to show Shorty the true meaning of pain.

Sue approached Shorty with a crazed smile on her face. Benny held the camera on Shorty to catch the entire ordeal on video. Shorty attempted to kick at Sue but Sue grabbed her leg, put a rope around her foot and pulled that foot as she tied it to a hook on the floor at one end of the room to Shorty's left. Then she grabbed Shorty's right foot, put another rope around that foot, and tied it to another hook at the opposite end of the room. Shorty's feet were about five feet apart.

Sue put on a black leather glove over her right hand. At the tips of each finger were 2 inch razor sharp knives. She ran the razors down the front of Shorty's jeans several times and then across her pelvic area, shredding the jeans. With her left hand she tore the jeans off of Shorty's body. She did the same with Shorty's tee shirt, leaving Shorty completely naked, with the exception of her Timberland boots.

Without warning, Sue closed her right hand into a tight fist, knelt in front of Shorty, then rammed it into Shorty's virgin pussy. Shorty's eyes widened and almost popped out of her head. She tried to scream, but no sound would come from her sealed lips.

Sue pushed further into Shorty.

Shorty pissed all over Sue's hand and arm.

Sue pushed even further until she was inside of Shorty almost up to her elbow. Then she started moving her hand savagely inside of Shorty's chest cavity.

Blood shot out of Shorty's nose.

All of a sudden, small bloody lines began to appear on Shorty's chest and stomach.

She lost control of her bowels, and as shit began to escape from Shorty's rectum, Sue's right hand emerged out of her chest. She had cut through Shorty's insides and right out of her body.

Sue pulled her blood covered arm out of Shorty, and as she stood up, she slammed her face into Shorty's torn, bloody and mutilated chest. She bathed her face in Shorty's blood. Then she turned to face the camera, blood running down her face.

Benny looked into the camera and shook his head in mock disgust.

12

"This is fuckin' ridiculous!" yelled Tiana. The police had discovered the bodies of Tyson and Chino inside of the house that they shared with Smurf. The bodies of Crystal and Carmen were also found in a house less than a mile away. Scientific's body was also found. The story was on all the news channels as the Atlanta Police were trying to convince the media and the public that a serial killer was not on the loose.

Especially since all of the bodies were being discovered without their heads.

"I can't believe this shit! In the past few weeks we have lost 6 of our people. That doesn't even include Divine. Nor does it include the twins who are still missing. And now Shorty is fuckin' missing. What? Have we stopped watching each other's backs in this cipher?"

What was left of Tiana's team had all met at Mecca's condo in Dunwoody.

"We can't be everywhere at all times T. Look at Tyson and Chino. Look at Big Head and Click. Crystal and Carmen. They were together when they got hit," said Smurf. "And what's fucked up is that we have no fuckin' idea who's at us. I mean, we running around layin' niggas to sleep, but evidently we ain't hit the right ones yet cause we gettin' slim as a motha fucka. I'll go to war with anybody but what the fuck we gonna do if the enemy is a fucking ghost?!"

"There's no such thing as ghosts. Just like there is no mystery God. We're gonna find out who it is that's at us. And when we do, we'll be at them. And when we come, you already know that we come hard. Until then, I want everybody to fall back a little. Keep your eyes and ears open at all times, and watch each other's backs a little better than we've been doing I might add. Other than that, I don't know what else we can do. Unless someone has a suggestion." Tiana looked at everyone in the room.

No one said a word.

Tiana's cell phone rang. She saw that it was her office. She answered it and listened for a minute.

"Ok. I'm on the way Kemya," she said then hung up.

"Look, please. Please be careful out there. Smurf is 100% correct. We can't see them but they damn sure are out there and they are getting to us. Stay on point at all times and nobody is to be out alone until we find out who we're up against. I've got to head to my office. If no one has anything else, I'll leave you all in peace."

"Peace," responded Mecca and Divinity.

****

At the exact moment that Tiana's meeting in Atlanta was ending, another meeting was about to begin in Queens, New York.

"One, two, three," the S.W.A.T team leader counted down. On three, the hundred and twenty-five pound battering ram made quick work of the front door of the Flushing, Queens two-story A-frame house. At the same time, scores of S.W.A.T, FBI, ATF, and NYPD officers burst through the windows and the back door of the house.

"On the ground! On the ground!" yelled officers as they stormed the house from every direction. Some of the officers ran up the stairs carrying their M-76 and M-16 submachine guns in front of them.

"Hands! Hands where we can see them mother fucker!"

No shots were fired.

Ninety seconds after 26 law enforcement officers from four different agencies entered the house, it was over and the house was secured. Six men were arrested.

Thirteen weapons were seized, along with an undisclosed amount of drugs and money.

****

"The messenger said that this package was for your eyes only Miss Brantz, and that it was imperative that you receive it as soon as possible because you would be contacted soon." Kemya handed Tiana the small package and relayed everything the messenger had told her. Tiana looked at the package. "Counselor Brantz" was written on it in black marker.

"What messenger service Kemya?"

"I don't know Miss Brantz. He didn't have on a uniform and he didn't ask me to sign anything. That's why I called you right away."

"You did good Kemya. Thank you. I'll be in my office, and I'm not to be disturbed." Tiana turned and walked towards her office.

"So does that mean I'll need to come back later?" said a man's voice from the door.

Tiana turned around.

Charles Clarkston was standing in the door. A laptop computer in his hands.

"Mr. Clarkston," Tiana said.

"Miss Brantz. I apologize for showing up unannounced, and I hate to sound so cliché, but I was actually in the area."

Tiana looked at the package in her hand, then at the laptop held by Clarkston.

"It's ok. Come in," Tiana said walking to her office, then to Kemya she said, "absolutely no interruptions."

"Yes ma'am."

Tiana entered her office with Clarkston right behind her.

"Now you do understand Mr. Clarkston," Tiana said to him. "That since you didn't let me know you were coming I haven't had the time to get your payment ready." Tiana didn't want to go into her office safe. "But if you'll stop by here first thing in the morning I will be sure to leave that with my secretary."

"That will be fine Miss Brantz," he said, then he handed her the laptop. "Everything you asked for is there. It is in the folder entitled '50 Grand' on the desktop. Call me if you need me again Miss Brantz."

"I will. Now if you'll please excuse me."

"Of course. Of course. Let your secretary know that I'll be here about 10 a.m. Is that good with you?"

"That will be fine. Please close the door behind you Mr. Clarkston. And thank you again so much."

When the door closed, Tiana set the package that Kemya had given her to the side, and she opened the laptop. She quickly found and opened the folder marked "50 Grand".

The face of Ben Djaper appeared on the screen. Next to his face was all of his personal information.

He was 33 years old. Vietnamese descent, but born in America. N.Y state birth certificate. A long criminal record which includes three stints in the N.Y. DOC. No known siblings or children. Moved to Atlanta 2 years ago and is the owner of a strip club in East Point called "Tit 4 Tat". Suspected involvement in gambling, prostitution, white slavery, pornography and drugs. Again, nothing confirmed. No present warrants, but subject of interest in several investigations.

Tiana scrolled through some more of Benny's information, then she picked up the small package marked "counselor Brantz". She tore the paper off of the package.

It was a CD case. It contained a DVD in it.

Tiana opened the case, took the DVD out, and inserted it into the laptop's player. She hit a few buttons and then pushed the play button.

Shorty's face filled the screen. In her eyes was horror.

As the camera's view widened to include Shorty's entire body, as well as a clear view of the predicament she was in. Tiana could not take her eyes off of the screen. She watched, tears streaming down her face as Shorty was violated and mutilated.

Then Benny's face appeared.

Tiana froze the picture.

That was when her cell phone rang.

She stared at the screen and ignored her phone.

After about ten more rings, she finally decided to pick it up, not bothering to check the caller ID display.

"Brantz," she said into her phone.

"Hello counselor."

Tiana didn't respond.

"By your silence I can only assume that you have had the opportunity to view the little video I had delivered to you. A rather disturbing short film wouldn't you say."

"Who is this?"

"Soon counselor. We will get acquainted very soon."

"You are a dead man is what you are."

"Please counselor, do not bore me with your frivolous and empty threats."

"Whatever. What do you want?" Tiana asked, still staring at the screen.

"Directly to the point. I can appreciate that. You killed a man named T.C. or Trey Clark over 2 years ago."

"I have no idea what you're talking about," Tiana answered.

"Please don't insult my intelligence counselor. The fact that you escaped conviction is irrelevant. You and I both know that it was you. That in itself means nothing to me. What does mean something to me though is the fact that T.C. had just taken possession of some merchandise of mine that very day. Merchandise that he never had the opportunity to pay for, because you killed him."

"What merchandise are you talking about?"

"I'm speaking of the 40 kilos of pure heroin that you removed from Mr Clark's house the night you killed him."

"You've got to be fucking joking right?"

"Look at the DVD I sent you counselor, and tell me if I am fucking joking. Now, I don't expect you to have my merchandise after all of this time, nor would I want it back. But since you prevented Mr. Clark from compensating me for my product, I expect you to assume that responsibility—with interest of course."

"What kind of interest are you talking about?"

"I was thinking somewhere along the lines of 25 million."

"25 million! Are you fuckin' insane!?" Tiana barked into the phone.

"Actually counselor, many would say I am. But that's neither here nor there. You see, that particular package was at the time the purest grade of heroin the United States had seen in three decades. Yes,

25 million is a figure that I literally took right out of mid-air, but, nonetheless, it's what I want."

"What if I decide not to pay?" Tiana stated defiantly.

"Then I will continue to systematically eliminate the last remaining members of your organization until you are all that is left. Then I will torture you for weeks, keeping you alive with antibiotics, and keeping you wide awake so that you feel every bit of pain that is inflicted upon you. You will become very intimately acquainted with the unsavory looking woman in the DVD. I will give you 24 hours to make your decision counselor. I will be in touch."

The phone went dead in Tiana's hand.

"Another fuckin' dead man," Tiana whispered.

She pushed play on the screen and the picture came to life again. Benny moved his face out of the way of the camera and for the next 15 minutes Tiana watched as the woman continued to cut and stab at Shorty's body, mutilating every inch of her until eventually she cut Shorty's body down. Shorty fell to the ground. Just before the video went black, she cut Shorty's head off.

13

When Mecca and Divinity walked into Tiana's home office, the first thing they saw was Benny Djaper's face looking at them from the screen of the 61 inch plasma TV on the wall.

After Tiana finished looking at the video, it took some time to get herself together. She gathered the laptop and the DVD and drove to her home, calling Mecca on the way. She wanted Mecca and Divinity at her house in an hour.

"You see that man right there?" Tiana asked the two cousins as they entered the office behind her. "That is the man who killed Divine, Scientific, and the rest of our people."

"That puny, punk motha fucka? Are you sure T? I just can't see him getting the best of us like he that," Mecca said.

"Oh, I'm sure. As a matter of fact, I've spoken with him. I'm about to show you a DVD that he had delivered to my office today. I'm gonna step out for a minute because I can't stand to look at it again." Tiana put the DVD into the player. "Push play when I walk out. I'll bring you back some drinks. You're gonna need them"

Tiana left the office and went into the kitchen. She leaned against one of the counters thinking about how much she should tell them. Nobody knew that she had got that heroin 2 years ago from T.C., at least not anyone who was still alive—other than Chen. Tiana believed that the man on the video and the man who called her were one and the same. She didn't realize that they were two different men.

After about 10 minutes, Tiana returned to her office carrying three mixed drinks. When she walked in she could see that the DVD had been turned off, and on the screen was the laptop image of Benny.

"Who is that Tiana?" asked Mecca.

"And where do we find him?" added Divinity.

In response, Tiana went to the laptop, hit a few buttons, and the plasma screen split in two. Benny's information appeared next to his picture.

"His name is Benny Djaper," began Tiana, reading out loud to the two cousins who were now her two top people. "He was a petty criminal who has decided to move up to the big leagues and figures on us to be his ticket."

"Why us?" asked Divinity. "What the fuck is his deal?"

"Money."

"Money?" Mecca questioned.

"Yes. He wants money."

"How much does he want? And why?"

"25 million."

"Dollars?!" exclaimed Divinity.

"It sure ain't cents."

"Oh shit!" said Divinity.

"It doesn't matter. He owns a sleazy little strip club in East Point called Tit 4 Tat. Tomorrow night I want him in our possession. I have a small house in College Park. I want him taken there. I want everybody there. Everybody gets blood on their hands on this one. Maybe we'll get lucky and the vampire bitch is in Tit 4 Tat. If not, we'll make sure he tells us where we can find her."

"Oh, he'll tell us. Believe that T," said Divinity.

"I'm putting the two of you on this. I'm getting you a panel van to pick him up in. The house you're taking him to has a garage that you'll be able to drive right into and shut the door behind you. The room you'll be taking him to is completely soundproof so we'll be perfectly safe there. You'll most likely wanna catch him coming out of the club when it closes. Do it quickly and as quietly as possible. No witnesses."

"We got this T," responded Mecca.

"Good. I hate to put so much on the two of you, but I need you to handle one more thing for me," stated Tiana.

****

Charles Clarkston walked out of Brantz and Brantz fifty thousand dollars richer than when he walked in. He was in and out in less than three minutes—most of that passed in the elevator. He stepped out of the Buckhead high rise office building with a smile on his face and a briefcase full of money in his hand. He walked across the street to where his car was parked.

There was a ticket on his window. He couldn't believe that he was issued a ticket and he was gone no more than five minutes. He took the ticket from under the arm of the windshield wiper, crumbled it into a ball, and threw it on the floor. He got into his car and pulled into traffic.

Four cars behind him, Mecca and Divinity pulled into traffic too. They stayed about thirty yards behind him.

Charles Clarkston drove without a care in the world, trying to decide exactly where he was gonna go for his week-long vacation. He had always wanted to take a cruise, but his ex-wife was afraid to get into any body of water that was over 2 feet deep. What a bitch, he thought. She left him right after he was arrested. Took everything she could pack into her brand new Yukon Denali and disappeared. A year later he got divoice papers delivered to him by the Sheriff's Deputy.

Good riddance to bad rubbish was how he felt about her.

He was lost in his thoughts when he made a right turn into his neighborhood.

That's when his back driver's side tire blew.

"Shit," he said as he pulled the car over towards the curb.

Directly behind him Mecca pulled over.

Clarkston got out of his car just as Mecca and Divinity both opened their doors. They both held their guns close to their sides so that Clarkston couldn't see them. By the time he did, it was too late.

It was Mecca who shot him first. Twice in the chest as Divinity went directly to the passenger side of his car, opened the door, and grabbed the briefcase. She stopped just long enough to open it and verify that it was the right one. Satisfied, she went around to where Clarkston lay on the ground clutching his chest. She shot him twice in his head. Mecca shot him two more times.

They got back into their car and made the U-turn to exit the neighborhood.

14

Chen Ayngen was born and raised in the Republic of Southeast Asia. His childhood was spent in an orphanage in the Quang Tri Province's Echo sector. It was operated by American missionaries. When the Vietnam War was in full swing the missionaries decided to relocate half of the orphans to the U.S. Chen was among those that were relocated.

He was 12 years old.

He was taken to a large orphanage in Chicago, and his dormitory was the size of a small gymnasium. He was just one of over two hundred children, both boys and girls of all ages in that particular dorm. Each week more children were brought in, and some were parceled out to families who didn't mind raising the Vietnamese refugee children.

When Chen turned 14 he was taken to the home of Mr. and Mrs. Anchors. Him and another child. A young seven year old girl.

Her name was Sue Wyn Ngo.

As a result of the chemical known as Agent Orange that was generously and constantly sprayed on her home village in Vietnam, Sue was born with deformed vocal chords and did not have the ability to speak. She could not even scream. That made her vulnerable to the older boys at the orphanage. She was first raped at the age of six and was raped or molested almost every day for over a year. When she was taken from the orphanage and placed into the home of the Anchors she felt as if God himself had lifted her out of hell and placed her in heaven.

She would soon lose hope that God even existed.

When her and Chen first arrived, Sue was very afraid of him understandably so. In a short period of time though she saw that Chen had no interest in taking advantage of her. It was Mr. Anchors who would eventually take a keen interest in her.

It started off very subtly. A soft pat on her rear end. An inappropriate rub between her legs. Later the rubs would linger and turn into caresses and fondling. Then he would take her hand and put it into his boxers. Sue never protested. Why would she? It was what she was used to. It was what she expected from men. And the less she protested, the further he went.

The fondling turned into oral sex. That turned into vaginal and anal sex. And Sue turned into Mr. Anchors' personal sex toy, to do with as he pleased. Once or twice he even brought some friends over to play with his "toy" while his wife was out of town visiting her sister in Phoenix.

Chen knew it was going on but he chose to ignore it at first. But he soon began to look at Sue as his little sister and he developed a protective nature over her. When Mr. Anchors noticed, that was when he started abusing Chen.

Mr. Anchors was a rather large man, so beating Chen took no more effort than simply swatting a fly. He would often beat Chen and then lock him in a closet. Or he would tie him to one of the bed posts and make him watch as he would rape Sue right there on the bed. Sue and Chen would stare at each other. Neither would shed a tear.

There were no more tears to be shed.

Chen was 17 years old when he had reached his breaking point. It wasn't any particular incident that set him off. It was the accumulation of years of abuse and having to see Sue abused and terrorized that did it.

One night he crept into Sue's room very quietly. He woke her and told her to get dressed. She got dressed and followed Chen into the kitchen. Under the sink was a toolbox. Chen quietly pulled the toolbox out and opened it. He found what he was looking for right on top. Two long Phillips screwdrivers. He put one in Sue's hands, and whispered into her ear. Sue did a strange thing then. Something she hardly ever did.

Sue smiled.

Chen took hold of Sue's hand and together they walked softly up the stairs. Chen pushed open the door to Mr. Anchors' bedroom. He was asleep, on his back, and snoring. They entered and Chen crawled to the far side of the room. Sue crawled up to the side of the bed and peeked her head up. When she saw Chen stand up on the other side of the bed, she stood up also. They both hovered over Mr. Anchors as Chen counted with his fingers to Sue.

Three. Two. One.

At zero, and at the same time, Chen and Sue plunged their screwdrivers into Mr. Anchors' ears, passing each other as they crossed a path through his brain.

Mr. Anchors' eyes shot open and he froze.

Then he sighed.

Then he died.

Without a word, Chen went around the room searching for anything of value that he could find. All the while, Sue was pulling out the screwdrivers and pushing them back into Mr. Anchors. Into his ears. Into his eyes. Into his nose. She tried making new holes, but she just didn't have the strength.

Chen found a large roll of money stuffed inside of a sock in the back of Mr. Anchors' underwear and sock drawer. He also found a gun. A .38 caliber Colt Revolver. In the closet he found a shoebox full of pictures of Sue engaged in all sorts of vile sex acts. He put the box on the dresser and he left the room. When he returned less than a minute later, he had in his hands a bottle of lighter fluid and a box of matches. He pulled Sue away from Mr. Anchors and told her to wait by the door.

Chen scattered the photos over Mr. Anchors' body, then he poured the lighter fluid all over them and his body. Chen took a step back, lit a matchstick, then threw it on Mr. Anchors. The lighter fluid ignited and Mr. Anchors was immediately engulfed in flames.

Chen and Sue walked out of the house and into the night. Eefore the sun came up, Chen and Sue were on a Greyhound bus to New York City.

In New York, Chen rented a room in a flop house in the Lower East Side of Manhattan for him and his "little sister". He found a job loading and unloading ships along the Hudson. Sue stayed in the room glued to the small television set that Chen bought for her.

Six months after Chen started working at the docks, a Vietnamese foreman saw how hard Chen worked and asked Chen if he wanted to make a little more money. Of course Chen did. The man said that he had a cousin who owns a couple of chop shops in the Bronx at the Hunts Point Market. If Chen was good with tools, he would recommend him to his cousin. His recommendations were like gold, he told Chen. Getting him the job would be no problem if Chen wanted the job.

Chen took the job, and soon after he moved him and Sue into another rooming house in the Hunts Point area of the Bronx. That way he didn't have far to go to get to the shop, and also so that he could get home quick when he was done for the day or night.

One day, while breaking down a Cadillac, Chen discovered a cache of money and drugs. His first thought was to keep what he discovered for himself, but he decided against that and instead, he called his boss and turned it over to him. So pleased with Chen's act of loyalty, the boss gave half the money to Chen. He also moved Chen out of the dirty chop shop and into one of the many drug houses that he ran. The drugs that Chen found turned out to be five kilos of pure black tar heroin.

Chen was moving up in the world.

Because of Chen's size, he was made a part of the security team at a shooting gallery on Dyre Avenue. His job, along with four other Vietnamese, was to make sure that no fights broke out, that no one was trying to sell any product on the low there, to keep the fiends in line basically.

The boss took a liking to Chen, and began bringing him along on different runs, or sending him on important errands or deliveries. Chen learned the ins and outs of the drug trade and got accustomed to being around large quantities of drugs and money. He wanted his own though. And he wanted lots of it. So when the boss offered Chen a promotion, running some of the drug houses, Chen could hardly contain himself.

In the years that Chen was in New York, Chen became an underboss in the Vietnamese Mafia. He only answered to the High

Council, and only needed to do so if a decision was to be made that would affect any of the territories outside of his own. For years Chen ran his territory with an iron fist. Nothing mattered to Chen more than Sue though. He provided her with everything she needed and wanted. He was very protective over her and allowed nothing to hurt or harm her.

She felt the same way about him. And he would come to see that for himself.

Chen was in his apartment discussing business with an underboss from a neighboring territory. The discussion became heated and turned into an argument. The older boss began yelling at Chen and criticizing his methods. He said Chen was too young to know how to rule over grown men. Soldiers, he said, who were veterans of the streets and much more qualified to rule over the streets that Chen had handed to him so easily. He was in Chen's face, yelling at him.

That's when Sue walked into the room. She did not acknowledge Chen at all. Instead, she walked right up to the man who was yelling at her older brother in a threatening manner. Out of nowhere she lashed out at him with her right hand. His throat opened in a bloody smile. He grabbed at his neck with both of his hands, but he couldn't stop the flow of blood. He dropped to his knees and the blood finally stopped flowing—when his heart stopped beating.

His lifeless body lay on the ground in a pool of blood and Chen looked at Sue. He knew then that she was different. Special.

She had a thirst.

Chen wrapped the body in a shower curtain and pulled it into the bathroom. Once the body was in the bathtub Chen ran the cold water and began to cut the body into pieces.

Sue helped him.

She was 17 years old.

Chen recognized Sue's affinity towards blood and violence. He didn't know if she acquired it from all of the violence and horror movies she was used to watching, or if it came from the violence of her own past. Either way, she liked it. It seemed that Sue was happiest when she was pulling someone's innards out of their body.

So Chen decided to make Sue a bigger part of his lifestyle. She was by his side at all times, and to shed blood is what she lived for. It was what she loved.

As the years passed, Chen and Sue developed a reputation as a ruthless duo not to be crossed in any way. And if Sue ever came calling alone, hers was most likely that last face you would ever see.

Chen and Sue's notoriety over the years became legendary enough for the High Council to extend an invitation to join the Council. But they wanted Chen out of New York—though they didn't put it so bluntly. They wanted Chen to take over the southern territories from Atlanta to Miami. But they ordered that Chen tone down the violence. Though Chen was not in the habit of taking orders—even from the High Council—he accepted their terms, and him and Sue moved to Atlanta.

Most of the Vietnamese community was concentrated in and around the Decatur, Georgia area, and so was the stronghold of the Vietnamese Mafia. There were several small Vietnamese gangs, but they all paid tribute to the VM, who in turn paid tribute to the High Council.

Chen and Sue's reputation preceded them, so the transition went relatively smoothly. Over the years Chen and Sue took control of the Vietnamese drug trade in the Southeastern United States.

15

Benny Djaper was a flunkie. He knew he would never be much more than that. But he was content with that position, because he was a well-paid flunkie.

And because he was Chen Ayngen's personal flunkie.

It was a job nobody really wanted—because no one ever lasted more than a few years at it. All it ever really took was one mistake for Chen to decide that he no longer needed you. And when he needed you no longer, Sue got rid of you. For good.

Benny was very subservient and eager to please at all times. He never tried to anger Chen or make mistakes. Oh, he would make a mistake from time to time, but he would kill as many as needed to cover up his mistake and blame it on someone else.

Benny was working for a man name Jordan Lau in North Miami Beach until about 3 years ago. Chen and Sue had to make a personal trip to Florida to find out why Lau was having problems making certain shipments in the middle Florida area on time. Lau worked for Chen and controlled from the middle district of Florida to the southernmost tip of the peninsula. Lau resented the fact that Chen came to Florida to chastise him. He felt that he could control his territory without Chen looking over his shoulders. He let it be known that he did not need an overseer and that he would seek a meeting with the High Council. He expressed this to Chen.

Thirty seconds later Jordan Lau was dead.

Chen offered Benny a job in Atlanta on the spot. Seeing first what Chen—and Sue—could and would do, he felt he had no choice. But it has never been a decision that he regretted.

The benefits of working for Chen were vast. Chen paid all of his workers very well at any level, and they were fully protected. At least they were supposed to be.

That's what Benny was thinking when his left ankle shattered from the impact of the shell that came from the Heckler & Koch G-3 SG-1 rifle that Smurf was shooting. Two seconds after he felt the ball joint of his left ankle completely obliterated, the female companion who was with him lost the upper right side of her head.

Benny was leaving Tit 4 Tat at 4:00 in the morning with one of the girls who worked at the club. He occasionally brought one (and sometimes two or three) of the girls home with him for a night of well-paid fun. Tonight, the fun ended early.

Benny fell back against the rear door of the club as Exotica's body grumbled to ground. That's when the Ford Econoline panel van pulled up and Mecca, Divinity and Young God jumped out, guns drawn.

"Get the fuck in the van nigga!" Young God barked as he ran up to Benny and pushed the muzzle of an Ingram Mac 10 under Benny's chin. Mecca and Divinity jumped out and opened the back doors of the van. Young God pushed Benny towards the van doors, hitting him in the back of head with the stock of the Mac 10. Divinity grabbed Benny and searched him quickly before shoving him into the van where Passion and Bitty Bit were waiting to tie him up. Young God jumped into the van behind Benny, the doors were shut, and Mecca and Divinity jumped into the front seats and pulled off.

Two blocks away, Smurf was climbing down from the roof of an Ace Hardware store. His rifle slung over his shoulders.

****

Tiana was on her way out of her house the following morning when her cell phone rang. She was about to go to College Park to confront who she thought was the man responsible for the murders of not only Divine, but the rest of her crew as well.

"Hello," she answered, knowing it was her office.

"Hi Miss Brantz." It was Kemya. "A letter arrived by registered mail a few minutes ago," she said.

"Who's it from Kemya?"

"It says, 'GBA Ethics Committee'."

"Open it and read it to me please Kemya," Tiana requested as she got behind the wheel of Divine's Lamborghini Murcielago. It was the first vehicle that Tiana had bought for him. She listened as Kemya opened the letter and began reading.

"It says that 'due to unprofessional conduct and the Committee's suspicions that you may be involved in questionable practices or with unfavorable persons who may be involved in continuing criminal activities, the Committee has no choice but to suspend your federal license to practice trial law in any courtroom within the state of Georgia for a period of 60 days. This decision is effective immediately." Kemya was in shock. "They suspended you Miss Brantz. Can they do that? What are you gonna do?"

"Well, it could have been worse I guess. What I'm gonna do is take a long needed vacation. Will you please set up a late meeting for six pm tonight. I'll need Roger, Anthony, and you there. The meeting is mandatory. No exceptions. Conference room 1."

"I'll inform them as soon as I hang up Miss Brantz."

"Good. Thank you Kemya. I'll see you all this evening."

Tiana hung up her phone and started the engine.

16

"I'm about 30 seconds away." Tiana said into her phone as she pulled the black Lamborghini into the College Park neighborhood off of Godby Rd. As she was nearing the house, she saw the double garage door rising, and the Econoline panel van came into view. The door was only half the way up when she slid the sleek sports car underneath it and pushed the button on her visor for it to close behind her.

Mecca and Passion came out of the garage door that led to the kitchen.

"Is everything ok?" Tiana asked. "Where is he?" she continued as she walked past the two women without so much as a hello.

"He's in the room playing darts with Smurf and Young God," replied Mecca as Tiana put her purse on one of the kitchen counters. She opened it and took out a .40 caliber Glock that belonged to Divine. She tucked it into the small of her back securely in the waist band of her Dereon jeans. Then she pulled a butterfly knife from her purse and walked down the hall towards the soundproof room where Benny Djaper was being held.

When she walked into the room, Benny was huddled in one corner of the room. He was naked and covered in blood. But he was alive. His left ankle was mangled and a makeshift tourniquet was tied just above his ankle. Bitty Bit tied it when he was thrown into the van so that he wouldn't bleed to death.

On one side of the room, Divinity held a sawed off .12 gauge shotgun and Bitty Bit held two 13-shot .9mm Daewoo DP-51 semiautomatics. All three weapons were pointed directly at Benny. Benny was not tied up or restrained in any way, and on the floor all around him were darts. Sitting across from Benny about 8 feet away, Smurf and Young God were taking turns throwing darts at Benny. Every time one would hit him, Benny would pull it out and throw it on the floor.

Benny hadn't said a word since he arrived at the house.

"Stand him up please," Tiana said to Smurf and Young God. They rushed over to Benny, grabbed his arms and stood him up so that he was standing on his one good foot. Benny didn't resist. When he lifted his head he saw Tiana standing there in front of him.

He smiled.

That smile infuriated Tiana. She walked to him, and with a few expertly maneuvered twists of her wrist she had the butterfly knife open and locked. When she got to Benny she grabbed him by his jaw with her left hand and pushed the knife into his cheek until it emerged from out of his other cheek.

"Who pulled the trigger on my husband?" she hissed. "And where is the chink bitch?" she added as she twisted the handle of the knife. Benny tried to speak, but he couldn't talk through the pain and agony of the knife in his face.

Tiana snatched the knife out of his cheek.

"You..." he gasped. "Y...you have no idea what kind of shit you have gotten yourself into do you?" Blood was coming out of his mouth and from the holes in his cheeks.

"Where is she?" asked Tiana again.

"Don't worry, she will find you soon enough," answered Benny.

"Tell me where she is," demanded Tiana.

"She's in hell. It's where she's from. It's where she lives."

"Oh yeah. Well, when you see her, tell her I'm coming for her head." And Tiana pulled the Glock from her back, put it to Benny's forehead and pulled the trigger, blowing the back half of his head all over the wall. The sound of the gunshot was deafening inside the room, but no one could hear a thing outside of the soundproof room. Smurf and Young God dropped Benny's body on the floor.

"We need to concentrate on Decatur. Someone knows who this sadistic bitch is and I want her found. Get rid of that piece of shit and get some rest. I know you all have been up all night. Get some rest and we'll meet up tonight. Good work people." As Tiana was about to step out of the room, she motioned for Mecca to follow her along with Divinity.

In the kitchen, Tiana washed the blood off of her knife, put her gun in her purse, then sat at the table.

Mecca and Divinity sat down across from her.

"What's good T?" asked Mecca.

Tiana looked from Mecca to Divinity. Passion and Bitty Bit walked into the kitchen, followed by Smurf. Young God was still in the room wrapping Benny's body in plastic so that they could dispose of him.

"Is this a private meeting?" asked Bitty Bit. "Or can we sit down?"

"No, sit down. All of you," responded Tiana. "I don't know if you guys are as tired as I am," she continued. "But I am tired. I'm tired, fed up, and after this bullshit is over, I'm done."

"Done?" asked Bitty Bit.

"Yes. Done. Over the years I have made millions upon millions of dollars. More than I could ever spend in ten lifetimes. But along the way, I've lost too much. I've lost the only family I've had since the death of my parents. Shabazz was my heart and soul and I loved him like a true brother. I couldn't have loved him more if we had the same blood running through our veins. His loss hurt me deeply, and then I lost the man who helped me through that loss, and that hurt. Divine was the first and only man who I have ever given my heart and soul to. He too was taken from me. He was taken from us. This life took him. He left me with a gift though. The gift of life. He left me carrying his seed. But that too was lost as a result of the stress lately."

"Oh shit Tiana!" interrupted Divinity. "You lost the baby? When?"

"It happened right after Divine's funeral. I didn't want to tell anyone about it. It happened at my house, and I really don't want to talk about it if you don't mind."

"I'm so sorry," offered Mecca.

"I'm fine," Tiana answered. "But anyway, I want to find the bitch in that DVD, put an end to this matter, and I plan to remove myself from this life completely. We have all lost too much, and I personally refuse to lose anymore. I make this decision on my own and for myself. Queen Mecca and Princess Divinity." Tiana stared at the two cousins.

"Of everyone left, you two have been here. You two were with Shabazz when I was still in Baychester and here you stand with me now. Always ready to do whatever needs to be done. I love the both of you very much. There are over 300 kilos in our stash spots right now. They now belong to the two of you. They are paid for in full and they are my gift to you. I will arrange for your supply to remain constant and consistent. All you have to do is keep doing what you've been doing."

"Thank you Tiana," said Mecca.

"No, thank you. It has been a pleasure and an honor to build this empire with the both of you."

"You're making it sound like you're leaving," stated Divinity.

"I am," replied Tiana, shocking everyone. "I'm gonna take the next 2 months to liquidate as much of my assets and property as possible, and I'm going to find somewhere very far away where I could relax and enjoy the sun for the rest of my life."

"I'm not mad at you T," remarked Passion.

"Yeah. For real, you deserve to chill for as long as you want. It ain't like you need this anymore," said Smurf.

"Any idea where you wanna go T?" asked Mecca.

"And can we visit?" added Divinity.

"I don't know exactly where I'm going, but when I decide, you'll be the first to know, and if you don't visit you will hurt my feelings. But look, I've got to take off and handle a few things. You guys got that?" She looked at Smurf, referring to the disposal of Benny's body.

"Yeah, we got that."

"Ok, I'm out. Mecca, you and Divinity walk me to my car. I have something I want to give you." She got up and walked to the kitchen door that led to the two car garage. Mecca and Divinity followed Tiana to her car.

Tiana went to the passenger side of the black Murcielago and opened the door. She reached in and took hold of two small Louis Vuitton handbags. She handed one to Mecca and the other to Divinity.

"Thanks Tiana, but you know we still gutter with our shit. We don't really be into that purse and heels look," said Mecca, joking.

"Well, next time I'll get you Timberland shoe boxes Miss Thugged Out. Would you both look inside please."

Mecca and Divinity both unzipped their bags and looked inside.

Each bag contained one thing.

A gold and diamond covered cell phone.

"Is this what I think it is Tiana?" asked Divinity as she pulled the phone out of her bag.

The phones were originally given to Tiana by Victor Maldonado as a gift. The phones were layered in 12 layers of 24 karat gold and lined in diamonds. They were custom made and there were no other phones ever made like the pair. There was a chip embedded in both phones to scramble any frequency that attempted to tap into the line. One of the phones used to belong to Shabazz. After Shabazz was killed, Tiana gave the phone to Divine. Both phones were turned off after Divine's murder.

Until now.

"I want you two to have them. I had them fixed so that they are only compatible with each other. They can't be reached from any other phone and you can't reach any other phone with them. All you have to do is push the send button and the other will ring. The phones never need to be charged and there is no bill. And for your own information Mecca, both of those bags are knock-offs."

"Ha! I can't believe you were able to say that with a straight face," yelled Mecca.

"Shit, I'll bet you don't even know where to buy a damn knock-off!" added Divinity.

"Whatever. Next time I'll get your bags at Thugs-R-Us! Bye ladies."

Tiana pushed the remote door opener and the garage door began to rise. She started the engine and backed out of the garage.

17

At five minutes before six Tiana walked into Conference Room 1 at the law offices of Brantz & Brantz. After she left the College Park house, Tiana went straight to her accountant's office. She had one basic order. She wanted to sell everything she owned. All of her properties, vehicles, stocks, mutual funds, etc...she wanted everything she owned liquidated into cash and transferred to an oversees account. Since Divine was technically Tiana's husband at the time of his death, Universal Realty, his real estate company, belonged to her. Tiana's net worth was well over 150 million dollars, and that didn't include the 40 or 50 million she had in cash stashed in various places.

Tiana also stopped at one of her banks, and left 30 minutes later with several cashier's checks.

She called Victor.

"I received word from the Ethics Committee Victor," she told him.

"That was fast. What was their decision?"

"They suspended me for 2 months. I thought you were gonna take care of that little issue," she asked, a bit sarcastically.

"I did. They wanted to take your license completely and permanently. I convinced them that 60 days would serve its purpose. Consider yourself lucky Tiana. You take that 60 days and reevaluate your priorities. Focus on what is important from this point on."

"Oh, that's exactly what I plan on doing Victor. Reevaluating my priorities. I have to go Victor." Tiana hung up the phone before Victor could respond.

Tiana once loved Victor like a father. That love was replaced by hatred the moment Victor put a gun to her head. She could not forget that, nor would she ever forgive it.

She walked into the conference room and headed directly for the head of the conference table. She sat her briefcase down and looked at everyone in attendance.

"Hello everyone. I'm sorry to keep you late, but this shouldn't take too long," she said as she opened her briefcase and took out a leather folder. Sitting around the table were Roger—the head of her paralegal teams. Anthony Crawford, Tiana's top attorney at Brantz & Brantz. And of course, Kemya.

"I'll get right to it. I'm sure by now that you've heard that I've been suspended by the Ethics Committee."

"What!" Roger gasped.

"When?" asked Anthony.

Tiana looked at Kemya.

"You didn't tell them Kemya?"

"No ma'am. You asked me to inform them that there was a mandatory meeting tonight. You did not ask me to tell them the nature of the meeting, so I didn't think it was my place to do so," responded Kemya.

"That's why I value you so much," Tiana said, smiling. "Anyway, yes. Effective immediately I have been suspended for 60 days. Roger, you know what I'll need you to do. I'll need all of my cases diverted. I want Anthony to handle as many as he can. The two of you should get together on that as soon as possible."

"We're on it Miss Brantz," Roger responded, writing furiously on his legal pad.

"I want the cases diverted on a permanent basis. I'll need you to draw up the necessary motions to remove myself from all of my active cases that are currently in, or about to go to trial. Kemya, you'll draw up letters apologizing to any clients affected once Roger and Anthony work out the specifics."

"Yes ma'am."

"Anthony. Were you aware that Kemya is under contract to work here until I retire?" Tiana asked.

"I've heard something like that. I've never had reason to ask if it's true or not."

"How do you feel about Kemya?" she asked.

"She's wonderful. I don't think this office could survive without her."

"So, would you keep her on if something were to happen to me?"

"Of course. Without a second thought," Anthony responded, looking at Kemya with a genuine smile on his face.

"Kemya, what about you? Would you stay here at Brantz and Brantz even if I was not here?"

"As long as Mr. Crawford would have me."

"What about you Roger? Do you see Brantz and Brantz as your home? Your permanent work home?"

"Of course Ms. Brantz. I love it here and wouldn't dream of going anyplace else."

"Would the two of you sign contracts to that effect?"

"Yes indeed," replied Roger.

"Yes ma'am. Gladly," answered Kemya.

"Good." Tiana opened up the leather folder in front of her and removed some papers. She stood up and walked over to Roger, placing some papers in front of him. She did the same to Kemya.

"What I have just handed you Roger and Kemya are employment contracts. They basically secure your employment here at Brantz and Brantz until such a time that you retire, which you may do any time after your 60th birthdays. Your salaries, bonuses and retirement packages are all clearly detailed. Take them home and read them carefully. If the terms are to your satisfaction, sign and date them and give them to Anthony for him to look over. Anthony, if the terms are to your satisfaction, you sign them and they will go into effect immediately."

Tiana stood up again and took three envelopes from the same leather folder. She handed one to Roger and one to Kemya. Then she stood next to Anthony. The envelope she had for him was a larger one. "Kemya and Roger. In the envelopes I just handed you are cashier's checks in the amount of 2 million dollars. Consider that a bonus from me to you, a token of my appreciation for your years of loyal service. Now you, Mr. Crawford." Tiana pulled a smaller envelope out of the larger one along with some more paperwork. "I first met you when I was 8 years old. My parents were just killed and you told me to call you when I turn 18. 10 years later I called you and you told me that I was a wealthy young woman. Here we are, so many years later, you're still here, and we are both wealthy. Well, for your many, many years of simply being an asset not only to the law firm but to my life in general, I not only want to give you this check for 7 million dollars, but I want to also tell you that in 60 days, when my suspension is officially over, I plan to retire—permanently retire. And in doing so, I am giving total control of Brantz and Brantz to you. Provided that you can agree to the terms in Roger and Kemya's contracts. Always treat them like family. And one more thing."

"What would that be Ms. Brantz?" Anthony asked, smiling.

"You can never, under any circumstances, change the name of this firm."

"I wouldn't dream of it." Anthony stood up and hugged Tiana warmly. "Thank you Tiana."

"You're welcome," she responded. "Ok, let me go. This outfit cost me over 2 thousand dollars and I refuse to let you cry babies get tears all over it!" They all laughed.

"Read over the contract I just gave you Anthony. I'll have some more papers for you soon, and you and I will need to get together for a serious talk very, very soon ok?"

"Whenever you're ready," he responded.

Kemya stood up and approached Tiana. She wrapped her arms around her. "I'm gonna miss you Miss Brantz," she said through her tears. "Thank you. For everything."

"You just take care of yourself and that son of yours."

"I will. God knows I will."

****

That evening, Tiana ate a meal at home alone. She sat at her dining room table contemplating the decisions she was making. She picked up her glass of red wine and emptied it. She stood up and made another decision. She needed to see someone. She needed to consult with her true best friend.

She walked out of the house through one of the back entrances and walked across her spacious and well-manicured lawn. About a hundred yards away from the main house was a smaller house. From the outside it looked like a small guesthouse or groundskeeper's quarters. No one had ever stepped foot inside of this house, and Tiana was the only person with the key. She held that key in her hand as she approached the door. It had been some time since she'd came here. After Divine's funeral she couldn't bring herself to come, but now she needed to.

She opened the door and walked inside, closing the door behind her and turning on the lights.

She was inside of her custom built, climate controlled family mausoleum. A few years after she had purchased her land and house, she commissioned a crypt maker to build her a mausoleum on her property. She wanted it to look like a real home on the outside, but the inside would be made to accommodate her family and offer them a beautiful final resting place. Tiana had her parents moved here from New York and placed inside of a massive memorial crypt that was partly underground and encased in the finest Italian marble. A year after Shabazz was killed, she moved his body from New York also. That was initially difficult since Tiana was not legally his sister, but as the old saying goes, everyone has their price. With Divine, his funeral was held at the Eternal Horizons funeral home, and then she had his body brought here. Home.

There were no real windows. There only appeared to be windows from the outside. On the far side of the "house" were the crypts of Tiana's parents. To the right of theirs was the crypt that held Shabazz's body. And to the far left was the newest edition to the house. Divine.

Each crypt stood three feet tall, even though the actual bodies were 7 feet underground. In front of each was a single reclining chair so that Tiana could sit and "talk" with her family.

Tiana walked over to her parents' section and placed a gentle kiss on each of their crypts.

"I love you," she said to them. Then she walked over to where Shabazz's body lay in rest. There were pictures of Shabazz of all sizes on the wall surrounding a large Universal flag—the emblem of the Five

Percenters—with the words "In The Name of Allah" around it. She sat in the chair facing him. Beside the chair was a small table. On the table was an ashtray, a lighter, and a very exquisite humidifier. She opened the humidifier and took out a pre-rolled blunt. She lit the blunt, took a long pull, and leaned back in the chair.

"Hi Beloved," she said as she exhaled the thick smoke in the direction of the crypt. Tiana didn't smoke normally, but whenever she came to see her brother she would allow the smoke to fill the area because it's what he liked.

"I know I'm fucking up brother," she said. "I don't know how I let this get so out of hand. We've lost so many people to this bullshit." She took a pull from the blunt and placed it in the ashtray. "I should have gotten out long ago. WE should have gotten out. We had millions upon millions. I mean, how much money is enough? But you know something Shabazz, it was my fault. Not yours. Not Divine's. You would still be alive if I didn't mess up. When I killed TC and took those 40 kilos of heroin it started a chain reaction that took the lives of a lot of good people, including the two men I love the most in my life. Well, it's over my beloved. At least for me it is. After we find that woman I'm done with this life. I've already set the wheels in motion. I'm turning over the reins to Mecca and Divinity. I gave them our phones today and though they don't know it yet I had the deed to the house changed. When I leave I'm giving them the house. I'll let them know that they have to smoke with you from time to time. They'll take good care of you. I don't know where I'm going yet, but it will be someplace nice and quiet. And don't worry, I'll come and visit you as often as possible." Tiana picked the blunt up and took another pull. "Let me go talk to Divine before I go. I love you Shabazz." Tiana walked across the "house" to where Divine lay. "Hi baby."

She didn't sit. Instead, she stood in front of the large picture of her husband.

"I know you know I lost the baby," she said to him, rubbing her now empty stomach. "I'm so sorry my love." That's when she began to cry. This was the first time that Tiana had visited with Divine since he was placed here, so this was the first time that she had had to really think about the miscarriage. It happened right after Divine was killed. She was laying in her bed crying when she felt the sharp pains suddenly, then the wetness came. She started bleeding badly, and she had no doubts what was the cause. She called her private doctor—he was someone she used to discreetly treat any gunshot wounds in the crews. He rushed right over, and after a preliminary examination told her what she had already knew and accepted.

She lost her baby.

The next day, Tiana went to his office for a full examination. Afterwards, she returned to her home, and seclusion. To deal with her losses alone. As she stood there in front of Divine's picture now, Tiana let her tears flow. After a few minutes, she gathered herself together.

"I think it was gonna be a little girl baby," she said. "I was gonna name her Divinely Beloved." Tiana almost started crying again. "You're disappointed in me aren't you? I know you are. As soon as I'm left to really run things on my own, more people start dying in such a short amount of time than ever before. But baby, once I find this woman and make her pay for what she did to you, to us, then I'm getting out forever. Just like you and I talked about. I'm giving complete control of everything to Mecca and Divinity. They'll have to rebuild their forces, but I have faith in them. I'm also hoping that they decide to one day take the same route I'm taking. Well baby, I'm gonna go and take a nap. Everyone is going on the hunt tonight and I want to be there. I want to look her in the eyes when she dies. I'll come back and tell you about it ok. I love you with all my heart Divine." Tiana kissed her finger and reached up to touch Divine's picture with it. She looked over at the crypts that held her parents and mouthed two words.

"Forgive me."

Tiana went back to the main house to rest before the hunt began.

18

Tiana walked out of the house at 1:10 a.m. She wore a black, two-piece Emilio Pucci casual suit with matching flat shoes. Under the blazer, her double shoulder holster held two silenced Desert Eagles. Smurf had just pulled up in an all-black, fully armored Suburban with tinted—and bulletproof—glass. Young God jumped out of the passenger side and into the back. Mecca, Divinity, Passion and Bitty Bit were also in the back. Tiana climbed in and shut the door behind her.

"Everybody rested? Everybody ready?" she asked. In response, everyone in the vehicle showed off their weapons. Smurf pulled out a mini Uzi submachine gun and 4 25-round clips. Young God had an Ingram Mac 11. Passion lifted her shirt to reveal a Metalife custom .357 magnum. Bitty Bit had a baby Glock 19 with 2 17-round clips. Both Mecca and Divinity carried SIG P226 .9mm automatics.

"Shit. It looks like we're all ready then," Tiana stated as she crossed her arms, stuck her arms into her blazer on both sides and pulled out her famed Desert Eagles. She put her guns back and began passing around small pictures.

"This is the bitch that we're after. Once we're in Chinatown, or whatever they call this place, it's all eyes and ears open. It's only a few blocks long and a couple of blocks wide, but nothing is in English there, except the street signs. We are gonna stick out like sore thumbs once we get there so it makes no sense to split up."

"T. Would you mind if I cut in?" Mecca interrupted, showing that she was ready to assume control.

"No, go ahead Mecca," Tiana responded with a smile.

"Ok. Tiana is indeed right. Not only will we stick out, but if we split up we'll be spreading ourselves thin. We already know that this bitch is ruthless so we can't slip up or underestimate her. What we need to do is flush the bitch out. Make our presence known. But be on the lookout for anything. We know this bitch can't roll alone so we should be ready for an all-out war tonight. Everyone watch everyone's back and at all times keep your eyes on Tiana. Let's handle our shit tonight yo, and please, try not to lose your heads to this bitch. Tiana, anything else?"

"Not really. Let's make some noise."

"That's what's up!" exclaimed Smurf. "Let's be out," he said as he turned the big SUV towards the street. He stopped at the end of Tiana's long driveway.

"Yo Tiana, you know the way there right?" he asked.

Everyone burst out laughing.

****

Two black men and five black women definitely did stick out at two in the morning in the small Vietnamese community in Decatur. Most of the stores were closed, but it was the ones that were opened that interested them. The clubs, 24 hour stores and late night restaurants were where they figured they would find the gothic looking woman who so boldly and brutally killed Shorty on that DVD. She just looked like a night person.

The first thing that everyone in the Suburban noticed was that, just as Tiana stated, all the signs were in Vietnamese. It was as if they were no longer in Georgia. Little 'Nam, as the community was called, was a culture shock, but that didn't stop Smurf from pulling the big battle tank into the first gas station he saw.

"Ok yo, let's wake motha fuckas up around here," he said, pulling right up in front. The doors opened and seven killers got out of the black SUV. Mecca went straight to the counter where an older woman stood, looking a bit frightened at all the black faces that just entered her store.

"Do you know this woman?" Mecca asked her as she placed the picture on the counter.

The woman looked at the picture and shrugged her shoulders.

"Do you speak English?"

The woman just stared at Mecca.

"Ayo!" Young God yelled from the back of the store. "Is this Coke or what?" he added, holding up a red and white can that looked like a Coca-Cola except that all the writing was Vietnamese.

"Fuck it!" he said, putting the can back when he saw that he wasn't getting any answers from the old woman.

"Let's go," said Tiana as she walked up to Mecca at the counter.

"Either she really doesn't speak English or she's just not talking to us."

As the group left the store and piled into the SUV, the woman behind the counter picked up her phone and dialed a number.

They stopped at one more gas station—with basically the same results—before pulling over in front of what looked like some kind of club.

"Look," Mecca addressed the crew. "If anything is gonna pop off, it's most likely gonna be here. So, be alert at all times."

People were lingering around the outside of the club—and staring at them—as they emerged from the large vehicle. The group of seven walked casually into the club, no one had a clue that they were probably seven of the most ruthless and deadliest killers in Georgia.

The seven of them didn't notice the two cars that pulled up and parked behind their black Suburban as they entered the club.

Smurf walked up beside Mecca.

"Yo Mecca, I know you and Divinity are in charge now, but can I make a suggestion?"

"What's that?" responded Mecca questioningly.

"The straight up and direct approach."

"Which is?" she asked.

"Want me to show you?"

"Go ahead. Do you," said Mecca.

"Gladly," said Smurf as he pulled his mini Uzi out. When Mecca saw his move she pulled her .9mm out, which caused a chain reaction amongst the rest of the crew as Smurf pointed his Uzi at the ceiling and emptied the entire 25-round clip. Chaos broke out in the club as people began screaming and laying on the ground. Smurf spoke loudly as he pulled the empty clip out and slammed another one home.

"Everybody shut the fuck up so I can have your undivided attention. We're looking for this bitch right here," he said, holding up the picture of Sue that he had. "She hangs out with Benny! We need to holla at her! Does anybody here know where we can find her?!"

The rest of the crew were waving their guns around in an effort to maintain control of the crowd.

They didn't see the eight Vietnamese enter the club until it was too late.

Bloc-ow!

Bitty Bit was the closest to the entrance of the club and unfortunately had her back to the door.

She heard and felt the shotgun at the same time as it tore through her back. All she could do was drop to the floor as her vitals flat lined.

"Noooooo!" Passion screamed as she pointed her .357 at the one holding the shotgun and tore a hole in his face with a hollow point shell. The next bullet separated the upper left side of his head with the rest of his body. Young God spun around and let loose a long burst into the other seven Vietnamese. They didn't have a chance to split up, and that was their demise as bullets tore through them.

Smurf and Young God led the charge as they let loose with their fully automatic weapons. The crew made quick work of the Vietnamese hit squad. Young God bent down and picked up Bitty Bit's petite body, throwing her over his shoulder while Tiana covered him with her two Desert Eagles.

They rushed out of the club before any Vietnamese reinforcements could show up. Bitty Bit's body was placed in the back while everyone else piled into the SUV. Smurf pulled a bag from under the seat and unzipped it. Inside were several M-26 grenades. He handed two to Passion and he took two. They pulled the pins and tossed the grenades towards the front entrance of the club.

The big SUV screeched off just as the sounds of the first explosions filled the air.

****

To avoid being implicated in the incident in Little 'Nam, the group agreed that Bitty Bit's body would have to be left somewhere for now. So her body was laid on a bench in front of the Decatur public library. Tiana assured everyone that her body would be claimed and she would be given a proper burial.

Mecca and Divinity were dropped off first since they lived right there in Decatur. They entered the house in a somber mood, not believing that Bitty Bit was gone. Everyone agreed to meet the next afternoon at Tiana's house to talk about and plan their next move.

The series of simultaneous explosions ripped through the house so quickly that by the time they realized what was happening, it was too late. Both of their bodies were virtually vaporized instantly.

19

"Santana," he said when he picked up the phone.

"Detective Santana, this is Special Agent Seaver with the FBI's New York office. You got a minute, cause I got something I think you'll be interested in."

****

"Hello." Tiana was still half asleep when she picked her phone up. It was a little after ten in the morning. As she listened to the caller speak, the small microscopic hairs on the back of her neck began to straighten. She slowly rose out of her bed. "This can't be real. This can't be happening." The tears began streaming down her face. "I'm on the way. Stay there."

Tiana got out of bed and dressed as quickly as she could, crying uncontrollably. She just couldn't believe what Smurf had told her. Evidently, Passion was supposed to be at Mecca and Divinity's house this morning to discuss how they were gonna arrange to claim Bitty Bit's body and give her a proper burial. When she got there though, the only thing left where their house stood just last night was a pile of smoldering ashes. One fire truck was still there spraying water on some of the still smoking areas of the house. The area was blocked off and the police were walking around the scene. Passion was able to get close enough to ask one of the officers what happened.

He said that the house had exploded in the early hours of the morning. He said that the explosives used were so intense that there was nothing left of the house at all, and that the explosives were placed strategically so that they were aimed inward and none of the houses on either side were harmed. Then the officer told Passion just what she didn't want to hear.

The charred remains of two bodies were removed from the scene. The officer then excused himself. Passion tried calling Tiana first but got no answer. So she called Smurf.

Tiana made the drive from Buckhead to Decatur in record time, parking the Lamborghini behind Passion's brand new Dodge Charger. Smurf and Young God were standing with Passion outside of the house. The house was no longer blocked off, so when Tiana got out of the car she slowly walked across the grass to the house. Passion, Smurf and Young God followed silently behind her.

The large house was completely destroyed. Reduced to a pile of ashes. As Tiana was walking through the rubble her telephone rang. She didn't want to answer it but with so much going on in her life at the time, she couldn't take the chance that it was important. She stopped and pulled her phone out, her eyes still surveying the damage around her.

"Hello," she said, her voice void of any emotion.

"Miss Brantz"

"Yes."

"This is Detective Santana."

"No offense Detective, but this really isn't a good time."

"Miss Brantz, we really need to talk," he persisted.

"Well like I said Detective. Right now is not a good time."

"When will be good for you Miss Brantz because this can't wait."

"I'll call you Detective," Tiana responded, irritated.

"But when..." Tiana hung up on Detective Santana before he could finish his sentence. She put the phone back into her pocket and walked around in the ashes.

"Yo Tiana, who the fuck is this bitch we're dealing with?" asked Passion.

"I have no idea Passion. But I do know that I want her head. She has to die....a slow and painful death."

Tiana had the look of death in her eyes. Death and vengeance. She wanted revenge so badly that it hurt.

"Yeah, but we gotta find her first," said Young God. "It's like she knows all about us, our moves, where we live, what we drive, everything. We don't know shit about her though. All we know is what she looks like."

What they also didn't know is that Benny Djaper was not the "boss", Sue Wyn Ngo was not all they had left to contend with, and their lives were about to get just a little bit more complicated.

"We'll find her," said Tiana.

"Yeah but will we find her before she takes us all out?" Smurf asked. "I mean look at us Tiana. Math don't lie. We're down to four of us, not counting the local motha fuckas we got working for us on the streets, and most of them really ain't build for this war shit."

"Are you built for this war shit?" Tiana asked.

"You already know I am. I was born for this shit!" he exclaimed. "I don't give a fuck who it's with. This bitch bleed just like the next."

"Ok then. Then us four need to make sure this bitch bleeds, along with whoever stands with her. We have lost a lot of good people. People we loved. I for one refuse to let any of these deaths be for nothing."

"Word is bond!" affirmed Young God.

"I think we need to stick together til we get this chick," said Passion. "We can't watch each other's backs if we can't see each other. What do you think Tiana?"

"I like that idea, but let me add this. Since it seems like she knows all our whereabouts, I think we need to lay low somewhere different. Not at any of our places anyway. I was thinking of maybe..." That's when Tiana's phone rang again.

"Hello," she answered.

"Who in the fuck do you think you are playing with counselor?"

At the sound of his voice Tiana froze. She thought she was talking to a dead man.

"Did you think killing Benny would hurt me? He was about to outlive his usefulness to me anyway. You did me a favor, but the fact remains that your flagrant disrespect could not go unpunished. Your actions last night were bold. Bold and brave. I respect bravery. It shows you have bigger balls than most."

Tiana realized that Benny Djaper may have been who was on that DVD, but he was not the man who had been calling her. She needed to know who this man was or she felt she would lose this war very quickly. She could never win a war against an enemy she couldn't see.

"You know who I am. You seem to know an awful lot about me and my organization. Is it too much to ask who you are and who the woman is?" Tiana asked, hoping to get some answers out of him. She was still standing in the middle of Mecca and Divinity's destroyed house. Passion, Smurf and Young God were looking at her, listening to her every word.

Chen was silent for a moment, but his arrogance was overpowering.

"I suppose that bit of information would be useless if not irrelevant since I am going to kill you anyway. And make no mistake about that counselor. I am going to kill you. How you die is the only choice you will have in the matter, because you still have an unpaid debt that you are responsible for. If you choose to pay it, your death will be swift. If you don't, I will make sure that you are kept alive and in extreme pain for months. You will be gang raped by every male in Little 'Nam old enough to get an erection. As for who I am. My name is Chen. Chen Ayngen. And the woman you are so intent on meeting is my beloved Sue." Then Chen went on to give Tiana an abbreviated version of their history. "Well counselor, I have business elsewhere which unfortunately demands my attention in another part of the country. That business will almost certainly take maybe a week. Until then, you may rest easy. I will come for you when I return."

"Come for me?" Tiana asked.

"Yes. I will come for you. I suggest that you get your affairs in order."

The phone went dead in Tiana's hand.

She looked at the phone then put it in her pocket. Tiana hadn't felt this helpless since Shabazz was in the hospital right after he was shot in the back of his head. She looked once again at the devastation around her.

"What's up Tiana?" Passion asked, concerned. She could see the look on Tiana's face. It was a look she'd never seen before.

Tiana looked afraid. But then she looked up at Passion, Smurf and Young God. Her expression changed. "We've got to tighten up," she said. "We've got about a week to get out shit together, find these mother fuckers, and kill them. If not, you can believe they'll be coming for us. Everybody go home and pack some things. I'm gonna find us a spot somewhere. The people we're dealing with know everything about us so we need to find someplace new to plan until this is over. I'll take care of it. I just need everybody to be reachable."

Tiana left Mecca and Divinity's house with an agenda. The first thing she did was secure a four bedroom condo in Stone Mountain for her and her crew. She had computer and alarm systems installed and updated. Then she went by her accountant's office to check on the progress he was making with her assets, as well as the transfer of ownership of Brantz and Brantz into Anthony Crawford's hands. She was definitely "getting her affairs in order". Once she had as much of her assets as possible liquidated and into cash accounts, then she wanted to put the life she had lived for over 20 years behind her.

****

She pulled up to her accountant's office still thinking about (and hurt by) Mecca and Divinity's deaths. She called him to let him know she was on the way. He was expecting her, and he was ready for her.

His name was Dawit Burroughs. He was one of the few blacks to graduate Magna Cum Laude in his class at Harvard. He had a dual CPA in Business as well as Scientific Mathematics and Statistics. He was one of the best numbers men on the East Coast, and that was why he managed all of Tiana's financial affairs—as well as Divine's when he was still alive.

Before Tiana got out of the car she called Passion to give her the address to the condo in Stone Mountain. She told Passion to let

Smurf and Young God know that she will meet them all there at about 8:00. The key was under the mat, she said.

"He's waiting for you Miss Brantz. Go right in," said Janeane, Mr. Burroughs secretary when she saw Tiana enter.

"Thank you Janeane."

When Tiana walked into the office Mr. Burroughs was on his telephone. He stood up when he saw Tiana walk in. He walked over to her and hugged her briefly, giving her a quick kiss on her cheek.

"Look Simon, a very important client just walked into my office so I'm gonna have to get back to you on that...yes, as a matter of fact she is more important than you," he said, then hung the phone up. "How are you this morning Tiana?"

"I'm exhausted Dawit. Please tell me that you've got some good news for me because I could sure use some in my life."

"Well then, you've come to the right place at the right time. First things first." He pulled a capital "T" shaped key chain out of a small velvet bag and handed it to Tiana. "Put this on your key ring."

Tiana looked at the gold "T", then looked at Dawit.

"Dawit, thank you, but I really don't do vanity initials." She put the key chain on his desk.

"Tiana, in all the years that you've been with me, have I ever done you wrong, lost you a dollar, or given you a reason not to trust me?"

"No, no, and no," Tiana responded.

"Ok then. Put it on your key ring so we can move on."

Tiana picked up the key chain and attached it to her key ring reluctantly.

"There. Now what?"

"Ok, now." He turned a laptop computer towards her. "I want you to type in a password twice, then press enter. Anything up to 16 characters." Tiana thought for a few seconds, then she hit the keyboard a few time and pushed enter.

"Ok, now what's next?" she asked.

"That's it. All of your accounts have been consolidated into two separate accounts. I haven't been able to liquidate all of your assets, yet, but most have been taken care of. The remainder will be taken care of as soon as possible, and as soon as they do the funds will be automatically transferred from a sub account into your two main accounts. All of your stocks and mutual funds have been sold. Some of your properties are gonna take a little longer than expected, but I've got someone really good on it. All of Divine's assets were transferred into your control and placed in the same portfolio. I've got a dealer interested in your vehicles. Which reminds me, what's the least you'll take for your Phantom?" He leaned back in his chair and smiled at her.

"Why? Do you have someone interested?"

"Well yeah. I am, if the price is right."

"I'll tell you what Dawit. I'll bring you the title and all the paperwork tomorrow along with the key fob. My gift to you."

"Are you serious?" Dawit asked, sitting forward in his chair.

"Of course I'm serious. I'm not gonna need it, and I can't think of anyone else I'd rather have it. But it comes with two conditions."

"Anything. What do you want?"

"First, I want you to store one of my cars."

"Which one?" he asked.

"My Saleen S7. Just keep it safe for me in case I decide to visit Atlanta."

"You got it. What else?"

"Tell me about that password I just entered, and this damn 'T' on my key chain."

Dawit Burroughs laughed a hearty laugh.

"The 'T' on your key chain is a carefully concealed memory stick. All you have to do is get on any computer, access the internet, then plug the mem stick into a USB port. You will automatically be connected to a highly secured account. Once you enter your passcode— that only you know—you will have access to all of your money. You can wire cash around the world or simply use your card."

"This may sound like a silly question," Tiana said, "but what if I lose this memory stick?" She held up her keys.

"Then you can call me and I'll get another to you. I have two duplicates," replied Dawit.

"So you have my passcode then?"

"No. I only have the ability to deposit into the accounts. I can't make any withdrawals or manipulate the funds in any way."

"So tell me Dawit. How much am I worth?" she asked.

"As of this morning, 215 million dollars. But there are still a lot of properties, and you've got some very high dollar vehicles that still have to be sold. Basically you are set."

"Yes I am Dawit. I'll have the Phantom and the Saleen delivered to you at your house tomorrow." She stood up to leave.

"I'll take care of them for you Tiana," Dawit said as he stood and walked from behind his desk.

"I know you will Dawit." Tiana gave him a quick hug.

"Just like you've always taken care of me. Thank you Dawit. I'll miss you."

"I'll miss you too Tiana. But we'll see each other again very soon. I hate to see you leave, but with such overwhelming events in your life lately—personal and business—a long vacation is exactly what you need. You take care of yourself."

"That's exactly what I plan to do."

****

For the next few days Tiana methodically planned her every move. She finalized all business at her law firm, putting it into the hands and custody of Anthony Crawford. She delivered her Saleen S7 and Rolls Royce Phantom to the home of Dawit Burroughs. Tiana also cautiously and quietly tried to find out all she could about Chen Ayngen.

Which was basically nothing.

What she did find out was that the people who lived in Little 'Nam were very tight lipped. They didn't talk much to people outside of their community, and they protected their own. And even though Chen claimed that he would be out of town for a week, Tiana was still careful not to make too much noise in her inquiries. She still recognized that Chen was a very formidable adversary and she didn't want to risk the lives of the few remaining members of her team.

Arrangements were made, funerals were planned and attended. Tiana had grown weary of watching those she loved and knew lowered into the ground inside of coffins. After the double funeral for Stacey Anderson and Tiffany Swanson, also known as Queen Mecca Earth and Princess Divinity Earth, Tiana was officially completely drained. She drove her late husband Divine's Lamborghini home from the cemetery. She planned to drive that car until she left Atlanta since she had already gotten rid of all her other vehicles. She intended to give the Lamborghini to Kemya's son the day she left.

She pulled up to her mansion, went through the gate, and parked right in front. She sat in the car for a couple of minutes reflecting on the past and on the journey she took to get where she was. It seemed like a lifetime ago that she walked out of Baychester Diagnostic Center where she was placed by the Bureau of Child Welfare after the murder of her parents left her with no family to care for her. She remained at Baychester from the age of eight until her eighteenth birthday. Baychester was a coming-of-age period for Tiana. It was also where she met Shabazz. Shabazz became Tiana's mentor, best friend and brother. Shabazz left Baychester four years before Tiana did, and from the day he walked out of Baychester Tiana didn't hear from him again. But he promised her that he would be there the day she walked out of those same gates.

It was a promise that he kept.

Just as she was about to get into a taxi in front of Baychester on the morning of her 18th birthday, Shabazz came running around the corner. That day Tiana told Shabazz the one secret that she had kept from him during all of their years at Baychester together. And that was that she was due to receive a large sum of money as a result of her parents' deaths.

She had grand plans. She wanted to buy Shabazz a car and she wanted to take care of him, just as he had taken care of her for all of those years. She also wanted to go to college and law school. Shabazz encouraged her, but he had one suggested change to her plans.

Instead of buying him a car and taking care of him, Shabazz suggested that she let him use some money to invest in his own drug business and let him build an empire so that they could be rich while she went to college and became a lawyer. She agreed and gave him two hundred thousand dollars.

20

Shabazz had been selling drugs since the day he walked out of Baychester with his 250 dollars, his food stamps and bus tokens. Not having anywhere to go, no family, and determined not to end up in a men's shelter for the homeless, Shabazz went to the Bronx, which was where he was born.

In the Bronx he sold his food stamps and tokens. He bought 200 dollars' worth of cocaine along with a .38 special snub nosed revolver and 30 bullets. The dealer he bought the coke from showed him how to bag it up into 10 dollar packages. Shabazz made about 350 dollars off of his first package. He kept putting money away and buying 200 dollar packages until his supplier suggested that he buy crack instead of cocaine. He said that the crack sells quicker so the money is made a lot faster.

For the next few years Shabazz went through many ups and downs. He took losses from time to time of course. He was even robbed once. Starting over was nothing new to him. He had taken several jobs over the years just to get enough money to "re-up". By the time Tiana got out of Baychester and put that 200 thousand dollars in his hands, he was a known hustler on the streets. It was said that Shabazz could wake up with ten dollars in his pocket and have a hundred by lunch.

He took the 200 thousand that Tiana gave him and put it away. The first thing he did was ask around to find the best coke at the best price. He wanted to buy a kilo to start with. He had learned how to cook the cocaine himself.

Shabazz met a Puerto Rican named George in Yankee Stadium Park who claimed he could get him a kilo for 18 thousand. He told Shabazz to meet him on 167th and Jerome at 11 o'clock that night with the money and that he would have the coke. When Shabazz showed up at 10:50, George was already there. He had a bag in his hand. When Shabazz pulled out the two rubber banded rolls of money, George grabbed them and took off running towards the Grand Concourse.

He got maybe 10 feet away before Shabazz pulled his gun and shot him in the back twice. George fell to the ground and Shabazz shot him three more times. He reached down and retrieved his money, then grabbed the bag George had with him. He heard the train coming on top of him so he ran up the stairs, jumped the turnstile and made it onto the 4 train just as the doors were closing. He walked to the back of the train and sat down in the last car. When he opened the bag he wasn't surprised.

It was just a two pound package of Dixie Crystals sugar.

Shabazz just laughed.

Eventually Shabazz started dealing with Migs and Louie. Their price began at 22 thousand five hundred a kilo until Shabazz started buying more than one at a time. Migs and Louie became Shabazz's supplier until they were gunned down one night in front of a salsa club called the Devil's Nest.

That was when Tiana decided to step up.

Knowing that her friend Victoria's father Victor Maldonado was a major figure in the Columbian drug cartel, Tiana approached him with an offer to buy 100 kilos of cocaine.

The rest, as they say, is history.

****

Tiana's thoughts were interrupted when she noticed about 7 or 8 figures standing around her car. She recognized Sue immediately, and she guessed that the large Oriental man standing next to her was Chen.

She took a deep breath. For a brief second she thought about reaching for the Desert Eagle that was mounted under her seat, but she decided against it. She lifted the driver's side door and stepped out of the car.

"Hello counselor. I told you that I would come for you," said Chen.

"Just like that?" Tiana said, shutting the Lamborghini's door.

"Just like that," he replied.

That's when Sue hit Tiana with the stun gun and Tiana blacked out.

21

1982—Baychester Diagnostic Center

Tiana had been at Baychester for four years. In those first four years she grew up quickly and she learned about life the way no child should have. She stuck to Shabazz like a lost puppy those first few years and she listened to everything he taught her. At the age of 12 she was very mature both mentally as well as physically. She was always asking questions, and one day she shocked him with one of her questions. They were in one of the yards early on a Saturday morning just walking and talking. Saturdays and Sundays were their favorite days of the week because they could spend the whole day together and not have to go to school.

This Saturday morning Tiana had something on her mind.

"Shabazz?" she stopped and turned towards him.

"What's up T?"

"Am I pretty?"

"Yeah you're pretty."

"Am I as pretty as the other girls?" she asked.

"What girls?"

"The other girls here."

"You're way prettier than the other girls. As a matter of fact you're the prettiest girl here. Why you ask me that T?"

"Because none of the boys here mess with me."

"What do you mean, mess with you? They all know that if they mess with you I'll kick their ass."

"I don't mean mess with me in bad way. I mean in a good way."

"What good way?"

"Like the boys and girls who hold hands and kiss," she replied.

"That's what you want? You wanna hold hands and kiss a boy? What do you want, a boyfriend?"

"No! Well, I don't know."

Shabazz took hold of one of Tiana's hands, then he kissed her on her cheek.

"There. You happy now? You held hands with a boys and got kissed."

"That's not funny Shabazz!"

"I don't care if it's funny or not. You ain't gonna be messing with none of these niggas in here."

"Why not?"

"Cause they ain't shit. They be messing with all the girls they can, then they talk shit about them, and I ain't gonna let none of them fuck with you."

"Why haven't you ever tried to mess with none of the girls here?"

"You don't know what I do," he said defensively.

"Yes I do. You're with me all the time."

"I don't like any of these girls."

"Do you like me?"

The question took Shabazz by surprise.

"What do you mean?" he asked.

"You heard me. Do you like me?"

"Of course I like you. But not like that. And besides, you're my sister."

"I'm not your real sister."

"That's how you feel?" Shabazz asked her. Tiana could feel the hurt in his voice and she felt bad about what she had just said.

"I didn't mean it like that. I'm sorry. You are my real brother. You're my brother and my best friend and I love you. I just don't know why none of the boys try to talk to me. It makes me feel like I'm ugly or something."

"You're not ugly Tiana. You're the most beautiful girl I ever saw, and that's why I don't let anyone talk to you. I don't want nobody to hurt you. You're my little sister and I love you too. So word is bond, I'm gonna protect you as long as I can."

"Ok, thank you Shabazz," she said. Then she thought for a second and asked him another question.

"What does word is bond mean?"

"It means anything I say to you is like an unbreakable promise. It's the truth, and you can count on it. Have you not heard that your word shall be bond, regardless to whom or what? Yes, my word is bond, and bond means life, and I shall give my life before my word shall fail."

"What was that?" she questioned.

"What?"

"What you just said."

"It was part of my lessons."

"What lessons? School lessons?"

Shabazz laughed, but he also realized that in the past four years he had never really formally shared this part of his life with Tiana. Shabazz was a member of the Nation of Gods and Earths, better known as the Five Percenters. When he first arrived at Baychester he was befriended by an older brother who was a Five Percenter. The older brother taught Shabazz the teachings and lessons of the Five Percenters. The lessons originated in the Nation of Islam. Shabazz was intrigued by the science and history taught in the lessons and studied hard. The older brother gave Shabazz a Five Percenter name—an attribute. His birth name was Shabazz, but the older brother gave him the name, Noble Shabazz Allah Majestic. Shabazz studied under the older brother for three years until the older brother was released from Baychester. But before he left, he gave Shabazzz all of his lessons, and Shabazz studied on his own.

"No, not school lessons. It comes from the Five Percenter lessons. That's the eleventh degree of the 1-14 Lost Found Lesson Number One. It's one of our lessons."

"What's a Five Percenter?" she asked, very interested. Shabazz took a deep breath and told her the history of the Five Percenters. After he was done, she of course had more questions.

"So I'm God because I'm black?"

"No. You can't be God because you are a girl. You are a Goddess. But you have to have knowledge of self to be called a Goddess or an Earth."

"What is knowledge of self?" she asked.

"It's what you get when you study the lessons."

"Can you teach me?"

"Do you want me to?"

"If you don't mind. Please."

"Ok, but I have to give you a righteous name," he said.

"Ok!" Tiana beamed.

Shabazz gave Tiana the attribute Beloved I-Shine Earth and taught her the lessons. One of the most important being that one's word should always be bond regardless to whom or what. A lesson that Tiana lived by her entire life.

22

"Maybe she's in the house," Smurf said.

"How the hell is she in the house and her keys were left in her Lambo? I talked to her when she left the funeral. She was fine. She said she was going by her house and then she was coming back to the condo. I'm tellin' you, something is definitely up," Passion said. It had been two days since Mecca and Divinity's funeral and no one had heard a word from Tiana. Her black Lamborghini was parked outside of her mansion, but the keys were left inside. Passion was worried. She knew that Tiana could take care of herself, but she also knew that they weren't up against any ordinary enemies. And Passion had dealt with plenty of different enemies in her years.

Growing up on the streets of Brownsville, Brooklyn, Passion was definitely no stranger to violence and death. By the age of 13 Passion realized something about herself, and that was that she was beautiful. At 13 she had the body of a voluptuous 25 year old woman. It drew the attention of the neighborhood boys. Attention she didn't want. One of her younger friends had been raped by some of the boys in the neighborhood, and ended up killing herself by jumping out of the window in her 11th floor apartment after people were saying that it was her fault. That she wanted the boys to have sex with her. By the age of 14 Passion had already fought several of the boys who tried to have their way with her, and by the age of 15 she was in New York's most notorious juvenile detention center—Spofford.

Spofford was for juvenile boys and girls between the ages of seven and sixteen. It was meant to be a temporary holdover facility until you were sent to a more permanent designation within the juvenile justice system. Spofford looked like a large white medieval castle. It was built on a high hill in Hunts Point in the South Bronx. A tall wall surrounded the facility and security screens covered all of the windows. Spofford held over three hundred juveniles.

Passion was sent to Spofford for assault and manslaughter after three girls tried to jump her because they said that Passion felt that she was better than the other girls in the projects. Passion cut one of the girls in her face from her temple to her chin. One of the girls ran, but the third wasn't so lucky. Passion stabbed the third girl in her chest, puncturing one of her lungs in the process. The girl bled to death by the time the police and ambulance showed up. Passion was sitting on a bench next to the girl's body—smoking a cigarette.

The girl who ran from the scene testified that the three of them tried to jump Passion which was how Passion's charges were downgraded to manslaughter in the third degree and assault in the third. She did a year in Spofford and came home to a warrior's welcome.

Soon after Passion came home from Spofford, her and a few other girls started the Lady Decepticons—a brutally violent female street gang that was the sister gang to the Decepticons. The Decepticons were one of the most violent street gangs in New York at the time. The Lady Decepticons, or Lady Decepts as they were often called, tried to emulate their male counterparts. Passion was one of the original members of the Lady Decepts and undoubtedly one of the most ruthless. Passion had a blood stained two by four with nails sticking out of it that she liked to use often. When she didn't carry her two by four, she still had her brass knuckles.

Passion was surely not one to be underestimated or taken lightly. Throughout the years she had beaten three murder indictments. Witnesses would either disappear or just forget what they saw—out of fear of course. Over the years, Passion's reputation became well known, so when she approached Shabazz and told him she wanted to be on his team and get money. He didn't hesitate. He put her on Mecca and Divinity's team.

Passion had never let him down during times of war. But with the disappearance of Tiana, and the loss of so many people, Passion was starting to question herself and her skills.

****

Word was spreading quickly that Tiana was missing and it had people talking and speculating. If it wasn't for the keys and Tiana's purse that were left in the Murcielago in front of her house, the people at Brantz & Brantz would have figured that Tiana just took off. Dawit Burroughs also knew better once he heard about the keys.

But where did she go?

Her telephone was turned off, and all calls went straight to voicemail.

Victor Maldonado was furious when he heard the news. Even though there had been tension between him and Tiana, he still loved her, and he didn't want her hurt.

"Who are her enemies?" he asked his daughter Victoria.

"I don't know poppy. Tiana's business is her business. She doesn't share things like that with me," she replied. "Not anymore anyway," she added with a bit of resentment in her voice.

"What about her people? Don't they know who her enemies are?"

"Poppy, most of Tiana's people are dead. She just buried her two girls Mecca and Divinity. The few people that she had around her that are still alive, I didn't know them that well," Victoria said. She was right. She didn't really know Smurf, Young God or Passion. It seemed that her and Tiana were starting to grow apart. Especially after Tiana was acquitted of murder. Victoria felt that she was losing her best friend.

"Well look mami, if you hear of anything, let me know, and if I can help in any way I will. Until we know she is safe, we must keep Tiana in our prayers, that God returns her home safely."

"Yes Poppy."

****

"Who's on the Brantz case captain?" asked Detective Santana as he walked into his captain's office at the Special Crimes Unit's homicide division.

"How should I know?" asked Captain Pendleton. "This is homicide, not missing persons. When her body shows up, then ask me that question. Until then, solve some murders and stay out of other people's shit."

Captain Pendleton was still bitter over losing Tiana's murder case, after the key piece of evidence went missing and the only witness in the case was gunned down.

"What the hell are you worried about her for anyway?" the captain asked.

"I'm still on her husband's murder. I just saw the story on the news and was curious that's all."

"Well, be curious about getting your stats up and leave that woman be. Maybe we'll all get lucky and her body will show up in a dumpster somewhere."

For some reason Santana didn't see that happening. He went to his desk, picked up the phone, and dialed a number.

"Brantz and Brantz," said the woman's voice who answered.

23

Tiana opened her eyes and looked around the room. She blinked, hoping that she was having a nightmare. She couldn't move her body much because she was bound to some sort of bench on an incline so that she was almost sitting straight up. She could move her head though, and what she saw shocked her.

She saw heads.

Scattered all over the floor, in different degrees of decomposition, were the heads of all of the members of her crew that she had lost. She even saw the heads of the twins.

The smell in the room was unbearable and it stung her eyes. She couldn't feel any pain in her body, and as far as she could tell, other than being tied up to the bench she was otherwise unharmed.

So far anyway.

Tiana was under no illusion that she might somehow escape her present predicament. Seeing the decapitated heads all over the place really drove that home for her. So she closed her eyes and leaned her head back, accepting the destiny that lay ahead. Whatever it may be.

Every now and then she would open her eyes and look around the room. She noticed that the only window in the room was painted over black. Other than the heads strewn all over the floor, there was nothing else in the room from what she could see. She looked at Scientific's decapitated head and mouthed the words "I'm sorry".

Scientific was a true warrior and a general in her army. It was Scientific who made it possible for her and Divine to relax when they all arrived in Atlanta after the war with Cashmere. Scientific, Mecca and Divinity took control, and the money flowed like never before.

Tiana's thoughts were interrupted by the door opening. In walked two Vietnamese men carrying guns. Behind them entered Sue and then Chen Ayngen.

"Hello counselor. I'm glad to see that you are up. I hope that the stun gun wasn't too painful. I would hate for you think I was a barbarian."

"Where in the world would I get that idea from?" replied Tiana, looking at the heads on the floor.

"Oh, I apologize about the mess," said Chen, waving at the floor and smiling sadistically. "But the maid and Sue just didn't get along well and she just up and quit. It's so hard to find good help, don't you agree? Well of course you do. Look at all of your help." He waved at the floor.

"How do you know so much about me and my organization?" asked Tiana. She was hoping she wasn't betrayed by one of her own, just as Shabazz was years before. She was hopeful but doubtful at the same time.

"Well, since you must know." He walked across the room, looked around, then picked up a head by its ear. It was one of the twins. "It was one of these two. The ones who look alike. After days of being pumped with heroin, and then witnessing the murder of his brother, he was happy to discuss the inner workings of your organization with me. Of course I killed him anyway, but I suspect that he already knew that. He died in shame and addicted to heroin."

"Why?" Tiana asked.

"You already know why. I told you, you owe me. You stole from me, and I don't take kindly to being stolen from."

"I didn't steal a thing from you. That heroin was TC's as far as I knew. I took it from him the night I blew his head away."

"Yes, well, you may have taken it from him, but it belonged to me. Until he paid for it it was still my property. So you took what was mine."

"You could have called me," she said, "before you started killing my people."

"I thought about that, but I have a certain flair for dramatics. Besides that, Sue was bored and needed some excitement. So I decided to send you the message. But you didn't heed my words. Instead you killed Benny. I'm assuming that Benny is dead, by the condition in which his female friend was left. Would I be correct in assuming that Benny is dead?"

"Yes."

"And his body?"

"It could be anywhere. I don't get involved in disposal."

"But you killed him personally?"

"Indeed," she answered coldly.

"Such a beautiful woman, but yet so deadly. So cold. Why?"

"It's a long story."

"Ah, and time is a luxury that unfortunately you no longer have counselor."

"Whatever. Do what you're gonna do and let's get this over with. I'm sure you've got other things to do," Tiana stated defiantly.

"Very spunky for a woman about to die."

"Fuck you! Why did you kill my husband?" Tiana spat.

"Your husband unfortunately…" He stopped in mid-sentence as the window shattered. He looked down at his chest where the first bullet hit him and touched his now blood soaked shirt. As the second bullet struck him, the door to the room burst open.

In rushed Young God and four other brothers along with Passion. Before the two armed Vietnamese could react Young God cut them down with two bursts from the MP-40 submachine gun he carried.

"Don't move bitch!" yelled Passion as she pushed her .45mm Hardballer into Sue's face. As Chen fell to the ground bleeding to death, one of the four brothers—who were unknown to Tiana—put a bullet in his head from the .40 caliber Glock he was carrying.

"Are you ok?" asked Young God as he untied Tiana.

"I'm fine now. Sure took you guys long enough though," Tiana joked.

"That nigga Smurf wanted to make a big entrance."

"Smurf?" Tiana asked, looking around. "Where's Smurf?"

"Across the street." Young God went to the window and threw up his fingers in a "peace" sign.

"Across the street?"

"Yeah. Where do you think that first shot came from? He'll be here in a second. I just gave him the sign that we got you."

Once Tiana was untied she gave Young God a quick hug. Then she looked over at Passion, who had the gun to the back of Sue's head. Sue was standing facing one of the walls. Tiana walked up to Passion and gave her a kiss on the cheek.

"You did good girl," Tiana said. "Thank you."

That's when Smurf burst into the room carrying an M-76 Smith and Wesson submachine gun.

"What the fuck did I miss!" he said, waving the automatic weapon around. That's when the smell hit him and he saw the heads all over the floor. "Damn, these motha fuckas are sick fo' real! You good T?" he asked.

"Yes, I'm good Smurf," she replied as she gave him a quick hug also.

"But I'll bet you'll feel better with this in your hand," he said as he pulled a Desert Eagle from his waistband and handed it to her.

"Look at you," she said, smiling as she took hold of her favorite weapon. "On some commando, S.W.A.T-type shit. What if you would have missed that first shot?"

"I never miss," Smurf replied proudly.

"How did you know where he was standing? The window is blacked out," Tiana asked, puzzled.

"Thermal imaging scope on my rifle. I could see everything like it was daylight."

"Well thank you. You did good. All of you."

Tiana walked back over to where Passion stood with Sue. She put her gun to Sue's head.

"Wait Tiana," said Passion. "Let me have her. I wanna check her fight game out. Woman to woman. Fighter to fighter."

Tiana smiled. She liked the idea. She searched Sue real quick to make sure she didn't have a weapon hidden on her. When she was satisfied that Sue was clean, she backed away from them. Smurf and Young God had already moved the heavy bench that Tiana was tied to from the middle of the floor.

"She's all yours girl," Tiana said. "Handle your business."

Passion backed away from Sue very carefully and handed her gun to Tiana.

Sue turned around and smiled at Passion.

"Don't smile bitch. Bring it," Passion said, positioning herself in readiness for an attack.

She didn't have to wait long.

Sue's right foot left the floor with lightning speed aimed at Passion's face.

Passion blocked the blow with two hands.

Sue tried again, and again Passion blocked it easily.

"That all you got bitch?" Passion said and hit Sue with a quick right hook.

Sue backed up a step then threw a front snap kick into Passion's midsection. A left hook of her own grazed Passion's chin and Passion countered with a three piece combination—two right jabs and a left hook.

Sue was dazed.

Passion followed up with a hard punch straight into Sue's solar plexus, knocking the wind out of her.

"Yeah, that's what the fuck I'm talking about! Do that bitch!" yelled Smurf.

Sue went down on one knee, but she was back up quickly. She charged at Passion, but Passion side stepped her and punched her in the back of her head. Then Passion grabbed a handful of Sue's hair and pulled her to her and began pummeling Sue's face repeatedly. Sue tried hitting Passion, but her blows had no effect. Then Passion grabbed Sue's head with both hands and smashed Sue's face into her knee. Sue fell to the ground and Passion kicked her in the face.

"Ain't shit without your knives are you bitch!" Passion said as she stood over Sue, kicking and punching her in her ribs and back. Sue was trying to crawl away, but with each foot she moved Passion kicked her harder. Sue couldn't escape Passion's attack, but she was trying.

She crawled over to where the body of Chen lay in a pool of blood. She tried to pull Chen's body over her to shield herself from Passion's blows.

Before anyone knew what was going on a shot rang out in the room.

Passion was hit in her chest. She was dead 3 seconds later.

While Sue was trying to pull Chen's body over her to shield herself from Passion's attack, no one could see her pull the gun that she knew Chen kept in his pocket. Not until it was too late.

One second after Sue shot Passion, three shots erupted in the room. They came from the door.

Standing in the open doorway, holding a .357 Colt Lawman pointed at Sue's now dead body, was Detective Edwin Santana.

24

After Detective Santana killed Sue, he told them all to leave. He said that he would deal with the police when they arrived. But he made Tiana promise to come see him the next morning at his house. He said that he needed to talk to her about something very important.

Tiana agreed.

Then she went to the condo in Stone Mountain with Smurf and Young God to try and piece things together. She couldn't believe that Passion was dead too. Another casualty of the life she wanted so badly to separate herself from.

The first thing she did when she got to the condo was to take a long shower. Smurf ordered some pizza and also some pizza because he figured Tiana would be hungry.

And she was.

After her shower, Tiana couldn't stop shoveling food into her mouth. She ate two slices of pizza and was on her third when she finally slowed down long enough to talk.

"How the hell did you guys find me?" she asked first.

"With this," replied Smurf, holding up an iPhone.

"With your phone?"

"No, with your phone," answered Smurf.

"What do you mean?"

"Your iPhone led us to you. It's got a built in GPS locator. Your girl Kemya hipped us to it. We were just glad your shit wasn't turned off."

"I put it on sleep for the funeral. They snatched me right after the funeral in front of my house. I never had a chance to take it off of sleep mode, and surprisingly, they left it in my pocket."

"No, luckily. If they would've shut your shit off, you would've been stuck like motha fuckin' Chuck," said Smurf.

"And who were the four new faces? I've never seen them before," asked Tiana.

"Just some local cats out of Decatur who was buying weight from Young God and them before all the bullshit jumped off. They aight. Just some young, hungry soldiers."

"What do I owe them?" she asked.

"You don't owe them shit. They did that on the strength of Sci. They was eatin' good off that nigga. They miss him. I know they still tryna eat though so I broke 'em off anyway."

"Well, the good thing is that this is all over with now. I'm gonna get some rest and plan my next move." Tiana grabbed another slice of mushroom and cheese pizza and started down the hall. Then she stopped and turned around.

"Hey," she said, "where's my Lamborghini?"

Smurf stood up and reached into his pocket. He pulled out her keys and lightly tossed them to her.

"That motha fucka rides smooth too," he said, smiling. "It's parked in the back."

Tiana looked at the initial. The "T" that Dawit Burroughs gave her. It represented her freedom. And she was about to take it.

"Thanks Smurf," she said.

Then she want to sleep.

25

In the morning, the first thing Tiana did was to make some phone calls. The morning news carried a story about the events of the night before. Their story was so far from the truth that Tiana had to laugh. Detective Santana sure did tell a tall tale. She hoped he didn't get himself into any trouble.

She called Kemya at the office.

"Brantz and Brantz." Kemya answered the phone.

"Well hello young lady."

"Ms. Brantz!" Kemya yelled. "Oh my God, it's so good to hear your voice! Are you ok?"

"Yes I'm fine Kemya. Just a little tired. But we'll get together and I'll tell you all about it. I promise. The reason I'm calling is to say thank you for your involvement. Smurf told me that it was you who alerted him to my GPS locator."

"Actually Ms. Brantz, it wasn't me."

"What? I don't understand. He told me that it was you."

"I was the one who called him, but that's because Detective Santana had called me and suggested the GPS thing. I bought the iPhone and showed Smurf how to locate you."

"Detective Santana huh."

"Yes ma'am."

"Ok. Well thank you Kemya. Tell Anthony and Roger and the rest of the staff I said hello. I'll call you later ok."

"Ok Ms. Brantz."

Tiana hung the phone up. Now she had even more questions for Detective Santana. She called him and said that she would be at his house around noon. Then she called Dawit Burroughs to let him know that she was ok. She called Vickie, but got her voicemail. Vickie was in court, so Tiana left her a message.

The last call Tiana made was to a travel agent. She booked a one way flight to the Cape Verdean Islands. She was going to get away for a while and even though she had no living family that she knew about, she did know that her father was black Portuguese and Cape Verdean, so she wanted to see where her heritage was. She didn't know how long she planned to stay, and that was why she booked the flight one way.

Her flight was 3 days away.

****

Tiana pulled Lamborghini Murcielago into the driveway. It was a small one-story home located in the historic section of Union City, just south of College Park. When she pulled up, the front door opened and Detective Santana stepped onto the front porch in a pair of jeans and a black T-shirt. When the driver's side door lifted and Tiana got out, Santana laughed and shook his head.

"Do you drive anything that doesn't cost two hundred grand or better?" he asked.

"Why would I?" she replied. "And look at you in your jeans and T-shirt. Chillin' are we?" she asked, following him into the house.

"Well actually, I've been suspended pending an investigation over what happened last night. They just didn't buy the story I fed them."

Santana told his superiors that he received an anonymous tip that someone was being held captive in a house, and he was in the vicinity of the house when he received the call so he decided to check it out himself. As he approached the door he heard a gunshot, so he burst in the door and was forced to shoot a gun-wielding woman. He couldn't explain how the window was shattered or who killed the three men in the room.

Basically his story was full of too many holes, and internal affairs got involved quickly. They asked him for his gun and badge pending a full investigation.

"I'm sorry to hear that detective," Tiana said, sitting at his kitchen table. "Can I ask you why you even gave a damn?"

"Because even though I know that you're no Mother Theresa, I also don't think you're a monster either. I think you're just a victim of a series of circumstances."

"Is that right detective? And where did you earn your psychology degree?"

"On the streets."

"Well, just so that you know, and of course, not admitting any guilt to any crime, I have chosen my own paths. Certain events or sets of certain circumstances may have contributed to my decision making over the years, but ultimately, I choose my own destiny."

"So you chose to be kidnapped and almost killed," he asked.

"Of course not, but that was an unfortunate event that took place as a result of my past actions."

"Can I ask what that was all about."

"You can ask, but you know I can't tell you. Suspended or not, you are still a detective to me. But you can tell me what it is that was so important that you needed to talk to me in person."

"I'll be right back. Let me get my files," he said, leaving the room to go to his office. He was back in a half a minute with a file in his hand. He sat down across from Tiana.

"Ok, let me start at the beginning. Remember I told you that the shots that killed your husband came from a mile away from the scene."

"Yes."

"I also told you that according to ballistic reports, the slugs taken from your husband's body were determined to have come from a very expensive sniper rifle, the Belgian FLN automatic rifle model 5-31. The serial number is 08457052."

"What? How can you know that?" Tiana asked.

"Because this," Santana took a picture and slid it across the table to Tiana, "is the weapon that killed your husband."

Tiana looked at the picture.

"You mean a rifle like this one?"

"No. Not like that one. That is the actual weapon that fired the shots that killed your husband."

"How do you know that?"

Detective Santana looked at another page of notes.

"About three weeks ago, in a joint operation, the New York offices of the FBI, ATF, S.W.A.T, and NYPD raided the house of known drug dealers. Six men were arrested, along with thirteen weapons, drugs and money. One of the weapons seized was the Belgian FLN that killed your husband. Now, you also remember that I told you that not many people could have made that shot."

"I remember." Tiana's curiosity was killing her.

"Ok, well one of the men who were arrested in that raid in New York just happens to have a history of being an expert marksman, and he could easily have made that shot. So, since he was arrested in the house that the weapon was seized in, I think it's safe to assume we could put two and two together and come up with this man." He pushed an 8 x 10 photo over to Tiana. "This is the man who killed your husband."

Tiana picked up the photo and stared at it.

His name was Sabastian Gustavo.

"Where is he right now?" she asked.

"The Federal Detention Center in Manhattan. When the Feds get done with him, then we get him. But not before. In other words, we may never get him," he said.

"I've got to go detective." Tiana stood up to leave.

"What are you gonna do Brantz?" he asked as she walked away.

"What I know to do." Tiana replied as she got into the Lamborghini and pulled away.

26

Tiana left Detective Santana's house and went straight home. Every time she slowed down or stopped for a light she would stare at the photo of Sabastian Gustavo that was on the passenger seat. She stared into his eyes. All of the hatred she had ever felt in her life was on the verge of exploding within her.

She pulled up to her house and got out of the car, leaving the door up. She went into the house and was back out in 2 minutes.

30 minutes later she was parked in front of the home of Victor Maldonado. She turned the engine off and stuffed the keys into her pocket. Then she picked the photo up and got out of the car. She rang the doorbell and ten seconds later Victor's brother, Manuel, opened the door.

"Tiana, como esta?" he said.

"Is Victor in his office Manuel?"

"Si."

"Ok."

Thpt...thpt...thpt...

Manuel never saw the silenced Desert Eagle in Tiana's hand. But he definitely felt the 3 .9mm slugs that tore through his heart.

He didn't feel them for long though.

Manuel fell to the ground and Tiana walked over his body as she pushed the front door shut behind her. Tiana walked down the hall until she got to Victor's office. The door was cracked a few inches and she could see Victor at his desk, looking down at something on the computer monitor. She pushed the door open with the barrel of her gun.

Sensing her presence, Victor looked up.

The first thing he noticed was the Desert Eagle in her right hand. She raised the gun and pointed it at his face.

"Tiana?" he said calmly.

"Why Victor?" she asked, walking towards him, not taking the gun off of him.

"Where is Manuel?" Victor asked, looking towards the door.

"Why Victor?" she asked again, ignoring his question.

"Where is my brother?" Victor asked again, raising his voice.

"Fuck Manuel! He's dead Victor!" Tiana yelled.

Victor stood up and raised a gun of his own, but before he could get a clear shot at Tiana, she pulled the trigger.

Thpt...

One shot into Victor's shoulder was all that was needed to make him drop his gun on the desk. Tiana walked up to the desk and grabbed the gun. She threw it across the room. Then she put the photo of Sabastian Gustavo on the desk.

Victor looked at the face on the photo and sat down, holding his shoulder.

"Why did you kill my husband Victor?" She had both of her Desert Eagles out now.

Both pointed at Victor's head.

When Detective Santana showed Tiana the photo of the man who he said killed her husband, she recognized him immediately. She recognized him despite the fact that she hadn't seen his face in over 2 years.

She knew that he was a killer. She knew that he was an explosives expert. At the time, she didn't know he was also an expert sniper, but it made sense that he would be. It was around 2 and a half years ago that Sabastian Gustavo slit Miriam Adebisi's throat from ear to ear.

Two hours later, he pushed Lazette Adebisi into the path of an oncoming F train.

Later that night Tiana killed Cashmere Adebisi while Sabastian Gustavo, along with four other Columbians, and Divine and Scientific killed all of Cashmere's bodyguards, ending a drug war that had claimed the lives of well over a hundred people in New York.

Miriam Adebisi was Cashmere's mother.

Lazette was his sister.

Sabastian Gustavo was sent to help Tiana in her war with Cashmere Adebisi after her brother Shabazz was killed in that war.

Sabastian was sent to help Tiana along with 4 other Columbian hit men.

They were sent by Victor Maldonado.

"I'm only going to ask you this question one more time," she said as she leveled both weapons at Victor's face. "Why did you kill my husband Victor?"

"I had no choice," said Victor, sadly.

"What the hell did you mean you had no choice?"

"I had no choice. I was losing you. After all that I had done for you over the years, you were leaving me."

"I wanted a better life Victor. I was pregnant. I wanted a family."

"But you forgot that it was me who gave you your wings. Your start in this life."

"But I didn't want this life anymore."

Ignoring her, Victor continued.

"Then when they tried to take your freedom, you showed no appreciation to me for saving you. You never even expressed gratitude or bestowed a simple thank you, even though it was I who had your witness killed and made your evidence disappear. Instead, all you spoke about was leaving."

"So you killed my husband!" she yelled.

"He was taking you away from everything we built together."

"We were trying to build something of our own! A family!"

"We were a family!"

"No! We were drug dealers! I don't want this anymore!"

"But you chose this life Tiana!" Victor was standing now.

"But I don't want it anymore Victor."

"You can't just walk away. It's not that simple."

"Watch me Victor."

And with tears in her eyes Tiana empties both guns into Victor's head and chest.

Thpt...thpt...thpt...thpt...thpt...thpt...thpt...thpt...thpt...thpt

She kept pulling the triggers until the bullets stopped coming.

Click...click...click...click...

"Nooooooooo!!" The scream came from behind Tiana.

Then came the gunshots.

Boom...boom...boom...

The first 2 shots hit Tiana in her back. The third shot missed. She spun around as she went down.

Victoria was running across the room with her father's gun in her hand.

"Poppy!" she screamed.

Victor's body was sprawled across his desk in a pool of blood. Victoria ran to him and cradled his body, crying.

"You killed my poppy!" she yelled at Tiana, holding her father's dead body and shaking.

"He killed...Divine...Vickie," Tiana whispered. "I'm so sorry."

Blood was trickling out of the side of her mouth.

"You killed my poppy," Vickie repeated. She picked the gun up again and walked over to Tiana.

"You killed my poppy," she said one more time, standing over Tiana.

"You killed my poppy." Vickie lifted the gun and pointed it at Tiana's head.

"Vickie...he killed my..."

Boom!

Tiana never finished her sentence.

Her face was covered in blood.

But it wasn't her blood.

Victoria dropped the gun that was in her hand. Then she fell over, half of her head missing.

Standing at the door was Stacey Aller.

In her hand was Manuel's Browning .9mm automatic.

Stacey Aller was Tiana's cellie when Tiana was being held at the Atlanta City Detention Center for the murder of Trey Clark. Tiana took an instant liking to Stacey, who was charged with armed robbery. After hearing Stacey's story, Tiana asked Victoria to look into her case and to see what could be done about getting her 4 year old daughter

Sierra back. Sierra was taken by Child Protective Services and placed into foster care after Stacey was arrested.

Victoria was able to get Stacey's charges reduced from armed robbery to second degree accessory. She was given time served and placed on two years of unsupervised probation.

As for her daughter. If Stacey was able to prove that she could take care of her daughter financially, then Child Protective Services agreed that Stacey could have her back.

So Tiana and Divine set up a bank account for Stacey. The account was set up to distribute a check to Stacey in the amount of three thousand dollars every month for three years. On top of that, Tiana asked Divine to give Stacey a home. Divine, who owned his own real estate company, had a 3-bedroom home in Marietta. The house was placed in Stacey's daughter's name.

They also gave Stacey a brand new SUV and over 15 thousand dollars in gift cards and certificates to various stores all over Atlanta.

Tiana gave Stacey a new life for her and her daughter.

Stacey had been waiting to talk to Tiana for a few weeks but could never get a hold of her. When she heard the news about Tiana's disappearance, she was really worried. She knew that Tiana had some strong people around her. She saw that when two of her girls got themselves locked up on purpose, just so that they could get to the unit Tiana was being held in to beat a girl half to death for giving Tiana a black eye.

Still, she was worried.

When she heard that Tiana was safe after her kidnapping, she decided to go to Tiana's house. When she pulled around the corner, Tiana was driving by. She looked so distressed that she didn't even notice Stacey.

So Stacey followed the black Lamborghini.

When Tiana got out at Victor Maldonado's house, she had such a serious look on her face that Stacey decided to approach her when she came out of the house. Stacey made a call to her babysitter to check on her daughter Sierra.

That's why she didn't see Tiana shoot Manuel at the front door. By the time she looked up Tiana was already inside the house with the door closed.

What she did see was her lawyer, Victoria Maldonado, arrive at the house. But when Victoria opened the front door, Stacey could tell that something was wrong. Victoria rushed into the house and left the front door open.

A few seconds later she heard 3 gunshots. So she jumped out of her vehicle and ran towards the house. At the door she saw a man dead inside of the house. Sticking out of his waist she could see the butt of a gun.

She reached down and took hold of it. That's when she heard the voice coming from down the hall, and decided to follow the voice.

When she arrived at the open door to Victor Maldonado's office, she saw Tiana on the ground. Victoria was standing over her with a gun in her hand. Then Victoria lifted the gun, pointing it directly at Tiana's head.

Without thinking twice, Stacey aimed the gun in her hand at Victoria and pulled the trigger.

Boom!

She hit Victoria in her head right above her ear. When Victoria fell over, Stacey ran to where Tiana lay. With the blood that was all over Tiana, Stacey thought she was dead.

"Tiana!" she screamed.

"Stacey...what are...you..." Tiana's breathing was very heavy and labored. Even though she was covered in blood, Vickie's blood, her own blood was oozing out of her mouth.

"Shhhh...don't talk Tiana. You're gonna be ok."

"Stacey...listen..." Tiana coughed.

Tiana slowly moved her left hand and dug into her pocket. She pulled out her keys. She undid the clasp that held the "T"-shaped memory stick on her key chain. She grabbed Stacey's hand and placed the "T" into her hand.

"What's this Tiana?" Stacey asked looking down at the "T" that Tiana had just placed in her hand.

"It's a...computer...mem...memory st..." Tiana could hardly talk and she was losing a lot of blood.

"A memory stick?" Stacey asked. "For a computer?"

"Yes. Bank accounts..."

"Whose bank accounts Tiana?"

"Yours...you and Sierra...passcode is..."

Tiana went into a coughing fit, spitting blood everywhere.

"Passcode is...Lady Scarface..."

Tiana coughed one more time, sighed, then closed her eyes.

****

One month later...

The Federal Detention Center in Manhattan was one of the most secure facilities in New York. Over the years it held some of the most notorious men and women in New York's crime history.

Today it held Sabastian Gustavo.

Gustavo was being held on multiple gun and drug charges. The chances were that he would never see the streets again.

He was returning to his cell from the shower. When he walked into his cell he was grabbed from behind in a choke hold. Then an arm reached around him and plunged a knife into his chest over and over again.

Gustavo dropped to the ground.

The man grabbed Gustavo by his hair and looked into his eyes. He spit a single edged razor out of his mouth and caught it in his hand.

He cut Gustavo's throat.

"A little present," he whispered into Gustavo's ear. "From Lady Scarface." He laughed as he walked away.

PART TWO

LS4

1

Little Supreme was young, but up and coming. He was 25 years old and had already done 4 years in the Feds. When he got locked up he was a Vice Lord. While on the inside he became a Five Percenter. Now he ran his own set of Hidden Valley Bloods in the Hidden Valley neighborhood of Charlotte, North Carolina.

Supreme was 5 foot 2 and all muscle. He feared nothing and no one, and was quick to pull his gun to protect his money, his hood or his reputation. Not only did he have a short man complex, but someone had circulated a rumor when he was first arrested by the Feds that he was hot—meaning he was cooperating with the Feds. He spent his entire 4 years defending his reputation. He never did cooperate with the Feds; it was just an unfortunate coincidence that 2 days after he was arrested, a sweep was done in his neighborhood and 23 Vice Lords were picked up with charges which ranged from drugs to guns. Even though Supreme's name never appeared on anyone's paperwork, the question and doubt was always in the air.....or in hushed whispers.

Most of the Hidden Valley Bloods under Supreme were young. Most were well under 18 years old. They were from the South Side of Hidden Valley. The North Side Hidden Valley Bloods didn't really deal with the South Side Bloods. It was a beef that went back many years when Big Mike, an OG California Blood first came to Charlotte and laid down the first Blood Set. That was when Hidden Valley was a Vice Lord hood. By the time Supreme got out of the Feds, everyone had turned Blood. The hood first split because all the Vice Lords didn't wanna submit, so the North was Blood and the South was Vice Lords. But eventually the South bowed down. Supreme gained the respect of the young Bloods on the strength that he had done Fed time.

Supreme and his young Bloods had the South Side of Hidden Valley flooded with crack cocaine. 24 hours a day, you could ride down any number of streets and purchase from five dollars' worth to a hundred-dollar slab. Nothing bigger. There was not much competition since the Bloods all shared in every dime made. And all money went to

Supreme. He controlled the flow of drugs because it was his connection.

His connection came from a Jamaican named Dookie that he met while in jail. Dookie liked Supreme's heart, and he told him that when he got out he should look him up. So when Supreme got out, the first thing he did was find Dookie. He gave Supreme five kilos on consignment and Supreme never looked back.

In the past few weeks though, Supreme's people had been hearing rumors that a new crew was floating around. Good prices and better product. But Supreme wasn't really concerned. The new crew could have all of Charlotte.

But the South Side of Hidden Valley belonged to him.

"Yo, I'm comin' to holla at you tomorrow..." Supreme was standing outside of his Lincoln Navigator talking to Dookie. "I'm probably gonna need about 15 o' dem thangs. I'll let you know fo' sho' in the mornin'."

Supreme's right hand man, Sizzle, was standing a few feet away from Supreme, talking on his own phone when he felt the spray of something wet on his face.

"Oh fuck!...Shit!" He said when he turned around and looked at Supreme. Half of Supreme's face was gone. A bloody mess was all over the side of the Navigator and on Sizzle's face.

Supreme dropped his phone, and fell to the ground.

Dead.

Sizzle jumped into the SUV and pulled his .40 caliber Glock. He never heard the shot that killed Supreme, but he expected more.

None came.

The streets were quiet.

About a half a mile away, Smurf was putting his H&K G-3 SG-1 rifle back into its case. He took the shot from the back of his Cadillac Escalade.

One shot. One kill.

"Let's be out yo," he said to Young God as he climbed into the Escalade and pulled off, "Run This Town" by Rihanna and Jay Z blasting from the speakers.

Hidden Valley was about to be under new management.

****

Soon after Tiana's funeral, Smurf and Young God did the only thing that they felt they could do. They gathered all of the drugs and money from the two stash spots the crews maintained. With everyone else dead, they felt that they should inherit everything. They left Atlanta with almost 400 kilos and a few million in cash.

Riding with Smurf and Young God were the four men who helped to rescue Tiana from Chen. They recognized a winning team and figured that wherever Smurf and Young God landed, they were gonna lock some shit down, and they wanted to be a part of that from the ground floor.

They rode in 3 vehicles. Smurf's brand new Escalade, a Range Rover and a Yukon Denali. They ended up in Charlotte, NC on account of one of the 4 new members of the team knew a hustler who was gettin' money in Charlotte, and he figured something could be worked out between them.

Once they arrived in Charlotte, a meeting was arranged and terms were discussed on how Smurf and his crew could have a small piece of Charlotte for themselves.

The piece that was offered was the South Side of Hidden Valley.

Who was offering?

Big Mike.

Big Mike said that they could have South Hidden Valley, but they would have to take out the existing competition. A young brother name Little Supreme.

"Done," smirked Smurf.

They also could never cross the line into the North Side.

So, Smurf and the crew laid low in a small apartment complex called the Merriam Arms and let Big Mike spread the word that there may be a new crew in town. He also put Smurf onto some young hungry cats who may be trying to put in some soldier work. He said they couldn't work for him because they weren't Bloods. That was another problem Big Mike had with Supreme. Supreme hired anyone to work for him. Big Mike only hired Bloods. And even though he liked the prices that Smurf could offer, Big Mike was loyal to Blood all the way, and he only copped from his Blood connect.

Smurf knew in his heart that eventually he would have to take out Big Mike. But before he did that he wanted to familiarize himself with who's who in Charlotte.

2

When Shaquan Butler walked into Club Black Ties, all eyes were on him. But why wouldn't they be? His clothes and jewelry ensemble cost more than most of the cars in the parking lot. Actually all eyes were on Q when he pulled up in his 300 thousand dollar Lamborghini Murcielago Roadster. He was definitely used to all the attention though. All eyes were always on him.

For years, Shaquan, AKA Quan or Q had been "that nigga" in the Raleigh-Durham area. His heroin empire kept the surrounding cities like Charlotte, Greensboro, Winston-Salem, and Wilmington on a serious dope fiend nod. But Raleigh and Durham were where he called home. He rested his head in Raleigh and his mother had a beautiful colonial style mini mansion that he bought for her in Durham 3 years ago.

Yvette Butler was Shaquan's mother and only family. Due to complications during his birth, she wasn't able to have any other children, so Quan remained an only child. He never knew his father, and since his mother never spoke about him, Quan felt he must not have been worth the breath it took to talk about him—so he never asked.

It was always just him and his mom, and he was ok with that. As he got older, Q grew tired of watching his mother struggle to raise him with at least decent clothes and food. Sometimes she wouldn't even eat for fear that there wouldn't be enough food for him. When Q got old enough, he took to the streets and vowed to take care of her. No matter what was going on in his life, unless he was out of town on business, Q made it his business to see her every day.

Club Black Ties was where Q went to wind down. It was a more laid back, mature setting, and just to get in you had to be known as a serious factor in the economic underworld of the Triangle area.

"Q, what's poppin' fam?" Said the large bald headed brother at the door as he undid the velvet rope to allow Q into the club.

"Maintaining Malik. What's good with you?" Q responded as he pulled out a roll of money, pulled off a hundred dollar bill and slipped it into the brother's hand.

"Same ole, same ole."

As Q made his way through the club and to his regular table in the VIP section upstairs, he couldn't take his eyes off the bar.

Sitting at the bar, all alone, was one of the most beautiful women he had ever seen in his life.

When he was finally into the VIP section and comfortably seated at his table, the waitress rushed over.

"Hey Q," she said. "Henny and Coke?"

"Yeah, that's cool."

"I got you coming," she said as she rushed away.

The waitress returned in less than 2 minutes with a double shot of Hennessey with Coke on the rocks.

"There you go Q," she said as she placed the drink on a napkin in front of him. "Anything else?"

"No, not yet," Q replied. "You got a pen on you?"

"I got one right here," she said as she took a pen out of her back pocket. Q grabbed a napkin off the stack on his table.

"Gimme about 5 minutes and come back, ok? Imma need you to do something for me." He gave her a fifty dollar bill and waved off the change.

"Thank you. I'll be back in a little bit," she said as she turned and left.

Q began writing something on the napkin. When he was done, he caught the waitress's attention and waved her back over to his table.

"Do me a favor ma. You see the female in the black dress sitting at the end of the bar?"

"The real pretty one?"

"Yeah, that's the one. I need you to find out what she's drinking."

"She's drinking Patrone Silver," the waitress interrupted.

"Cool. Bring her a bottle of Patrone Silver on me and give her this note." He handed her the napkin.

"Do you need me to wait for a response?"

"No. I'll get a response if she's gonna give one."

"Ok."

The waitress went straight to the bartender, grabbed a bottle of Patron Silver and walked it over to the woman in the black dress.

"I didn't order a..." the woman started to say when the waitress sat the bottle in front of her, but she was cut off.

"It was sent," the waitress said. "I'm guessing this should explain it." She handed her the note and walked off.

She stared at the bottle and the note, puzzled. Then she read the note:

"No disrespect intended, but when I walked in a few minutes ago I couldn't help but notice that you are the most breathtaking woman in the club. I also couldn't help but notice that you are sitting alone. I would be honored if you would join me in the VIP section. If not, then please accept the drink with my apologies, and have a nice evening. Q"

She read the note once more, then she turned her body so that she could see towards the VIP section. Since she had her back the door while she was sitting at the bar, she didn't notice him when he walked in.

When Q saw her looking in his direction he lifted his glass and nodded his head slightly.

She nodded back at him and thought to herself, "what the hell." She finished the drink she was on, grabbed hold of the bottle of Patron Silver, her purse, and made her way to the VIP section.

As she approached his table, Q stood up to better admire her class and beauty. She wore a strapless Dolce & Gabbana dress that ended right in the middle of her thighs and hugged her flawless 36-22-38 figure perfectly. The matching Christian Louboutin 5-inch stilettos she wore complimented the dress just right.

"Hello," he said as he pulled out a chair for her. "I'm glad you decided to join me."

"Thank you," she said as she took her seat. "Do you make it a habit of always sending a 400 dollar bottle to invite a woman to your table?" She asked, holding up the bottle that Q had sent to her.

"Actually, no. Usually I come here to be alone. I turn my phone off, have a few drinks, and basically just maintain. I like the atmosphere here. And the music's real mellow. Calming. But as much as I come in here, I've never noticed you in here before. And as beautiful as you are, I would have remembered."

"Well, thank you for the compliment. The reason you've never seen me in here is because I've never been here. I just moved in this area. So..." She held up Q's note. "Is your name really 'Q'?"

"It's short for Shaquan. But most people just call me Q. And what's your name?" He asked as he poured her a fresh drink from the bottle of Patrone Silver.

"It's April. Short for April. But people just call me April. Pleased to meet you Shaquan." She held her hand out and Q took hold of it softly.

"The pleasure is all mine April, short for April," he said, smiling.

"So, you said that you come here to be alone. To mellow out. Do you mind if I ask, what is it that you do that is so hectic that you need to get away on such a regular basis Mr. Shaquan?"

"I try to do as little as possible," he joked. "No, but seriously, I'm an entrepreneur."

"Would that be the street-type of entrepreneur?" She asked, looking him in his eyes.

"Yes. Since you asked. Yes."

"I admire your honesty."

"I sell heroin, not lies or dreams. I've never been too good at lying."

"Is that right?" She asked.

"Yes it is. So, what is it that you do Ms. April?"

"I don't do a thing right now. I just moved from Atlanta. I'm staying with my cousin until I can get on my feet. I have a degree in business that I'm hoping to put to good use."

"That sounds like a plan," Q remarked.

"So, I know that you street entrepreneurs have loads of women fighting over you all the time. Should I be watching my back while I'm with you?"

"No, don't worry. I got your back when you're with me."

"Hmmm, is that right?" replied April, catching the sexual overtone.

"Yes, that's right."

Shaquan and April talked like old friends for a couple hours, getting to know each other and just enjoying each other's company.

"Listen April. Can I make a suggestion?"

"I'm listening."

"Why don't we grab a bottle to go, get ourselves a suite at the Ritz Carlton, and continue this conversation and lovely evening there. No pressures. Just two adults enjoying each other's time and company. Whatever happens from this point on is entirely up to you. No pressure at all."

"No pressure huh?" She questioned.

"At all."

April thought about Q's proposal as she looked at him. She definitely liked what she saw.

"Ok, let's do it," she said.

"You wanna follow me?" Q asked.

"My cousin dropped me off. I was planning on taking a taxi when I left here."

"No, that's cool. That just means you get to ride with me."

They stood up to leave and Q put 3 one hundred dollar bills on the table for the waitress. They walked out of the club and Q led the way to the side of the club where his metallic blue Murcielago was parked.

"Wow. This is your car?" April asked, impressed.

"Yeah. This is my baby right here, but I don't take her out much. I normally drive something a little less flashy, so please don't think I'm one of those bling bling type of niggas cause I'm not."

"I'm not saying a word," she said, smiling, as Q lifted the passenger side door for her to climb in.

Once Q got in, he took his phone out.

"Do you mind?" He asked April before hitting the power button.

"No, go ahead. Do your thing."

Q turned his phone on and checked his messages while he drove. He made two phone calls, all business.

"April, I've got to make one quick stop. It's on the way and won't take more than 2 minutes ok."

"That's cool. Handle your business."

Ten minutes later, Q pulled up into the driveway of a 2 story A-frame home in the Spruce Acres section of Raleigh. He left the car running and said that he would be right back. He ran into the house, and true to his word was back in about 2 minutes. He had a blue bag in his hand as he got back in the car. He put the bag behind April's seat.

"That didn't take long did it," he asked as he pulled off.

"Not at all."

15 minutes later Q pulled up in front of the Ritz Carlton. The valet saw him coming and moved a rope barrier that blocked a special parking section reserved for exotic vehicles. Q drove through and parked next to a titanium-colored Mercedes Benz SLR Mclaren, leaving about four feet of space between the two vehicles. He grabbed the blue bag as he got out of the car, and ran around to the passenger side to let April out.

"Thank you very much," she said when he lifted the door and she stepped out of the Lamborghini. "I could live in that thing."

"Maybe I'll let you drive it sometime," said Q.

"No thank you. That's a little too much car for me."

They walked into the lobby of the Ritz Carlton and Q told April to meet him by the elevators. "I'm gonna go get us a key," he said.

"Ok," replied April as she headed towards the elevators with her purse and a bottle of Patrone Silver in her hands. 5 minutes later Q arrived with a key card in his hand.

"Ok, let's go," he said, pushing the button for the elevators. "Room service is 24 hours here so if you're hungry, we can order something when we get to the room ok."

"That's fine. I am a little hungry too."

Once in the room, April went to the restroom while Q ordered two appetizer platters and some soda from room service. After room service arrived April and Q sat at the small table and resumed their conversation.

"So Mr. Shaquan, why don't you have a woman? Or do you?"

"No I don't. Real women are hard to find around here. The only things around here are chicken heads, hood rats and gold diggers. I don't have time for either. Just because I do what I do doesn't mean I want or need to be surrounded by a bunch of women with nothing on their mind but a quick come up. I don't even keep a bunch of niggas around me. Most niggas in the game around here have no idea that the nigga they coppin they weight from is most likely coppin his weight from me."

"Well I really doubt that anyone around here thinks you work at the Super Wal-Mart. Not driving a Lamborghini."

"Oh they may know something, they just don't know what. I keep my circle real close, and my name don't come out of nobody's mouth."

"The silent boss huh," remarked April.

"Yeah, something like that. Let me ask you a question."

"Go ahead."

"Would you ever consider dating a nigga in the game?"

"I never have, but I won't say that I'm completely closed minded against the idea. Maybe if I met the right one I might consider it."

"Maybe I'm the right one," Q said.

"Maybe. You never know."

"Can I kiss you April?"

"Only if you come get it," she replied.

Q stood up, took hold of April's hands and pulled her to her feet. He wrapped his arms around her as their lips met. Their tongues danced around in their mouths as Q began to massage April's breast. Then he reached around and took hold of the zipper to April's dress, slowly pulling it down.

April pulled away.

"Wait," she said as she walked over to the dresser, picked up the 'Do Not Disturb' sign and went to the door. "We don't need housekeeping trying to wake us up early," she said in a seductive tone as she opened the door and hung the sign on the outside knob. "We might be up late," she said as she turned around and let the dress drop to the floor. "Where were we now?" she asked, walking towards Q with nothing on but a black lace thong and a strapless matching bra from Victoria's Secret that could barely contain her 36D breasts.

"Right here," responded Q, pulling April towards the bed. He laid April on the bed with her legs hanging over the edge. Q knelt on the floor between her legs and softly looped his fingers into the sides of her thong. He was just about to pull her thong down when he heard the click. It wasn't a loud sound, but he heard it and he knew what it was.

The door to the room was opening.

By the time he turned around and was about to get up it was too late because two men rushed into the room. A tall brother with long dreadlocks rushed Q, hitting him across the back of his head with the butt of his .40 caliber Glock.

"Lay on the floor nigga!" He growled.

The second man grabbed April's dress and threw it to her.

"Get dressed," he said.

April ran into the bathroom with her dress while the one who threw the dress at her looked through Q's blue bag.

"We got loot!" He said to the dreadlocked brother holding the gun to Q's head.

"That's all I got yo," Q declared. "That and a few stacks in my pocket. You niggas can have that."

"Shut up nigga!" said the dread.

April came out of the bathroom, dressed and with a different look on her face. The bigger brother reached behind him and pulled out a Glock 19. He tossed it to April.

"What the fuck took you niggas so long?!" she exclaimed. "I almost had to give his bitch ass some pussy!"

"It's all good. You know how much I love seeing you half-ass naked."

"Fuck you Lungee!" she spat. "You're just mad cause you'll never get none of this pretty ass!"

"Would you two quit fuckin' off!" yelled the dread.

"So you wit' this shit huh?" said Q. "I should've known."

"Shut the fuck up, soft ass nigga," she snapped.

"Look," said Q. "Take the loot and the Lambo. It's all I got. I ain't seen none of you."

"We look stupid nigga? We want the real loot," snarled the dread.

"Call Five yo," he said to Lungee.

"I got it." Lungee pulled out his phone and dialed a number. After one ring it was answered. "Yo, you niggas good?" asked Lungee into the phone. "That's what's up. Yeah, we good. Hold up." He handed the phone to the dread.

"What's good my nigga?...That's what's good. Just hold on." The dread pushed the gun harder into the side of Q's head. "Look here nigga," he said. "We know about the safe at yo mom's crib. I'm gonna let you talk to her real quick so you know we ain't on no bullshit. Don't make it the last time you hear her voice." Then into the phone he said, "yo Five, put that bitch on the phone for a sec." He put the phone to Q's ear.

"Hello?" he spoke into the phone.

"Shaquan! Who are these...?" He heard the voice, but the phone was pulled from his ear.

It was his mother's voice.

"One time nigga. You got one time to act stupid or tell a lie and I tell those two retarded niggas at yo mom's crib to air her ass the fuck out. Just like that. So, what's the combination?"

Q knew he was beaten and he was pissed off that he let himself get caught slippin—over a piece of pussy. He could only hope that he lived through this, and that they didn't hurt his mother.

Shaquan's first mistake was allowing April, whose real name was actually Honey, go into the bathroom with her purse to send a quick text message to her crew—who followed them from Club Black Ties—informing them what room number she and Q were in. Then, he didn't notice that when she grabbed the 'Do Not Disturb' sign, she also picked up the key card to the room that was on the table, and before she hung the sign on the outside doorknob she stuck the room key to the back of it with the small piece of gum that was hidden in her mouth.

Q knew he had to cooperate.

"3607," he whispered. It was the electronic code that opened the safe he had stashed in his mother's house. It was where he kept the bulk of his cash.

"Yo Five," said the dread into the phone. "Try 3607."

"A minute later he received confirmation that it was the right code. "That's what's up. Handle yo business. One," he said as he hung the phone up. He tossed the phone back to Lungee. "We good," he said. "Let's be out."

Honey grabbed a pillow from the bed and put it over Q's head to muffle the sound as much as possible.

She pulled the trigger.

Q's body jerked once and was still.

"Just like that," she said as she went through his pockets.

"Yeah. Goon style," whispered Lungee as the three walked out of the room.

****

30 minutes away, in the Golden Ages luxury retirement community of Durham, Five and Mook were handling their business at the home of Yvette Butler—Shaquan's mother.

They emptied the contents of the safe that was nestled in the back of the large walk-in closet in her bedroom. When they were done filling two large bags full of money and jewelry, Five, the larger of the two, approached Q's mother. Mook held her at gunpoint as she sat on the floor at the foot of her bed.

"This is only gonna hurt for a second moms," said Five as he lifted his silenced .9mm to her head.

She closed her eyes and said a silent prayer.

He pulled the trigger.

Twice.

3

That's what they called themselves. The Goon Squad. Four men and one female. All of them fearless, and all of them deadly. They loved each other like family, would kill and die for each other without a second thought, and their sole purpose in life was to get paid. How they did it, what they robbed, and who they killed didn't matter.

They lived together in a large five bedroom house in a quiet suburban neighborhood called Devonwood, in Fayetteville, North Carolina.   They never brought anyone to the house, and they rarely did any dirt on their side of Fayetteville. They each had their individual reputations around Fayetteville, but as a unified squad, they were a ghost. They didn't exist.

The Goon Squad was a ghost crew because anyone who had the unfortunate displeasure of meeting them didn't live to talk about it.

They never left witnesses.

****

The leader of the Goon Squad was an older brother by the name of Five.

Five was 34 years old, 6 foot 2 and about 210 pounds. Five was originally from New York, but had moved to Greenville, North Carolina when he was about six years old. Most of his family still lived in Queens, N.Y. and in Queens is where he spent most of his summers growing up. At the age of 18, Five was sentenced to 6 years in the North Carolina prison system for stealing a BMW right off of a car lot. He served 2 years off of that bid, got released, then one year later caught a five year sentence in the Federal Bureau of Prisons for illegal possession of a firearm by a convicted felon. While he was in the Feds, Five met a woman through a prisoner pen pal service.

They hit it off pretty fast, and when Five was released he moved in with her—to Fayetteville, North Carolina. When that relationship didn't work out, he moved out of her house, but stayed in Fayetteville anyway and he started selling crack and weed out of home in the Hollywood Heights neighborhood of North Fayetteville.

Five was a very intelligent brother, but he also was very mean spirited and short tempered. He was quick to pull a trigger, but he had no problem giving a brother a fair one either.

One evening, Five was walking through the parking lot of the Hardees on the corner of Raeford Rd and Skibo drinking a 40 ounce Icehouse. As he crossed the lot, he heard an argument coming from between two cars. There was a female sitting on the ground crying, and two men beefing. The female was getting beat by one of the men—her boyfriend—and the other brother—a stranger—stepped in to save her. Now the female's boyfriend and the good Samaritan were beefing. Five stopped to watch the beef with the rest of the crown that had gathered.

While the two were arguing, a third brother crept between the two cars and came up behind the good Samaritan. He punched the good Samaritan in the back of his head, and when the good Samaritan dropped to the ground he was jumped on by the other two.

Five, not liking to see anyone jumped, walked over to where the two were punching and kicking the good Samaritan.

He smashed the 40 ounce bottle over the head of the sneaky one, knocking him almost unconscious. While that brother was on the ground in a daze, Five hit the girl's boyfriend with a flurry of blows that kept him off balance until a serious uppercut finished him off completely. By this time, the good Samaritan was on his feet and stomping the sneaky one into the pavement.

When they heard the sirens in the distance, the good Samaritan turned to Five.

"Good lookin my nigga. What you driving?"

"I ain't driving shit. I was steppin' it," responded Five.

"Come on, ride wit me. We need to be out," he said, and walked over to a brown Toyota Camry. He jumped in and popped the locks so that Five could get in on the passenger side. Five jumped in and look over at the good Samaritan.

"Yo, somebody gon' get your plate, you know that right?"

"Fuck em. This shit is stolen anyway." He laughed as he pulled out of the parking lot onto Raeford Rd., just as two police cars were about to pull in off of Skibo Rd.

The good Samaritan was Mook.

****

Mook was one funny looking brother. He was 5 foot 4 and about 280 pounds. He had a grotesquely large head, unusually small ears, and no neck. But make no mistake about it, at the age of 28 Mook had killed more men than he could remember.

Mook was from Boston. Born and raised. He killed his first man at the age of 15. He wanted to get a tattoo on his arm that said "Monk". Monk was his nickname when he was growing up. It was short for monkey. His family said that he looked like a monkey, so they called him Monk for short.

He paid a known junkie named Tattoo Man for the tattoo, but when Tattoo Man was finished, the tattoo said MOOK. He misspelled it. Monk was so pissed that he stabbed Tattoo Man in his neck. He was arrested and locked up until he was 21.

That day he changed his nickname from Monk to Mook.

While he was locked up he never hesitated to put that blade in someone, and he often had to since the older inmates picked on him all the time. Once he realized that until he turned 18 he could kill as many people as he wanted and still only be kept locked up until he turned 21, he really started acting up. By the time he was released at the age of 21, Mook had a serious reputation built up.

Once out, his rep earned him a top spot in one of Boston's most ruthless street gangs as an enforcer for the boss. But one day the boss was a little too drunk and started being a little too disrespectful for Mook's tastes. So when he finally got fed up, Mook shot the boss in the face 3 times, robbed him of his money, jewelry and car, and he just drove south until he got tired of driving.

He exited Interstate 95 South at exit 56. Fayetteville, North Carolina.

****

Dreads was from Baltimore. He ended up in Fayetteville after he got arrested on I-95 coming from Florida with a car full of stolen credit cards. He was sentenced to one year in a halfway house in Fayetteville. But that year caused Fayetteville to grow on him and he never left.

He made a name for himself by selling weed and credit cards, but his gun was quick to go off too.

Dreads was about 5 foot 10, 185 pounds, dark skinned, with dreadlocks that dropped below his waist. He started growing his dreads when he was about 14.

Dread gained notoriety after he killed a man in the parking lot of Cross Creek Mall, in broad daylight, then beat the charges when the arresting officers completely forgot to read him his Miranda rights.

****

Lungee was Five's cousin. Five told Lungee on one of his visits up north how sweet the money was in North Carolina and that he wanted someone he could easily trust on the team he was trying to put together. He knew without a doubt that he could trust Lungee with his life at any given time. But there was one other thing about Lungee that he knew—Lungee was a stone cold killer.

To look at Lungee you would never believe that he would even know how to shoot a gun straight, much less actually kill a man.

Lungee was an even 6 feet tall and stocky as hell. He wasn't fat though, just big. But he wasn't intimidating or menacing. He always had a smile on his face, and you couldn't be around him for more than five minutes without laughing. But as quick as he was to put a smile on your face, he was just as quick to put a tear in your eye and a hole in your head. One young Fayetteville hustler found that out the very hard way soon after Lungee arrived in Fayetteville.

151

Lungee was shooting dice behind the Suburban Mart on Murchison Rd one night, about 3 months after he came from N.Y. At the time he was living in Foxfire, a neighborhood off Yadkin Rd., with his cousin Five, but he liked hanging out of the Murk. That's where all of the action was.

Lungee was losing that night. Everybody was losing that night. They were losing to a new shooter. Someone who nobody knew. There were already some sinister glances exchanged as the new shooter stuffed his pockets. Lungee wasn't a sore loser, and the 4 thousand he had lost wasn't a reason to act up. No, Lungee didn't act up until the new shooter went to pull some money out of his pocket and accidentally let a die fall out of his pocket. By the time the die had stopped dancing around on the concrete, Lungee had his .44 Magnum out and in the unlucky kid's face.

"What the fuck is that son?!" he growled. He picked it up and looked at it.

"Empty yo pockets bitch!" he said.

"Look bro…" the kid began, but Lungee leaned into him with a left jab that knocked him on his ass.

"I said empty yo pockets nigga!"

The shooter started emptying his pockets, and just as Lungee suspected, his pockets were filled with dice. Three different colors. All of them loaded. Everyone had their guns out now.

Boom!

Lungee shot the kid in his neck, almost taking his head completely off.

"I lost four G's to this nigga," he said, going through the kid's money and counting out 4 thousand dollars. "Yall niggas can have the rest of that shit."

Lungee walked away with his money—plus about a thousand extra for his troubles.

That was a little over 5 years ago. When Five finally put his team of Goons together, he looked to his cousin to keep them in good spirits. He said it made no sense to walk around with a sour look on your face all the time. He felt that nothing scares a nigga more, or catches a nigga more off guard than to see you pull your gun and put it in his face with a smile on yours.

****

Five assembled the Goon Squad with one agenda in mind, and that was to get that money. The only way you could get money and not be a target is if you lived and did business in Fayetteville, because the Squad didn't do dirt in the 'Ville. But if word got to them that you were clocking major money anywhere outside of Fayetteville, they were coming for you.

The first time they pulled a caper together, it went so well that Five knew he had put something serious together.

One of his cousins in Greenville was coppin' weight from a Jamaican named Rico. Rico lived in a one story house in Shady Oaks, a dangerous subdivision just inside of the Greenville city limits. Everybody in Greenville who was getting any real money was getting their work from Rico. Rico hardly ever came out of his house, and not only kept to himself surrounded by five very deadly bodyguards, but running loose in his yard were 4 very mean and hungry Bull Mastiffs.

Five's cousin Eddie gathered as much information as he could for Five, including when Rico had the most money and drugs in the house. Five got the address and went online to get the blueprints to Rico's house. Something else that interested Five was the rumor that Rico kept millions in cash in the shed next to the house. The shed doubled as a large dog house for the monsters that roamed the yard.

After 2 months of planning, Five and his crew were ready. They arrived in Shady Oaks at 1 o'clock in the morning in a hunter green Yukon that they "borrowed" from the parking lot at Womack Army Hospital on Fort Bragg. They drove by the house three times. Each time, they tossed a few balls of dog food, mixed with steak, ground beef, and enough Ambien to put a herd of elephants to sleep, over the fence.

The house that was two doors down from Rico's was owned by a retired electrician and his wife. They hated living in Shady Oaks, but they had lived there before it became drug-infested. The one thing that was good about living on the same block as Rico was that it was the one street that no one in Greenville dared to harass.

Noone relayed that bit of information to Five and the Goon Squad.

The Yukon pulled into the driveway and Lungee jumped out. Dreads was right behind him. They walked onto the front porch and Lungee unscrewed the light bulb over the door so that it wouldn't come on if the occupants tried the switch from the inside.

Dreads grabbed the doorknob, put all his weight on the door and pushed inward until the door gave. They entered the house and ran down the hallway to the master bedroom. When they got to the door, it opened, and a large but older black man stood in the doorway with a bewildered look on his face. Lungee shot him 3 times with a silenced .9mm, then stepped over his body into the room and shot the wife while she slept.

She never felt the 3 bullets crash into her skull.

She went to sleep and never woke up again.

As Lungee and Dreads were securing the house, Mook walked over to Rico's yard.

All four dogs were fast asleep.

Lungee and Dread came out of the house and followed Five over to Rico's house. Dread and Lungee climbed over the fence into the backyard and made their way to the house. They quietly walked onto the back porch and Dreads tried the back doorknob.

The door was unlocked.

Lungee peeked into the house through the back window and could see two very large men at the kitchen table playing dominoes. The window was cracked and Lungee could hear the music playing. Perfect.

Lungee put the gun to the screen and stroked the trigger 4 times. Him and Dreads rushed into the house just as the front door burst open and Five rushed in with Mook at his side. Rico and his other bodyguards were in the living room smoking weed and watching Shottas for the hundredth time. The bodyguards were caught completely off point and never got a chance to pull their weapons before Mook cut them down with a long burst from the silenced MP-40 submachine gun that he held. Dreads and Lungee went towards the back of the house to make sure no one else was there. They found one girl asleep and naked in one of the bedrooms. That was how she died.

Asleep and naked.

Rico stared into the barrel of the Glock 17 that Five had in his face.

"Where's it at nigga?" Five asked him in a calm voice.

Rico spat on the floor at Five's feet.

"Ya gwan 'afta dead me bwoy!"

Five shot Rico in his knee.

"Aaaarrrggghhh!" Rico screamed and grabbed his knee.

Meanwhile, Dread and Lungee went into the backyard and into the shed. Behind two large toolboxes were several boxes.

They were full of cash.

They climbed over the fence and walked over to where the Yukon was parked 2 houses over. They grabbed 3 oversized duffle bags and went back to Rico's house. Dreads took two of the duffle bags into the shed to fill them up and Lungee went into the house with one of them.

"Yo son," he said to Five. "The shed is on the one. Word." He tossed the duffle bag to Mook and headed back out of the house to help Dreads load up.

"Where's the rest nigga? Where the dope at?" Five asked Rico.

Rico wasn't talking.

Mook took off to search the house.

Five shot Rico in his shoulder.

Mook came back into the living room, lifted his MP-40 and unloaded the rest of the clip into Rico's chest.

"Fuck that nigga," he said. "I found his stash."

Five followed Mook into one of the bedrooms. Mook opened the drawers in one of the dressers. Each drawer was filled with cash and kilos of cocaine.

"Damn, this nigga was too comfortable," said Five. "Let's load up and be out of here."

There was so much cash and so many kilos of cocaine that they had to take two pillowcases off of the bed to fit everything because the duffle bag wasn't big enough.

By the time they were done and rushing out of the front door, the Yukon was pulling into Rico's driveway. They tossed the duffle bag and pillowcases full of drugs and money into the back with the other two duffle bags filled with money, and they drove straight to the highway, headed back to Fayetteville.

"Goon style nigga," said Lungee as they drove away.

4

Five and the crew pulled 4 more job over the course of the next 7 months. They hit a drug dealer in Sanford, who was so easy they only had to plan for a week before they moved in on him. They hit a pair of twins just over the South Carolina border who kept all of their money at the bottom of a freezer in their basement. They also knocked off a furniture store when they heard that the owner had a big walk-in safe full of cash in the back of his office in the store. That turned out to be bullshit. When the owner opened the safe for them there was only about 40 thousand, some crack, and a pipe. They killed him and stuck him in the safe. They killed another mid-level dealer in Spring Lake just because he boasted that he couldn't be got. By far, the hit on Rico netted them the most money and drugs.

Over 2 million in cash and 19 kilos of cocaine.

The crew was doing well. They each still had their own individual ventures and hustles going on, but whenever they pulled a job together, they split everything down the middle. They also lived together in a large 4 bedroom home off of Morganton Rd and they split all the bills 4 ways.

They were chillin the basement of their house watching "Set It Off" on the big screen when the scene played where Queen Latifah's character, Cleo, drove the big SUV through the bank's front window.

"That's what the fuck I'm talking about right there!" exclaimed Lungee. "We need a bitch like Cleo on the team!"

"What the fuck for?" asked Mook as he passed a blunt to Five.

"Cause for real, a bitch can get into certain shit without attracting a lot of attention," replied Lungee.

"Yeah. And what happens when it comes time to split a nigga's shit? Then what?" questioned Mook.

"Then she just gotta split a nigga's shit. Just like that. She gotta put in that work."

"That sounds good," said Mook. "But I don't know no bitches that put in work like that."

"I do," said Dreads.

"Get the fuck outta here," said Mook.

"I'm serious. I know a bitch who ain't 'fraid of shit and she'll definitely put that hot shit in a nigga quick. Plus she fine as hell too."

"Let's meet her," said Five, blowing out a giant cloud of smoke, the wheels in his head spinning.

****

She was a Georgia peach. Born and raised in Atlanta, Georgia, she was raised by her father after he took her away from her heroin addicted mother. She never knew her mother, and it was her father who raised her and taught her all she needed to know growing up. Including how to fight and shoot a gun.

She was 23 years old, had a light golden complexion and a body that could start a traffic accident at 5 foot 3, 135 pounds. Her hair was as black as a raven's feathers, and it hung down just past her shoulders. Her hazel eyes set everything off perfectly.

Dread knew her because he had included her in a few of his credit card schemes in the past. So when she got a call from him about a business proposition, she was all ears.

"North Carolina?" she said after Dreads laid out an elaborate scam involving rebate checks.

"Yeah. This here's a military town. There's plenty paper here. You could come up, hit for about a hundred thou, and then head back to the 'A'."

"You got the ID connect already set up?" she asked.

"Of course. I'm fuckin wit some Mexicans. 300 a pop. Legit shit. So what's up? You wit it?"

"Yeah, I'm wit it. Let me hit you up later and give you my flight info." She always flew, and always first class.

"That's what's up. I'll be waiting."

The next day she arrived and Dread picked her up at the Fayetteville airport. The whole story about the rebate checks was of course all a lie just to get her to come to Fayetteville. Five wanted to meet her and see if she was everything Dread claimed her to be.

When Dread saw her walking through the terminal towards him, he saw that she looked even more beautiful than the last time he saw her. But she was all about her business.

"Hey girl," he said as they exchanged a quick hug. "You're still looking as good as ever."

"Thank you. I see the dreads are still growing. Let me get my bag before somebody tries to steal it."

They made their way over to the baggage carousel just in time to see a full-sized Louis Vuitton bag make its first appearance.

"It's the Louis bag," she said, pointing to her bag.

"Damn," said Dreads as he pulled the bag free. "What the fuck you got in here? A dead body?"

"Not yet. But you never know," she joked.

Dread smiled at the thought.

He drove her to her hotel, the Marriott, so that she could put her bag up, then he told her that they were going to a club called "Nikki's" to meet the man with the checks.

"Does this spot wand you when you go in?" she asked.

"Naw. It's not that type of spot," he replied.

"Good," she said, pulling her Glock 19 out of her bag and tucking it into a holster hidden at her hip. Dreads saw the move and smiled again.

When they arrived at Nikki's they walked right through the quiet club and into a private room in the back. The only things in the room were two sets of couches facing each other with an oversized table sitting low between them. Dreads was about to close the door behind them when three men rushed into the room with their guns drawn. The short fat one turned his gun on Dreads, while the tall bigger of the three put his gun in her face. The third brother was the tallest but not as big as the second.

"Who the fuck are you?" the one holding the gun on the female asked her.

"Who the fuck are you nigga, and why do you have a fuckin' gun in my face?" she retorted.

"I'll ask the motha fuckin questions here. Who the fuck are you?" he repeated.

"Look, if you're not gonna pull that trigger then get that goddamn pistol out of my face before I smack the shit out of you," she said with a deadly coolness.

"You hear this fuckin broad," he said as he looked over at the short one holding Dreads at bay. When he looked away that gave her all the time she needed.

With her left hand she moved the gun out of her face as she took a half step forward, pulling her Glock 19 and pushing it under the chin of the brother who had just made the mistake of looking away for a brief second.

"You know what," she whispered. "My daddy used to tell me that 8 out of 10 niggas who pull their gun and talk a bunch of shit really ain't ready to pull that trigger. I'm not one of them 8. Now who the fuck are you niggas," she said as she relieved him of his gun.

"Oh shit! Yo Lungee," the fat one said, taking his gun out of Dread's face and tucking it away. "You ain't never gonna live that shit down my nigga. Word." He was laughing.

"I told you," said Dreads, taking a seat on one of the sofas. Mook sat down next to him. The female, still holding the gun under Lungee's chin, was confused.

"What the fuck is up? Dreads, talk to me before I light this nigga up," she said.

"Calm down beautiful," said the tall brother. "Ain't nobody here to do a thing to you. Put the gun away. You're among friends here." He walked over to her.

"I've never had a friend put a gun in my face."

"Just checking to see where you heart is."

"Who said I have one?" she responded, taking the gun away from Lungee and putting it back into its holster. "You're lucky," she said as she gave Lungee back his gun.

"I like that," said Five. "You're gangsta with your shit for real. What's your name?"

"They call me Honey."

160

"I'm in love," said Lungee.

Honey rolled her eyes at him and took a seat.

"Look, I didn't fly here to play games. Dreads said there was some good money to be made here. Well, I'm all about getting' my paper, so I would appreciate it if you wouldn't waste anymore of my time and tell me exactly what's going on."

"Straight to business. I like that. Mook, you wanna grab us a bottle of Louie?" he said. Mook walked out of the room. "Look Honey. We each do our own thing here in Fayetteville. We get good paper doing what we do, but every now and then we'll pull a lick for a serious come up. Always enough for all of us to eat good. We don't shit where we lay our head, and Fayetteville is where we lay our head. When we hit a motha fucka, it's always outta town. We hit fast. We hit hard. We get paid. And we leave no witnesses. Ever." Five looked at Honey to see what her reaction was gonna be. Mook walked back into the room carrying a 16 hundred dollar bottle of Louis XIII cognac and five glasses.

"So you had me fly all the way from Atlanta to tell me that?"

"No, I had you fly here because Dreads seems to think that you would fit in perfectly."

"Is that right?" She looked over at Dreads.

"Yeah, I said it. We could use a female on the team and you are the most gangsta female I know. To top it off, you fine as hell wit it. A motha fucka will never see you comin."

Honey looked around the room at the four brothers. She considered everything that Five had told her. She poured a round of drinks from the bottle that Mook sat on the table.

"What the fuck," she declared as she lifted a glass. "I'm in."

Everyone else grabbed a glass from the table and lifted them.

"To family," said Five.

"To family," everyone else repeated and touched glasses in a toast.

"To the Goons," added Lungee.

Everyone touched glasses again.

****

Soon after that meeting, Honey moved in with the others and a few months later they moved into a five bedroom house in Devonwood. It was always strictly business with Honey, and she made it known when she first moved in with the four men that she had no interest in getting involved with any of them. But they all grew to love each other as only a family of killers could.

"Where you been?" asked Lungee one night. Honey had been out for a few hours.

"It's none of your goddamn business where I been. Don't be fuckin' questioning me!" Honey snapped.

"Come 'er. Lemme smell your breath, see if you been suckin' dick."

"Fuck you nigga! Let me smell your breath and see if you been suckin' dick."

Dreads laughed out loud.

"Yo Honey, why don't you just give that nigga some," said Five. "That way he'll see that he can't handle that cat and leave you alone once and for all."

"I don't even want none," lied Lungee.

"Stop lying nigga!" Honey shot back.

"Come put it in my face, and I bet you I don't do shit."

"You wish nigga!"

They all laughed. They joked like that all the time. Lungee loved Honey to death, and though he often joked with her on a very sexual level, he would never cross that line with her, and she knew it. They all knew it.

5

"Wilmington," said Five, walking in the room.

"What about Wilmington, son?" asked Lungee.

"That's where we're headed next."

"What's in Wilmington?" questioned Dreads.

"Nigga named Malik. Owns a little nickel and dime store in the middle of the hood. Opens up around 10 at night. Sells loose Newports, blunts, and Jamaican beef patties."

"So, what the fuck we gonna hit 'em for?" asked Mook. "A pack of Newports and a beef patty?"

"Naw, simple ass nigga. I was thinking more like the loot he got stashed at his crib. Word is, the nigga got Wilmington sewed up as far as that weed is concerned. He lives alone with 2 big ass pit bulls. No bank account. He bought a big safe 4 months ago that he keeps all his loot in."

"That's what I'm talking about dog," exclaimed Lungee. "I was damn sure tired of just sittin' around this bitch."

Four months had gone by since their last hit and the anxiety was thick. The crew was far from being broke, but they lived for the thrills. Even Honey fell in place just perfectly. The Wilmington job was just what the crew needed to take the edge off.

"So when do we hit 'em Five?" Honey inquired.

"I'm gonna get some more info on this nigga first, but it shouldn't be too long. Probably no more than a couple o' weeks at the most.

Since Five had a thriving weed market in Fayetteville, he always kept himself informed on any major players in the Carolinas. He didn't too much concern himself with any of the competition in the 'Ville because he felt that there was entirely too much money to go around. He had stopped selling crack altogether and left that to Lungee and Mook. Dreads stil fucked with credit cards and counterfeit bills just for something to do. Honey was involved in that with Dreads from time to time, but for the most part, she just lived for the next hit.

****

A 6 foot 4, 160 pounds, Malik wasn't much to look at. His dreads hung just past his shoulders, but did nothing to increase his intimidation factor. But though he didn't look like much, Malik was a 3rd degree black belt in karate and deadly with his hands. He didn't carry a weapon. He was a weapon.

But everyone liked Malik. He had the only store in the hood that stayed open late. Actually, the "Hot Spot" didn't even open until late. He showed up around 9:45 every night to open his doors. The "Hot Spot" was just an oversized shed. Once he was inside, he served his customers through a window on the side. He had a small microwave oven that he used to heat up the Jamaican beef patties that he sold for 2 dollars and a cooler full of ice so he could keep the sodas cold. A 12 ounce can of soda sold for a dollar. But his bestselling items were the loose Newports, Phillie blunts and dime bags of weed. He sold major weight in the Wilmington area, but after 10:00 at night he was at the Hot Spot, and it was strictly dime bags from there.

There were 4 customers at his window when Honey walked up. Malik was talking to one of the customers about his bill. Malik gave credit to some of his regular customers. The ones he felt were able to pay their bills.

"Come on Malik. You know I'm good for it."

"When am I gonna see you bro," asked Malik. "Cause you already owe me $23."

"Imma hit you tomorrow, even if I gotta pawn my chain," he said, tugging on his necklace.

"If you're gonna pawn your shit, bring it here first. I'll do something for you," Malik said, handing the man a dime bag of weed. "You need a blunt?" he asked, holding up a Phillie blunt.

"Naw, I'm good. I got papers. Thanks Malik. I got you," the brother said as he walked away from the window and down the street.

Honey waited her turn the stepped up to the window.

"Beef patty and a Sprite please," she said as she pulled a five dollar bill out of her pocket and handed it to Malik. He took the bill, put a beef patty in the microwave for 30 seconds, dug a Sprite out of the cooler and handed it to her.

"Here you go," he said, putting the soda and 2 dollars into her hand.

"Patty'll be ready in a second."

"Ok, thank you."

A few seconds later the microwave beeped and Malik took the beef patty out, wrapped it in a few napkins and handed it to Honey.

"What's your name sweetheart?" he asked.

"It's not sweetheart," she replied. "And since I hate to be called sweetheart, this conversation is over."

Honey left the window and started walking away.

"You have a good night...sweetheart!" Malik called out to her sarcastically.

"I got your sweetheart," she whispered as she walked away. "Mark ass nigga."

****

Malik's house was isolated behind a Food Lion supermarket. It sat on a large plot of land, and littered all over the property were close to 20 vehicles in all degrees of deterioration. The house itself was a small, one-story, 2 bedroom, rather unimpressive house with a porch that wrapped around the front and one of the sides. One of the bedrooms was where his two dogs—Bodie and Monster—lived. Bodie and Monster were what was left of a pit bull breeding venture that Malik dabbled in for about a year. They were almost as big as Mastiffs. Monster's head was about as big as a keg of beer. They were both loyal to Malik and heeded his commands without hesitation.

Malik pulled his minivan onto his property at about 3:20 a.m. He turned the engine off and pushed the button to unlock the back door so that he could unload his things. He grabbed a bag of leftover beef patties, his phone, and walked around towards the back.

From behind a sky blue Nissan Pulsar 10 feet away, Lungee and Mook emerged. Lungee held an Intertec Tec 9 machine gun in both hands and Mook was cradling a Mossburg 12 gauge pump shotgun.

"Don't move nigga," Lungee ordered.

When Malik heared Lungee's voice he was about to turn around and try to make a run for it, but when he turned he saw Five, Dreads, and Honey come from behind a Ford Econoline van.

"Where the fuck you going?" asked Five, pointing a silenced Mac 11 at Malik. Dreads had a Glock 17 and Honey held a Heckler and Koch .9mm.

Malik froze when he saw that he was outnumbered and surrounded. His dogs, sensing something wasn't right outside, went into a barking frenzy.

"Aight nigga, you know what the fuck this is," Five roared, keeping the Mac 11 in Malik's face. "Where's the safe at?"

"What safe? I ain't got no safe."

"Stop lying nigga," snapped Honey, smacking Malik in his head with her .9mm. Malik fell to the ground at the back corner of his minivan bleeding from his head. He looked at Honey and recognized her from the store earlier in the evening. He looked around and weighed his options. One man with a gun up close would normally be no match for Malik's lightning fast speed and superior fighting skills. But he had five weapons on him. The odds against him were astronomical.

"One more time. Where's the safe?" repeated Five.

"In my dog's room, but they'll never let you in there yo."

"Oh, don't sweat that shit cause I'm 'bout to take care of them right the fuck now," said Mook. "Gimme the keys to the crib, nigga."

Malik gave Mook the keys that were in his hand and Mook walked towards the front door with Lungee while the other 3 kept Malik covered. The dogs were going crazy.

"Yo, them sound like some big ass motha fuckas!" observed Mook.

"Yeah I know. How we gonna do this?"

"When we get the door unlocked, Imma get down low and you gonna crack the door a little. Just make sure you hold onto the fuckin doorknob."

"Whatchu gonna do, put your little dick through the crack so one of them can give you a blowjob nigga," laughed Lungee.

"Fuck you. Just don't let go of the door."

They stepped onto the porch and the barking was thunderous. Mook tried a couple of keys. The third one he tried unlocked the deadbolt. He held the shotgun in front of him and crouched down.

"Aight, open the door," he told Lungee. "Just enough so I can get the shotty in the crack."

"I got you nigga. Stop bitchin 'for I kick this bitch wide open." Lungee knew that Mook was scared to death of pit bulls. He grabbed hold of the doorknob and turned it. Mook was ready, the shotgun barrel at the door jam. Lungee eased the door open about an inch. The dogs were frantically trying to squeeze their noses into the crack. He slowly opened the door another inch and Mook pushed the barrel through the crack.

Monster grabbed hold of it and tried to rip it from Mook's hands.

Ba boom!

Mook pulled the trigger while Monster had the barrel of the shotgun all the way in his mouth, sending the back of Monster's head and upper back spraying into Bodie's side. Bodie backed up, startled by the loud sound. That gave Mook the chance to chamber another round.

He stuck the barrel into the door again, but instead of holding the door, Lungee pushed it wide open. Bodie saw Mook crouched down holding the shotgun at the same time that Mook saw Bodie.

Mook froze.

Bodie didn't.

Neither did Lungee.

When he pushed the door open, he was ready to let loose with the Tec 9 in his hands.

"What the fuck!" yelled Mook when the door flew open and he saw the 190 pound dog less than 6 feet away. Bodie crouched down and prepared to leap at Mook, who was closest.

Bodie never made it off the ground.

Lungee unloaded his entire clip into the freakishly large pit bull. It looked like it took the whole clip to take it down.

"That was some fuckin bullshit nigga!" Mook cried, getting up and trying to regain his composure, after receiving one of the biggest scares of his life.

"Man chill out. I told you I got you."

In the yard, Malik heard the shotgun blast, then the tat-tat-tat-tat...of the Tec 9. When the shooting stopped he knew his dogs were dead.

"Yo, we good!" yelled Lungee from the front porch. "Come on!"

When Five heard Lungee he grabbed Malik by his shirt.

"Get up nigga. Come on."

Dreads and Honey backed up a little to let Malik and Five pass them. With Malik leading the way, the four of them walked onto the porch and into the house. When Malik saw the bodies of his two dogs he was filled with rage. But there was nothing he could do.

"Back here!" yelled Mook from down the hallway.

"Go get the whip Dreads, and bring the bags in." Dreads rushed out of the house to get the Suburban that was parked in one of the loading docks behind the Food Lion.

Malik entered the room that used to be the dogs'. In the corner of the room was a 5 foot tall safe that was just covered with a black sheet. The sheet was lifted to reveal a large combination.

"Open it nigga," said Five, pushing Malik towards the corner.

Malik stumbled towards the big safe. He grabbed the dial and spun it around a few times. He turned it in the opposite direction, then back again, stopping at 15. He took hold of the handle and pressed down.

The safe opened.

He pulled the door and stepped back.

The safe was completely filled with money.

"That's what I'm talking about," exclaimed Lungee when he saw that the safe was full.

Honey walked up to Malik.

"The name's Honey nigga," she said as she lifted her .9mm and put it to Malik's temple and pulled the trigger. "Not sweetheart."

Dread ran into the room with a pair of black duffle bags.

"Damn!" he said when he saw the contents of the safe. "We gon' need some more bags."

The crew filled both duffle bags and then a trash bag that they found in Malik's kitchen. They completely emptied the safe, and even went into Malik's bedroom and cleaned out his jewelry box.

"Straight like that," declared Lungee as he climbed into the big Suburban. "Goon style."

They pulled away from Malik's house at 3:50 a.m.

6

After Supreme's killing, placing Smurf and his crew in place was going to be a sensitive issue. So Big Mike had to pull some underhanded moves. The first thing he did was put out a rumor that Supreme's killing was retaliation for him snitching on a New York cat that he helped the Feds get a few years back. To add weight to that rumor, Big Mike had some fake paperwork created with Supreme's name all over it. Supposedly, it was Smurf's brother who Supreme had set up. That smoothed things out with the Southside Bloods somewhat.

The next thing that Big Mike did was set up a meeting between Smurf's team and Supreme's old connect, Dookie.

Dookie came up in the Charlotte drug game by being in the right place at the right time. He was locked up in the Mecklenburg County Detention Center on a murder charge that stemmed from a shooting at a Charlotte nightclub called Flames. Dookie was guilty, but the state's evidence was shaky. So was Dookie's lawyer—an overworked and underpaid public defender.

But while Dookie was awaiting trial in the max unit at the MCDC, he came to the aid of a Hispanic man who was about to be jumped and robbed of his commissary by a couple of block bullies. That Hispanic man happened to be the head of a 16 man federal conspiracy case and he controlled a vast majority of the drug flow in North and South Carolina. He was so grateful to Dookie that he hired the best attorney in Charlotte to represent Dookie in his murder trial. Once Dookie was freed, the Hispanic gentleman arranged for him to receive a shipment of 50 kilos of cocaine. His gift to Dookie. He also arranged for Dreads to have a steady supply of cocaine at reasonable prices. With this new good fortune, and his freedom, Dookie went straight to the top.

The Hispanic gentleman got life in Federal prison.

Dookie liked Supreme, so he was a bit skeptical about meeting with the men responsible for his murder. He listened to Big Mike tell his story of Supreme's past betrayal, and since Supreme was no longer around to defend himself, he had no choice but to take what Big Mike told him on face value.

So he let Big Mike arrange the meeting with Smurf.

They met at "Coco's", a Jamaican restaurant in downtown Charlotte owned by Dookie. The place was completely surrounded by Dookie's men, so he felt safe.

Smurf and Young God arrived alone. They pulled up to the front of Coco's and were met by 4 very large Jamaicans. One of them quickly frisked the two, then they were escorted to a table, where Dookie sat in front of a spread of various island dishes.

Smurf and Young God introduced themselves to Dookie, who sat alone, and they sat down.

"Eat," said Dookie. "We eat and talk."

Youn God looked over at Smurf, who gave him an approving nod. "Go ahead. Eat," he said, grabbing a beef patty with one of the napkins on the table.

"To da business," Dookie said through a mouthful of curry goat and rice. He swallowed, then looked at Smurf. "You da boss?" he asked.

"We both run our squad."

"Only one boss. You da boss?" he asked again.

Sensing that Dookie only wanted to discuss business with one of them, Smurf stepped up.

"Yeah, I'm the boss."

"Take a plate," Dookie said to Young God. "Excuse yourself please."

Young God looked at Smurf.

"Go 'head. Wait in the whip. I got this," Smurf told him.

Once Young God was out of the restaurant, Dookie spoke to Smurf.

"No disrespect. You see I sit alone. No more ears than necessary. Bloodclot police come, no doubt who do da talking. No me. Must be you. You tink same ting. If not you, must be me. Simple." Dookie put his fork down, grabbed a bottle of Cola champagne to wash down his food, and leaned back in his chair.

"So, what can we do for each other?"

"I need a steady connect. I need good prices. I need good shit. But I don't need it right now."

"Den why we talking now? Who ya dealing wit now?"

"Nobody. I come with my own work. But I wanna know I can cop from you when the time is right. Since I took out Supreme's snitchin' ass, I now control the South side of Hidden Valley. I got enough work to last a little while, but I don't know how long."

"Supreme used to buy 20 kilos a week from me. You deal wit me, you buy at least half of that. 10 kilos. Beginning in one month. I don't want all money to stop immediately. You killed Supreme. You buy half from me what he was buying."

"What happens when I need more than 10 a week?"

"Then you buy more than 10," replied Dookie.

"And then when I need more than 20?"

"Ha. A week?"

"Yeah, a week. Something funny about that?"

"Don't know how you tink you gwan sell 20 kilos a week in da South Valley."

"Supreme was doing it wasn't he?"

"Supreme barely sell 15. Him put 5 away every week."

"Oh yeah?"

"Yeah. You need more than South Valley. I know people. Let me make some calls. Leave your number and gimme 2 days."

"Why you tryna help a nigga?" asked Smurf.

"Because I help you, then you help me. You need a good supply. I got the best. The more of Charlotte you control, the less people I deal wit. If I deal wit you only, the better. But you gwan hafta take it. No one gwan give you a ting," replied Dookie.

"I ain't sweatin' that shit. I rather take my shit anyway. It make a nigga think twice 'for he try and step to my squad."

"Ok," Dookie said, taking the number that Smurf wrote down for him. "I'll call you in 2 days. Maybe less."

"That's what's up."

"And Smurf?"

"Yeah."

"I tell you, you really wan take dis city, you know where you hafta start?"

"Where?"

"North Valley. South not nuff."

7

"Dreads can't even fit all that shit in a ski mask!" joked Lungee.

"Yeah. Nigga'd look like close encounters of the black kind," added Mook. They all laughed.

The crew was discussing the reasons why they don't wear any masks to do their hits. Five felt that five people leaving a scene wearing ski masks would draw too much attention.

"Plus," said Five. "Cowards wear ski masks. Nigga put a ski mask on to hide who he is. I'm a motha fuckin Goon. And when a bitch see me comin, I want my face to be the last thing he sees before I put his ass to sleep forever. The reason why ain't nobody talkin' bout us is because we don't leave nobody around to talk about us. We wear our gloves and we always change gats. The white boy Rick keeps us in new hammers. As long as we do our shit right, be smart, and don't slip up, we're gonna stay ghosts. And we'll never need any fuckin punk ass ski masks."

"I feel you my nigga," said Dreads. "But lemme ask you this. Last week you were talking about hittin a bank. I don't know if you was for real or if you was fuckin' around. You know I don't give a fuck either way. When the time comes, I'm ready to get it. But banks got cameras all over the fuckin' place. How you think we gon' get in and out without gettin' caught on camera. When we start hittin' banks, we fuckin' wit the Feds."

"I was in the Feds wit some of the best bank robbers ever did it…" said Five.

"Shit," interrupted Lungee. "They couldn't've been that motha fuckin good. They was in there with you." He laughed.

"Anyway, like I was saying, them niggas like to talk, and a nigga like me likes to listen. I picked up on a few things. We might be able to hit the right bank, with no masks, and get away from it without getting caught on tape. Trust me, I'm not tryna see my face on the 6 o'clock news."

"I kind of like the idea of a bank," said Honey. "It would be on some 'Set It Off' shit."

"Yeah, you could be Jada Pinkett," exclaimed Lungee.

"And you could be Cleo," retorted Honey.

Everyone erupted in laughter.

"Y'all doin' a whole lot of laughing," Five said. "Y'all think you ready to take a bank?"

Everyone saw that Five was serious and the laughing stopped.

"I'm ready for whateva," responded Mook.

"You already know what's up wit me cuz," added Lungee.

Dreads and Honey remained silent.

Five noticed.

"What about you two?" he asked, looking at them.

"I already told you," replied Honey. "I like the idea."

"I'm like this Five. If you can lay it out proper like and let me know how we're gonna do it, without ski masks, and it looks good, then I'm with you 100%. Just lay it out proper. Cause you already know that the Feds ain't no joke. One slip and they comin for us."

"I hear you Dreads. Don't worry, I'm working out all the details. When we hit, we'll be ready."

"That's what's up then. Let's set it off!" Lungee exclaimed, hyped up.

8

Over the course of the next few weeks, Five planned. The first thing he wanted to do is find the perfect bank. He knew, from listening to the many bank robbers he'd run across in his short time in the Federal Bureau of Prisons, that one of the most important aspects of a successful bank robbery was the getaway. What happens inside of the bank was equally as important, but the getaway was just that—the getaway.

Never, under any circumstances, should you have a getaway vehicle parked directly in front of the bank with the motor running. That was a tell-tale sign, and as nervous as this world we live in is, some good Samaritan is bound to call 911 if he spots a car idling in front of a bank. Plus, your tags would almost certainly be on You Tube and Facebook in minutes.

You should be able to get in and out of the bank's lot with little or no problem, and without attracting any undue attention. Having a residential neighborhood very close to the bank is helpful, especially if you could drive through the neighborhood and exit onto a major traffic expressway. If you could time your exit from the bank just right, your getaway vehicle could pick you up and roll out—sort of like a taxi.

Leave the tellers alone. The window tellers are for crack heads and dope fiends. Plus, the tellers' drawers are full of dye packs and alarms, and the last thing you want is to jump in your getaway ride and your money explode on you. But contrary to popular belief, hundred dollar bills covered in red or blue dye are not completely useless. Strippers will take them, and so will a crack dealer at 2:30 in the morning.

Five's main problems were gonna be the amount of people in the bank. How would a crew of 4 be able to keep everyone in the bank from activating an alarm and alerting the police to the robbery? How could the 4 person crew control the situation from the moment they enter the bank, keeping any stray phone calls from some back office somewhere?

Before the 4 man crew killed everyone.

That was something he would have to figure out.

As for the problem of the cameras, that was actually no problem at all. It never was.

After a couple of weeks, Five was ready to lay out his plan to the rest of the crew. The bank, because of its layout, was gonna be the High Point Industrial Credit Union in High Point, NC. It stood on a hill directly adjacent to the highway that took them out of High Point, so the getaway, if timed right, would be perfect.

The HPI Credit Union was a one story bank, Five explained to the crew. It wasn't a very big bank, but it did serve a greater portion of the High Point Industrial Park, and on Fridays it would carry a lot of extra cash. There were 4 tellers and a drive through window. One of the tellers served merchants. The bank had one double door entrance, and directly to the right of that was the bank manager's office.

Five went on for a half hour, detailing every aspect of his carefully laid out plan. It seemed foolproof. But there was one thing that he refused to mention.

"What about the cameras?" asked Dreads. "The whole shit sounds tight as hell, but you haven't mentioned the cameras. What do we do about them?"

Five smiled.

"I've been waiting on you to ask me that," he said, and he stood up. "I'll be right back." He left the room and went into his bedroom. He returned a few minutes later carrying what looked like a surveillance camera. He unraveled the cord, plugged the camera into the wall outlet, then he plugged the RCA jacks into the big screen's video and audio in. He grabbed the remote and turned on the big screen and changed the input selector to Video 1.

Honey appeared on the screen since Five had the camera pointed on her.

Lungee didn't miss a beat.

"Hey Honey," he said. "I'll bet that's not the first time you've ever been in front of a video camera."

"I'll bet you can kiss my ass, fat ass motha fucka!" she snapped back.

"Ok," said Dreads, ignoring Lungee and Honey's foolishness. "What are we seeing?"

"Watch," said Five. He moved the camera from person to person, each person was clear on the high definition plasma screen. Five sat the camera on its stand and left it pointing at Dreads. He took a pair of black shades out of his pocket and walked over to where Dreads was sitting, coming into view of the camera as he walked. His back was to the camera. When he was at Dread's side, he turned around and faced the camera.

His face was a complete blur.

Everything on the screen was crystal clear, except Five's face. His face was a completely unrecognizable blurry mess.

It was like he was invisible. Or at least his face was.

"Yo, how the fuck you do that?" asked Lungee in amazement.

"It's the glasses ain't it?" questioned Dreads.

"Come here," said Five. "I'll show you." He led the way back to his bedroom with Dreads right behind him. About 5 minutes later they returned, and Dreads walked right into the camera's view. Just as Five's was earlier, Dread's face was invisible to the camera.

He smiled when he saw himself on the TV's screen. He didn't have glasses on and all he could see were his eyes.

"What the fuck nigga? How y'all do it?" asked Lungee. "Let us in on the secret."

"Hairspray," said Five. "Simple hairspray."

"Hairspray?" Now it was Honey's turn to be confused.

"Yeah. Hairspray. Aqua Net. I used to hear that if you spray hairspray on yourself you won't show up on the cameras. All we gotta do is tape our eyes shut, spray Aqua Net all over our faces real good, and when it dries, pull the tape off and throw on a pair of shades. The cameras don't pick us up."

"Oh shit!" exclaimed Lungee. "Invisible Goons. Yo, that's some ghost shit for real."

"So, when we gonna do this shit," Mook asked.

"Soon," Five responded. "Real soon."

****

The High Point Industrial Credit Union wasn't too crowded on this Friday morning. It was only 9:15 and there were only two tellers open. There were 3 customers: a white man who had just stepped up to a teller's window. One black woman was waiting for her turn at the window since the other teller had walked away momentarily and put her "Be Right Back" sign up. Another black woman was at the center kiosk filling out a withdrawal receipt. The bank's assistant manager, Carver Mead, had just sat down at his desk with a fresh cup of coffee. The manager, David Medlock, was late—again. Carver Mead would make bank manager if Medlock kept showing up late.

Those were Carver's thoughts when he noticed the three black men enter the bank. Unfortunately he didn't notice the black woman at the kiosk when she put her pen down and pulled out two silenced Detonics .45mm automatics. With one shot from each, Honey took out both of the customers in the bank.

The black woman who was standing, waiting for the 2nd teller to return felt the bullet slam into the back of her head, but only for a brief second. She never felt it exit her forehead, the greater portion of the front of her brain along with it. The white man dropped to his knees at the window when the .45mm shell penetrated his heart from behind.

"Three minutes!" yelled Five as him, Lungee and Dreads entered the bank. Dreads jumped over the counter and pumped two shells into the head of the teller who had already started yelling. Then he quickly located the second teller and shot her three times in the head and chest. Lungee ran into one of the other offices and found two more employees. He made quick work of them with a pair of bursts from the Ingram Mac 10 he carried. Five had ran straight into the assistant manager's office.

"Don't get up," Five said as Carver Mead was about to stand. Five shot him 4 times with his .40 caliber Glock.

Lungee had a backpack on. He took it off and took two duffle bags out of it. Five grabbed one and Dreads grabbed the other.

"The vault," he said. Then, "2 minutes 15 seconds."

The three men entered the vault while Honey kept an eye on the door. A block away, Mook was in the parking lot of a Bojangles. He was listening to Five on his Bluetooth, and monitoring police action on his handheld scanner.

Five, Dreads and Lungee filled both duffle bags and the backpack.

"90 seconds!" said Five. When Mook heard that he pulled out of his parking space and made his way towards the highway entrance. Less than 300 yards onto the highway, he pulled off to the side, turned the hazard lights on in the Ford Explorer, and waited.

"Let's go!" Five announced once the bags were completely full. Honey had already unplugged the dye pack activator that was at the front door on the floor.

The three men walked out of the bank calmly, Honey right behind them, and they walked into the short section of woods next to the bank. Through the 20 yard stretch of woods, they emerged at the top of the highway.

Mook was at the bottom of the hill on the shoulder.

"Here we come Mook," Five said into his Bluetooth. When Mook heard him he turned off the hazard lights and unlocked the doors. Traffic was light at 9:17 in the morning.

The four of them came down the hill, threw the bags into the back of the SUV, then they all climbed in and Mook pulled out onto the road.

Three miles later, and still with no police activity directed at the bank on the scanner, they pulled off the highway. Behind an abandoned warehouse they parked a Monte Carlo S5. They transferred the bags from the SUV into the trunk of the Monte Carlo. Five took a can of gasoline out of the trunk and poured its contents all over the inside of the Explorer. He lit a piece of paper.

"Goons," he said as he threw the lit paper into the SUV.
Whoosh!

9

Beeeep beeeeep.

"Damn, this bitch ain't never ready when I get here," Lungee uttered under his breath. He lit a blunt and turned up the volume on the car's stereo system. Jay Z's "Brooklyn, We Go Hard" blared through the speakers. Lungee was driving his new burgundy Dodge Challenger.

He was parked in front of Lot 17. A singlewide trailer at the Galaxy Courts trailer park off of Bragg Blvd. He was there to pick up Tiffany. Tiffany was a white girl that Lungee paid on a regular basis when he wanted to get away and get his freak on.

Tiffany was down for whatever—as long as the price was right. And Lungee paid well.

Lungee was about to pick up his phone and call her when the door to her trailer opened up.

Tiffany was about 5 foot 6 and petite. Probably 120 pounds. She wasn't that bad looking. She had a slight tan, long light brown hair, hazel eyes and unbelievably perfect teeth. Especially for a crack smoker. But even though Tiffany smoked crack, she kept herself in shape. She was always clean, and her bills were always paid.

"I'm sorry baby," she said as she got into the passenger side. Her short skirt just barely covering her. She threw her bag in the back seat.

"It's all good now," said Lungee as he reached over and put his hand under her skirt. She pulled the skirt up and spread her legs wide. She didn't have on any panties. Lungee pushed two fingers into her pussy.

"Mmmmm..." she moaned. "Come on baby, let's get out of here."

Lungee pulled his fingers out and put them in her mouth. As she sucked his fingers clean she reached her left hand over and tugged at Lungee's zipper. When she released Lungee's manhood from the confines of his True Religion jeans, she pushed his fingers out of her mouth and bent over the seat, taking him into her mouth.

"Ok then," exclaimed Lungee. "Let's get this party started then!" He turned the volume up a little more, put his right hand on her head, and pulled out of her lot.

Lungee had been picking Tiffany up for over a year now. He tried to see her every 2 weeks or so. He had other "working girls" who he would pick up for a blowjob in the car or a quickie fuck behind a store somewhere. But when he felt like an all-nighter, Tiffany was his go to girl. He made sure that Tiffany got tested once a month and all of her other clients had to use a condom. Mandatory. Lungee and Tiffany did all kinds of perverted sex acts over the past year. Tiffany didn't mind since Lungee paid her well whenever they got together.

Lungee already had a room at the Ambassador Suites on Skibo Rd paid for. He went by earlier in the day and took his portable DVD player to attach to the TV in the room. He always had a "special" movie or two that he would watch while him and Tiffany went at it. Tonight's movie was called "Animal Farm". Lungee never let Tiffany know where they were going until they got there. Even though he'd been "seeing" her for over a year, he didn't care. Lungee didn't trust anyone.

No one except the Goons.

Once in the room, Tiffany knew the drill. She removed all of her clothes—not that she had much on to begin with. She tossed her skirt and t-shirt on one of the chairs next to the bed, then she laid on the bed. Lungee had a routine of his own. He lit a blunt, changed into a pair of shorts and turned the air conditioner on full blast. Then he left the room, walked over to the vending machines to fill up the ice bucket and get some sodas out of the machine. When he returned to the room, Tiffany was just finishing up on the phone with Domino's Pizza.

"They said about 25 minutes," she said when she hung the phone up.

"Cool. Go soak that good pussy in the tub til they come," he responded as he spread her legs and rubbed her pussy.

"Let me go daddy before you start something you can't finish," she joked, jumping up out of the bed and heading to the bathroom.

"Oh, don't get it fucked up. If I start, I'm damn sure gonna finish! Fuck that pizza," he said, lightly smacking her on the ass as she ran past him.

The pizza was delivered 20 minutes later. Lungee and Tiffany ate a few slices each, drank some ice cold soda, then Lungee was ready to play.

"Come here," he said as he laid on his back. Tiffany crawled towards Lungee, stopping to take his dick into her mouth just long enough for it to get good and hard. Then she climbed on top of Lungee's 300 pound body, positioned herself over his pole, and slowly took him into her pussy.

"Mmmmmm daddy!" she squealed as she began to ride him, grinding herself onto his throbbing manhood. "Gimme that dick daddy...aaahhhh!" Tiffany was very loud. She knew that it was a big stroke to Lungee's ego, so she laid it on thick for him. In reality, Lungee really didn't do a thing for her sexually. Actually, some of his perverted sexual likes really turned her off. She was hoping he would keep it simple tonight.

She could only hope.

She did have plenty of orgasms when she was with Lungee, and that only added to his ego boosting. The truth of the matter was that Tiffany just had an overly sensitive clit. Tiffany would get an orgasm if she ran 50 yards in a pair of tight jeans. It was that sensitive.

But she never told Lungee that.

Let him dream.

She rode him hard for about 2 minutes, then she felt the first orgasm building up inside her.

"Oh shit daddy!" she said, slamming her hips onto his dick. "I'm cumming daddy! Ohhh daddy...I'm...oh shit!...It's a big one daddy!"

As she slammed harder and harder onto Lungee's dick, he started thrusting back at her, matching her, stroke for stroke, feeling his own orgasm starting to rumble inside of him.

"Oh shit bitch!" he said. "Yeah, slam that pussy on me! Take that big dick! Whose pussy is this?!"

"Oh…it's yours!" she exclaimed, slamming harder.

"I said, whose fuckin' pussy is this bitch!"

"It's yours daddy!"

"Whose?" He grabbed her hips and slammed into her as hard as he could.

"Oh…it's…yours…daddy…fuck me…daddy!" She was putting on one of her Academy Award winning performances, and Lungee was loving it.

"Yeah, I'm bout to cum…take all that cum bitch!" he said as he was about to fill her pussy.

"Give it to me daddy! I'm cumming too!" she screamed.

"Yeah…here it comes! Cum with me!"

"Oh, I'm cumming daddy! Aaaaagghhh!"

"Cum all over that big dick bitch!"

"Ooooh, there it is daddy!"

"Oh yeah, feel that hot cum!" he grunted back as he exploded deep inside of her. He felt her pussy muscles tighten as her own orgasm began.

"Oh yeah! Cum all over that dick! Yeah, suck that cum off baby!" he said as he lifted her off of his dick and spun her around so that she could take his dick in her mouth.

"Yeah, take that dick. Suck it clean bitch! C'mere, bring me that pussy. Lemme taste it," he ordered.

Tiffany swung one of her legs over his head and put her pussy, filled with her pussy juices, her cum and his own cum, over his face. Lungee grabbed her ass cheeks, spread them wide, and then covered her pussy with his mouth, sucking out all of the creamy liquids that her pussy had to offer in the 69 position.

While Lungee was busy sucking his own cum out of Tiffany's pussy, she was sucking his dick dry. As she was expertly servicing his dick, Lungee's legs began to rise and bend upwards. She knew what that meant. She knew what he wanted.

Tiffany filled her mouth with saliva, then let it pour out of her mouth onto Lungee's now exposed asshole. She rubbed the saliva onto his asshole with two fingers, then slowly pushed a finger into Lungee's

185

not-so-tight hole. Lungee lifted his hips to receive the anal penetration. Tiffany pushed deeper into Lungee's ass as his hips rose.

Lungee began licking Tiffany's asshole, at the same time he pushed two fingers deep into her warm and wet pussy.

"Oh daddy!" she whimpered as Lungee began to finger fuck her in her pussy and tongue fuck her asshole. Then he pulled his fingers out of her pussy and pushed both of them into her asshole.

"Aaaaahhh…" she gasped. Then she pushed two more fingers into Lungee's asshole, pushing them deep into him.

The both of them went into a strange frenzy, finger fucking each other's assholes. Lungee pushed his face deep into Tiffany's pussy while two of his fingers fucked in and out of her ass. On the other end of the bed, Tiffany now had four fingers pushed deep into Lungee's asshole and was deep throating his dick as she slammed her fingers into him.

They bucked and fucked against each other until they both climaxed into each other's mouths.

"Get on your knees," Lungee said as he pushed Tiffany off of him. "Lemme fuck that ass." He rolled her onto her knees and he got behind her. Once he pushed his dick into her asshole, he started to slow grind her, until she began to push her hips back at him.

"Gimme that dick daddy!" she growled at him. "Fuck that tight ass!" That's all he needed to hear. He started to really pound away at her, pulling his dick all the way out, them slamming it as hard as he could all the way back in. Whenever he pulled his dick all the way out of her, he could see that her asshole was stretched so far open that you could drop a golf ball straight into it and not touch the sides. Lungee pounded away at Tiffany's asshole for about ten minutes.

Then he got a thought. He slowed his strokes down a little bit.

"Hey Tiff?"

"Oh yesss daddy…" she purred.

"Can you tighten your asshole up?" he asked, still stroking at a slow, steady pace.

"Like this daddy?" she asked, then, when he was all the way into her she tightened up all her ass muscles and her asshole gripped Lungee's dick.

"Oh shit!" he replied, enjoying the new feeling. "Yeah, just like that! Do that every time I'm deep in your shit."

"Ok daddy," she replied.

So, for the next few minutes, every time Lungee sunk his dick into her, she would tighten her asshole. He was loving it. Then he got another idea.

"Yo Tiff?"

"Mmmm hmmm?"

"Let me give you a pink sock," Lungee said.

"What the hell is a pink sock?" she asked. She had never heard of a pink sock before. Knowing Lungee's perverted ass, it could be anything. But she was curious.

"You never heard of a pink sock?" Lungee said, still slow stroking her.

"No, tell me already."

So Lungee told Tiffany what a pink sock was. When he was done, Tiffany pulled away from him, letting out a long airy fart when Lungee's dick came out of her asshole.

"Oh hell no!" she said, jumping out of the bed, letting out a long series of sputtering farts every time she moved. "You are one sick fat fucker!" she yelled as she ran to the bathroom, farting all the way.

Lungee let out a long fart of his own as he sat on the edge of the bed and lit a half piece of blunt that was in the ashtray.

"Fuck it," he said to himself. He heard the shower turn on in the bathroom. Ten minutes later Tiffany came out of the bathroom wrapped in a towel. She sat on the other end of the bed drying herself off.

She stopped and looked at Lungee.

"You just gonna sit there smellin' like butt and nut perv boy?" she asked.

"I got your boy right here," Lungee said, grabbing hold of his dick.

"Well, you're gonna be suckin' your own dick for the rest of the night if you don't go wash that shitty thing off."

Lungee stood up and walked to the bathroom naked. He stayed in the shower for about 15 minutes, masturbating himself once while he was in there. Once he was done he grabbed a towel and walked out of the bathroom.

Tiffany was gone.

Lungee would have considered the fact that she could've ran to the vending machines real quick, except that not only was she gone, but so were all her clothes, his clothes, his keys, even the pizza. Everything was gone.

"No this bitch didn't!" Lungee shouted and ran out of the room.

His car was missing too.

"Fuck!" Lungee yelled, standing outside of his room naked.

"What the fuck you lookin' at?!" he said to a man and woman who had just walked out of their room. He went back into the room and slammed the door. Tiffany had taken his money, phone, and car. He picked up the hotel phone and dialed Tiffany's number.

"This is Tiff. You know what to do. Beeeeeep."

"Bitch, you got 10 minutes to bring my shit back!" he yelled into the receiver. He dialed his own phone. It rang a few times then it was sent to voicemail.

"Yo, this is Lungee. If it don't make a dollar it don't make a damn bit o' sense. Holla at ya boy. Beeeeeep." He hung up. He waited about five minutes then tried Tiffany again.

"Yo Tiff," he said right after the beep. "I ain't playin' wit you. Bring my shit back right now and I won't split yo shit!" He slammed the phone down again. He noticed that his cigarettes were gone too.

Now he was really pissed off.

He picked the phone up and dialed another number.

"Hello." She picked up after two rings.

"Honey." He was relieved that she answered. "I need you girl."

"Nigga, stop playing on my phone," she said.

"No, Honey I'm for real. I need you to come get me."

"What?" Honey was alert now. "What's up bro?"

"This bitch took off with my shit."

"Look, where you at?"

Lungee told her where he was, and Honey said she would be right there.

"Oh and Honey."

"Yeah."

"Can you please go in my room and grab me some clothes?"

"The bitch took your clothes?"

"Yeah."

"I'm on the way bro," Honey said as she hung up.

10

When Honey arrived, Lungee opened the door wrapped in a blanket.

"Go put some clothes on boy," she said, handing him a bag of clothes.

"Thanks girl," he said, taking the bag and heading into the bathroom to get dressed.

"I drove your Caddy out here," she yelled towards the door, referring to his Cadillac Escalade. He came out a few minutes later.

"Why the Lac?"

"Cause we gonna go find the bitch who got your shit, I'm gonna drive it back to the house for you," Honey said.

"Ok, let's roll," Lungee said, leading the way out of the room, the keys to his Escalade in his hand.

****

"I can't believe this bitch just took my shit and went home," exclaimed Lungee when he pulled into the Galaxy Courts trailer park and saw his Dodge Challenger parked in front of Tiffany's trailer.

"Just drive by," Honey said.

Lungee drove by Lot 17 and noticed that the lights were on inside of the trailer.

"Ok look Lungee," said Honey. "Lemme do this my way. Drop me off at the end and go home. I'll be there a few minutes behind you."

"You sure?"

"Hell yeah I'm sure. I got you bro. Just drop me off and go. Your shit is there, so it ain't gonna be no problem getting' it back. Just go. I got this."

So Lungee pulled up to a trailer at the end of the road and turned around. Honey got out.

"I'll see you at the house. Go," she said and shut the door. She watched Lungee's Escalade disappear up the dirt road and she started walking in the direction of Tiffany's trailer.

It was just past midnight now.

****

Tiffany was sitting on her couch putting a flame to the tip of the crack pipe in her mouth. Next to her was her friend Melissa and Melissa's boyfriend Joe. She passed the pipe to Melissa when she heard the knock at the door.

"That's probably Lungee," she told her guests. "All pissed off cause I left him at the room naked. If he's real pissed, y'all don't trip. He'll probably just take his shit and go."

She opened her trailer door and saw Honey standing there.

She didn't know Honey.

"Can I help you?" she asked, blocking the entrance.

"Yeah," said Honey, pushing her way into the trailer and shutting the door behind her. "I'm here for my brother's things. You Tiffany?" she asked.

"Who the hell are you?" asked Melissa from the couch. "Just barging in here like that!"

Honey pulled her 17 shot M82 Llama .9mm with a silencer on it and pointed it at Melissa's face.

"Who the fuck are you bitch?" Honey snapped at Melissa.

"She ain't nobody!" interrupted Joe. "That's Tiff right there!" he declared, pointing at Tiffany.

All three of their buzzes disappeared just that quickly.

"Shut the fuck up," he whispered to Melissa.

Honey directed her attention to Tiffany.

"Where are my brother's keys, clothes, his phone and his money?"

"It's all right there," uttered Tiffany. She pointed to the counter. Lungee's clothes were folded neatly on the counter. His phone and keys were on top. Tiffany dug into her pocket and pulled out a roll of money. She handed it to Honey.

"It's all there except two hundred."

Honey put the roll of money in her own pocket.

"Are you fuckin' crazy, or just stupid bitch," Honey asked her.

"We ain't gonna be too many more bitches in here!" said Melissa, standing up now.

She should have kept her mouth shut.

Honey pointed the gun at her face.

Thpt...thpt...thpt...

She stroked the trigger three times, sending three hollow shells directly into the middle of Melissa's face and head. Then she turned the gun on Joe.

"Oh shit!" Joe said, throwing his hands in the air to protest the inevitable.

Thpt...thpt...thpt...

The first bullet tore through Joe's left hand and found a home in his throat. The next two tore into his heart.

Tiffany pissed on herself when she saw what Honey had just did to her friends.

"Oh my God!" she cried, urine running down her inner thighs. "I wasn't gonna keep his shit! I swear! He wanted me to do some fucked up shit with him, so I just wanted to teach him a lesson. I was gonna give him his stuff tomorrow. I swear! I would never steal from him! He knows that."

Tiffany was openly crying now.

"What kind of fucked up shit?" Honey asked out of curiosity.

"He wanted to do a purple sleeve or a pink...shit...a pink sock...that shit is nasty and perverted!"

"What the fuck is a pink fuckin' sleeve?"

"He said that he wanted to fuck me in my ass, then, when he's cummin' in my ass I'm supposed to tighten my ass up as tight as I could, then he wanted to punch me in the back of my head."

"What?!"

"Yeah, when he punches me in the back of my head, he's 'pose to knock me out. My whole body tightens up, then he yanks his dick out, pulling my asshole inside out."

"You're bullshittin' me!" said Honey trying to hold in her laughter.

"I swear to God I'm not! Then when I told him no, he said instead of him knocking me out with a punch to the back of the head, he could just hit me with a stun gun. No disrespect, but your brother is a pervert."

"Is that right?"

"Yeah, he's always wantin' me to do nasty shit to him. One time he made me go buy a big ass strap on dick and fuck him in the ass with it. He's real sick with his sex shit."

"So why you fuck with him?" asked Honey.

"For the money. He always pays me really good."

Honey really did feel sorry for her a little.

"Put all his shit in a trash bag for me," said Honey. Tiffany went under the kitchen sink, took out a bag and put all of Lungee's things in it. She handed the bag to Honey.

"Here you go. Please tell him I said I'm sorry."

"You've never seen me right?" asked Honey, grabbing a rag from the kitchen sink.

"No, I swear! I don't know you! I've never seen you! I'll tell 'em that some white guys came in and did that."

"You won't mention me to the police?"

"No, I swear! On my momma!"

"I know you won't."

Thpt...thpt...thpt...thpt...

Honey grabbed the doorknob with the rag and walked out of the trailer.

****

Honey pulled up next to Lungee's Escalade. She grabbed the bag with his things and walked into the house.

193

"Here," she said when she walked into the living room and threw the bag at Lungee along with his keys.

"Good lookin' sis!" he said, looking into the bag.

"Whatever," she said. Then she pulled her pistol and threw it on the couch next to him. "Get rid of that," she said as she walked past him. Then she stopped, looked at Lungee, and said, "You are one sick ass nigga."

11

The story of Tiffany, Melissa, and Joe's killings made the headlines, but not for too long. The police didn't have any suspects, but one neighbor in a trailer across from Tiffany's saw a car in front of the trailer for a couple of hours that night, then it was gone. What kind of car? She couldn't say. What color? Maybe black. Real dark. The police couldn't put much into her statement. She was really no help at all. The police didn't put many man hours into the investigation at all. They just filed it away as a drug-related killing and left it at that, what, with all the drugs that were found on the scene.

Even though the police weren't digging too hard and neither Honey nor Lungee were in any real danger, Five was still pissed. Everyone in the crew knew that they never did any bodies in Fayetteville unless it was absolutely unavoidable.

"That was some fuckin' bullshit!" yelled Five. "You sent Honey to smoke some crack head bitch, all cause you got caught slippin' and let her take your shit? Are you fuckin' stupid?!"

If Five wasn't Lungee's cousin he would never be allowed to get away with talking to him like that. But Lungee knew he fucked up so he just stood there and took the verbal lashing that Five was dishing out to him.

"What if somebody would have gotten your plate number? What if Honey would've gotten stopped? You don't think sometimes Lungee."

"Lungee didn't send me to do those crack heads," Honey said, defending Lungee. "I was just supposed to go and pick up his car. I'm the one that fucked up."

"Look, I'm gonna stop trippin'," said Five, still directing his attention at Lungee. "Get rid of the car though."

"My car!"

"Yeah, your car. And where's the gun Honey?"

"I gave it to Lungee to get rid of," she replied.

"It's already gone," Lungee added. "Recycled."

"Aight man. Y'all stop fuckin' slippin'. I know we each have our own lives to live, but keep in mind that shit you do could still affect us as a whole."

"Got you Five," replied Honey.

"My bad cuz."

"Aight. Stay on point cause we may be heading to Charlotte."

"Just say when."

"I'll let you all know. I'm working on it now."

12

With Big Mike and Dookie backing Smurf's moves, he was able to take control of the South side of Hidden Valley with little or no resistance at all. He dropped his prices as an added incentive to keep Supreme's old crew happy. Dookie did make some phone calls, as promised, and informed Smurf of which areas were weak enough for a takeover. But he also let Smurf know that until his crew controlled all of Hidden Valley, they wouldn't be a real force. Hidden Valley was the largest neighborhood, and even though Supreme controlled the South side, it was the North side that got most of the money.

Smurf was far from stupid. He knew that Dookie was planting the seeds in his head to move on Big Mike because he had his own agenda. He figured that if he controlled all of the Valley, he would be buying all his weight from Dookie. And that was Dookie's objective....to control the Valley through Smurf and his crew. The other spots he was putting Smurf on were just icing on the cake.

Linwood Oaks was one of those spots. It wasn't a very large complex, but it was unique because it had two back exit routes that led right into a wooded section of mazes that could take you into about 6 different neighborhoods. And all of those neighborhoods came into Linwood to buy their drugs. So, as small as it was, it was a goldmine.

Once Dookie laid it out to Smurf, he knew he had to have Linwood Oaks.

Casper owned Linwood Oaks.

Casper was a 28 year old white boy who had grown up in Linwood and thought he was black. He became a Gangster Disciple at the age of 17 and a six star general by the age of 21. He was the first one to really bring any good dope into Linwood and he was well respected.

Well, Smurf was about to test Casper's gangster. When he told some of the Bloods who he wanted to hit, they were with it. Not just because Casper was white, but because he was a GD.

From one minute to the next, Linwood Oaks became a warzone.

Linwood Oaks was comprised of 3 buildings set into a U formation. The open end was the main entrance, and at the back end, between the buildings led into the woods. Smurf, Young God and his four man Atlanta crew came into the front entrance in the Range Rover. At the same time about 20 Bloods came through the back way. All dressed in red, bandanas covering their faces, and all sorts of machine guns in their hands.

As soon as they got into the clearing past the buildings they opened fire on everything moving. People took off running in every direction, but the Bloods showed no mercy. Bodies began to fall.

Casper wasn't hard to spot. He was the only white face in Linwood. He was leaning against the open trunk of an old Buick. When the shooting started, without hesitation he reached into the trunk and pulled out an AK-47. At the same time that he ducked behind the Buick, Smurf spotted him. He stopped the Range Rover and him and his team jumped out. They had Casper pinned down, but Casper was so occupied with the Bloods that had swarmed the Oaks from the back that he really didn't pay attention to the Range Rover that pulled up 30 feet behind him.

Casper jumped up from behind the Buick and let out a burst from his AK-47 in the general direction of a group of about 4 Bloods who were shooting towards one of the buildings. His shot went wide, missing everything but air.

Unfortunately for him, Smurf didn't miss. He walked up behind Casper.

"What's up white boy?" he said.

"Who the fuck…" was all Casper was allowed to say before Smurf's .40 caliber Glock barked twice in his face, forcing a closed casket funeral. Casper fell to the ground and Smurf picked up the AK-47, emptying it at a group of Casper's people before jumping into the Range Rover and hitting the horn several times, signaling that it was time to go. The gunfire slowed down, then stopped as the Bloods made their way back out of Linwood Oaks, through the woods, and into several waiting cars.

"We'll come back and set up shop later," Smurf said as he pulled out of Linwood Oaks.

13

"Look here Blood, I know what I'm talkin' bout. I seen it before."

"Man, I'm the one put them niggas on here. I just can't see it," replied Big Mike.

Sizzle, who was Supreme's right hand man until Smurf came along, was trying to explain his suspicions to Big Mike that he didn't think Smurf was gonna stop until he took over all of Hidden Valley.

"That nigga knows that the North Valley is too deep for him. He would get slaughtered up in here. I just don't see that nigga being on no suicidal shit. But, I'm definitely gon' keep my eyes open. That nigga cross Lewiston Blvd one time without an invitation or announcing himself first and I'm gonna light his ass up myself. And that's on Blood!"

After the shootings in Linwood Oaks, Smurf let it die down before he put a crew of about 10 young Bloods, working around the clock, selling his product, into the Oaks. Smurf also set up shop in another small apartment complex, but that was a lot less complicated since no official crew had laid claim to that area.

Big Mike was indeed keeping an eye on Smurf's rise in Charlotte. He was also keeping his ears open. And from what he was hearing, Dookie was feeding Smurf his intell on Charlotte. Big Mike also knew that Dookie harbored some ill feelings because he refused to buy weight from him. So yes, he was keeping himself on point, and wondering if he had made a mistake in fucking with Smurf in the first place.

Did he have a snake in his midst?

Maybe two?

Either way, Big Mike wasn't too concerned because not only did he live dead in the center of North Valley, and getting to him would be damn near impossible, but even if Smurf was to get to Big Mike somehow, there would be a war in the streets of Hidden Valley like never before. All of Big Mike's people were loyal, die hard Bloods, and some were already whispering about Smurf and the South Valley. All he had to do was let go of the leash and let the dogs loose.

"Good lookin' out on the heads up though Sizzle."

"Blood is Blood my nigga. I told you before, I never really was on the North side bullshit. Blood is Blood. Soo woo!" Sizzle said, throwing up the Blood sign.

"Soo woo!" responded Big Mike, returning the sign.

****

Every spot that Smurf and his team took over increased his number strength. No one wanted to go against him. Besides, with him and his crew in control, everyone was eating. His supply was flowing smoothly and he had virtually no competition.

None except Big Mike and the North Valley Bloods.

"Ayo my nigga," said Young God. "All you got to do is say the word. We'll pull all the troops and run up into the North side deeper than a mutha fucka yo! Them nigga'll think they was in Iraq. Word bond! All you gotta do is make it so."

Him and Smurf were discussing their rise and expansion in the Charlotte area. Smurf did feel that they would definitely need the North side of Hidden Valley to solidify their position as the dominant force in Charlotte. And eventually they would take the North Valley. But he didn't feel that the time was right.

"Don't sweat that shit right now Young God. The North side already belongs to us. We just haven't taken it yet. Be patient, because when we do take it, you gon be the nigga in charge of that side. So you better be ready to get what you ask for.:

"Oh, I'm damn sho ready my nigga," Young God declared, rubbing his hands together like a mad scientist.

"Yeah, but you gonna be able to handle it when you get it?" Smurf asked.

"Watch and see."

****

"How long you gonna let this nigga run wild?"

"Him only run cause I allow him to run. I can pull him leash whenever I get ready to. Or, if him gets too wild, I can put him down like we do wit all wild animals."

Dookie and one of his Jamaican associates were talking about Smurf's team also. It seemed as if Smurf and his crew were the talk of the town. Some of the smaller dealers who controlled some of the yet untouched areas of Charlotte were wondering when and if they would be next. It really didn't matter much to Dookie though because he didn't sell on the streets. Most street level dealers didn't even know that Dookie existed since he didn't sell anything less than 10 kilos at a time. So the more of Charlotte that Smurf controlled, the more he would be needing to buy from Dookie—especially when his own supply was exhausted.

"Right now him good for business. Later, him better. Let da boy do him ting. What we need to be keepin an eye on is dat slick ass fat nigga Big Mike."

"Why you say dat boss?"

"Tink bout it. Like we see tings, Big Mike see tings. Him know only matta o' time fo' dat crazy nigga Smurf wan' more o' da Valley. North Valley is where da gold be at. Big Mike know it. An he know Smurf know it too. Him sittin' scary. Matta o' time. Matta o' bloodclot time. Dat lil' ugly nigga be ready soon."

"What we gon' do boss?"

"Do? We sit back an get paid." Dookie laughed.

14

"Ok, this is what I got so far," said Five to the rest of the crew. "It looks like this New York nigga named Smurf just stepped into Charlotte and started taking over shit. He smoked this cat named Supreme who supposedly snitched on his people with the Feds. After he took over 'Preme's hood, the nigga just went ballistic. Takin' over shit all over Charlotte."

"By his self?!" asked Lungee.

"Naw. He showed up wit a small crew, but he's deep as fuck now. Plus, he got some big time Jamaican nigga behind him call himself Doogie or Dookie. Some shit like that."

"This nigga sounds like he might be a little out of our league Five. You said he's deep as hell. How the fuck we supposed to get at him? It's only five of us," Mook questioned.

"We ain't goin after his whole crew, retarded ass nigga, we just want the loot. I got a nigga up there that's tryna find out as much as he can for me. All we really need to know is where the nigga keep his shit at—money and dope—and how many niggas be watching the stash at all times. Once we find that out, we'll figure out the best way to hit this cat. It sounds like this nigga is caked the fuck up."

"Charlotte, here we come," said Honey.

****

"My people are ready nigga," said Five into the phone. "I just need you to tell me more yo. We ain't going nowhere blind."

"I got you. I'm tryna find out where the nigga keep his shit at but it's hard as fuck. He stay moving around. It's like he a ghost sometimes. The nigga just showed up outta nowhere, smoked my nigga 'Preme right next to me! I was there, standing right next to him when his face just exploded! But the bugged out shit is that the nigga Smurf was nowhere around! Got my nigga on some serious sniper hit man shit. Nobody knows where the nigga came from, where he be at, where he lay his head, or where he keep his shit at. But believe me, I'm on that shit."

"Aight, just let me know when you got something for me."

"As soon as I got something, I'll get at you."

"Aight," replied Five. "One."

"One."

****

"I just wish you would bring your ass home boy! You know your mom is worried sick about you."

"I'm good cuz. We up here takin' over shit. Niggas don't fuck wit us. I'm cool. Ballin' outta control cuz!"

"I wish you wouldn't talk like that. I'm not one of your little thuggy ass friends. And you're only 18 years old. What do you know about 'ballin out of control'?"

"Your old boss used to ball outta control, drivin' Bentleys and Benzes and givin' away loot like it grow on trees."

"Yeah well, my old boss is dead now! That life that you're trying so hard to live put bullets in her back! I'm not trying to see the same happen to you Chris. And neither is your mom."

"Look Kem, I'm ok. We bout to have one last big beef, and when that's over we'll own this town."

"And what if something happens to you during your little beef?"

"I told you, we cool. I'm cool. Smurf got the local cats doin' all the real beefin'. We just be sittin' back pickin' up the pieces when it's over."

"Just come home Chris. Get out of those streets and come home. You know Boo Boo misses you."

"Tell him I said what's up. Look, I gotta go cuz. I'll call you."

"Chris wait…"

The phone went dead.

Kemya put her phone into her purse and placed her face into her hands. Her aunt called her and asked her to talk to Chris. Chris was

Kemya's cousin. He was 18 years old and as much as his mother tried her best to keep him off of the streets, the attractiveness and adrenaline rush of fast money and even faster women was too much of a temptation for him, and eventually the streets took hold of him. So much so that he fell in under Young God and Scientific back when they were doing their thing in Decatur. Chris was one of those new faces involved in Tiana's rescue when Chen kidnapped her.

Kemya looked up at the large oil painting of her former employer—Tiana Brantz. As much as she loved Tiana, deep down she knew Tiana and her siege on Atlanta was responsible for her cousin being so far gone into the streets. Tiana brought into Atlanta a team of some of the most ruthless killers the streets had ever seen. Chris took to Scientific's team like a fly to a pile of shit. Kemya did everything in her power to keep her own son, Booker, off of the streets, and so far she was doing a good job. Boo Boo, as she liked to call him, was about to graduate from high school with good enough grades to get into any college he chose to. Funding was not an issue. Tiana placed money into a trust fund account for his college years ago. Kemya was always thankful for all that Tiana did for her and her son over the years. Tiana left Kemya with a lot of money to take care of herself and her son, along with a place to work for life. She owed Tiana so much gratitude for all that she'd done for her. But as she looked up at Tiana's smiling face on the wall, the thoughts that were going through her head were how much she wished Tiana was there.

****

Smurf, Young God and almost 2 dozen Bloods laid a path of destruction through Linwood Oaks and gunned down everything that moved when they claimed the three building complex and dethroned Casper. They never expected that someone else would try and take it from them so soon. Especially not 4 shabbily dressed crack heads.

But everything is not always what it seems.

The four of them came through the woods and between two of the buildings laughing and joking with each other. The seven Bloods standing in the doorway to one of the buildings didn't pay them much attention. They noticed them, but only briefly.

What they did notice was the dark green Ford Excursion that had crept into the front entrance.

"Yo, heads up," one of the Bloods said, putting the others on point. They watched the dark SUV get closer, and paid no further attention to the 4 crack heads as they got closer.

Big mistake.

All four of the crack heads pulled out mini Uzis when they got within 10 feet of the Blood crew.

"Soo woo!" one of them screamed as they opened fire. None of them had a chance to pull a weapon as the "crack heads" emptied their clips into the seven Bloods. When they were done the "crack heads" jumped into the Ford Excursion and left Linwood Oaks. All seven of the Bloods lay dead in a large pool of blood.

****

The same thing happened in the other two spots that Smurf had taken over in the past few weeks that night. When Smurf heard the news, he was furious.

The next day, he called an emergency meeting at his own house.

"Yo, how the fuck none o' you niggas don't know shit 'bout who's steppin' to us?!" yelled Smurf.

"I told you who I think it is yo," said one of the young Bloods.

"And I already told you, Big Mike ain't trippin' on us! If I thought Big Mike was feelin' some kinda way about us, we'd of been hit that fat nigga! Naw, this is some other shit!"

"It just happened, so really we need to just hit the streets and see what we can find out."

"What the fuck we need to find out! We just lost like 20 something niggas out there! All we need to find out is who the fuck did this shit! Throw some niggas out the window or some shit in this motha fucka!"

"You're right Smurf," said Sizzle. "We're gonna find out who did this today. Come on, we out," he said to a group of Bloods as he got up to leave.

Once he was in his car, Sizzle pulled his phone out and punched in a number from memory.

It was picked up on the second ring.

"What's good?"

"Yo, I know where the nigga Smurf lay his head," he said into the phone looking up at Smurf's house. "I'm here right now."

"Ok, that's what's up. Lemme hit you back later to get the details from you."

"Aight, yeah hit me later."

"One," said Five.

"One." Sizzle closed his phone and pulled off.

15

"I've got your back Smurf. Meet at Mecklenburg High School, tomorrow at 6:00 pm. Football field. Be there."

Smurf didn't know what to make of the text message. It came from a private number, so he couldn't even respond to the message. He didn't like it one bit though, especially with all that was was going on around him right now. It could have been an attempt to ambush him and his crew, but he doubted anyone would believe that could work. But if that was the case, he was gonna be prepared.

He talked to Young God about the text, and Young God felt the same way as him. They should go, but be prepared.

"We need to have a few niggas posted up at the football field all fuckin' day, that way we know if niggas is tryna lay for us."

"Yeah, I like that," said Smurf. "Nigga say he got my back, so if somebody tried to show up mad early to post up, we gots to come in blastin'."

"Who you think it is?" Young God asked.

"Don't know. But we damn sure 'bout to find out. And if a nigga ain't bout no serious business, we gon leave his ass laying on the 50 yard line."

"Word bond my nigga!"

****

"I talked to that nigga a little while ago. He knows we ain't had shit to do wit hittin' his people."

Big Mike was talking to one of his top generals about the hits on Smurf's spots. He called Smurf and assured him that his people had nothing to do with it. But Big Mike wasn't so sure himself. A lot of the Bloods under him really weren't happy with the way Smurf and his team came up all of a sudden, and out of nowhere. Some of them could have did the hits on their own. He expressed that to his guy.

"I don't know Blood. None of our people be on that renegade shit."

"How can you know that for sure?" asked Big Mike.

"Cause that's what you got me for Blood. Niggas know better than to make moves like that on their own. That's on Blood OG. If I find out any of our people was behind that, shit, I'm personally gonna smoke those fools. Whoever was wit it."

"I feel you Blood. But stay on top of that shit real close. Cause I wanna know who was behind it anyway. Imma keep a close watch on that nigga Smurf though, cause he acts like we all cool, but he could flip. He lost a lot of his people from what I heard. That nigga's ready to take some heads, and he doesn't care who."

****

"Aight, look," said Five. "This nigga got a whole lot on his plate right now. His people are gettin hit and he has no fuckin' clue who's behind it. He's spooked, and he's vulnerable like a mother fucker. He already made a big ass mistake and exposed where he stay. That's how fucked up his head is right now."

"Yeah, but you know his main stash ain't at his house. If we gon' hit this nigga proper, we need to hit his stash," commented Dreads.

"I'm feelin' what Dreds is talkin' about," added Mook.

"You know we ain't no petty niggas Five. If we gonna hit this nigga, we need to hit his ass real hard."

"Oh yeah, we definitely gonna hit him hard. I'm thinking that we need to take a trip to Charlotte and scope this nigga and his team out for a sec. Just to see what we're dealing with."

"You don't think we'll draw attention to ourselves?" Honey weighed in. "Just popping up out of nowhere like that. New faces do tend to stick out."

"I don't think so in this case," replied Five.

"Why not?" questioned Dreads.

"Because Charlotte is so big that everybody don't know everybody. We'd most likely just blend right in. And my people there tell me that there's so much tension in the streets right now that niggas don't know which way to look."

"So when we heading to Charlotte," Lungee asked.

"I'm already working on that," Five replied. "So pack."

16

The next day, Smurf prepared for the unknown. At a little after 1 o'clock in the afternoon, he dropped off 4 of his South Valley Bloods at the Mecklenburg High School. Two of them were to remain outside of the school keeping an eye on the school grounds so that no one can creep up on the school. The other two were to chill in the stands and just keep their eyes open all day. If anything moved on or off the school grounds, Smurf was to be contacted immediately.

At 5:45 pm, 18 vehicles pulled into the parking lot of the Mecklenburg High School. Smurf had just talked to all four of the people at the school and they hadn't seen a thing all day.

Each vehicle contained 4 to 6 heavily armed soldiers who were ready for anything. All 18 vehicles circled the school once, just in case, before pulling into the parking lot reserved for the football stadium. Once the cars parked, each man got out carrying everything from .12 gauge shotguns, to Uzis, to AK-47s. They were being extra cautious, looking in every direction as they made their way through the turnstiles at the ticket booths with Smurf and Young God leading the way. They got to the home team's end zone and Smurf stopped.

"Y'all niggas keep your eyes and ears open and be ready for anything. We don't know what the fuck is up so don't nobody jump the gun. This could be some bullshit so just chill. Spread out some," he said, pointing to the area behind the end zone. "That way nobody could get in this bitch without us knowing it. Light em if you got em, but stay on point."

All those who smoked began lighting up cigarettes and blunts. Smurf and Young God pulled away from the crowd to talk in private.

Everyone heard it at the same time.

A slight rumble in the air.

Then they saw them coming.

"What the fuck!" exclaimed Young God.

All around him Smurf heard shells being chambered and shotguns being pumped and at the ready.

"Y'all hold up," he said as he held out his hand to his people in an effort to keep them calm and from overreacting, as he walked out onto the field.

Everyone was looking to the sky.

Looking at three helicopters heading in their direction. As they got closer it was obvious what their intentions were.

They were about to land on the field.

They got closer and lower.

"Y'all just chill," said Smurf over his shoulder as the three helicopters lowered themselves and were about to land at the opposite end of the field. "Let's see what's up." Young God stepped to Smurf's side as the first of the three choppers touched the ground, followed directly by the other two.

Two people emerged from the middle helicopter.

Four each from the other two.

All three helicopters quickly lifted off the ground and took off in the direction they came from.

All ten people began walking in Smurf's direction. Smurf and Young God began walking towards them, one by one, all of the soldiers fell in behind them. Guns in front of them, and ready for a war.

As they approached each other, one lone figure stood out. Smurf's eyes remained glued to the person in the middle of the group. As they got closer, Smurf noticed that person was wearing a full length white trench coat over a white suit and a pair of very large sunglasses.

It was a woman.

"Oh fuckin' shit!" Smurf said. Him and Young God recognized her at the same time.

It was Tiana.

She took her shades off when she got within 10 feet of Smurf and his army.

"I can't leave you alone for a minute," she said with a huge smile on her face. Her Desert Eagles at her side.

"I can't believe this shit," replied Smurf as he hugged Tiana.

Standing next to Tiana was Edwin Santana.

Detective Edwin Santana.

17

Six months earlier...

"What are you gonna do Brantz?"

"What I do."

Tiana got into the black Lamborghini Murcielago that belonged to her late husband and pulled away. She was at the home of Detective Edwin Santana. Santana was suspended from the force for his involvement in Tiana's rescue after she was kidnapped by Chen Ayngen. She was at Santana's house to get some long awaited answers as to who killed her husband.

What Santana told her shocked Tiana beyond belief. She left his house on a mission. The person who Santana said killed Divine worked for Victor Maldonado. She knew that for a fact because Victor sent him to New York to help Tiana once in the past.

But now she learned that Victor also sent the same man to kill Tiana's husband. On the very day of her wedding.

Her mission was revenge.

She left Santana's house and went to her own house, where she picked up her two favorite weapons—her silenced .9mm Desert Eagles. Then she left her house and drove to Stone Mountain.

Using the GPS tracking device that he planted in her car, Santana followed her.

Tiana drove to the home of Victor Maldonado.

But Santana wasn't the only person following Tiana. She was also being followed by Stacey Aller.

Stacey was a friend of Tiana's. Tiana had helped her out in the past. Actually, Tiana gave Stacey a new life for her and her daughter. Stacey came to talk to Tiana, but Tiana sped past her looking very distraught. So instinct told her to follow Tiana.

After Tiana pulled up to the large Stone Mountain home, a few minutes later, Tiana's best friend (and Stacey's lawyer) pulled in. Less than a minute later she heard 3 gunshots.

Stacey rushed to the house.

At the front door lay the brother of Victor Maldonado.
He was dead.

Stacey reached down and took hold of the gun sticking out of his waist and walked into the house. When she got to the back office, standing over Tiana, pointing a gun at her, was Victoria Maldonado.

Stacey shot her in the head.

She rushed over to Tiana's side, who was shot twice in the back. Tiana gave Stacey a computer memory stick with access to all of Tiana's money.

Then Tiana coughed blood out of her mouth, sighed, then died. Or at least, Stacey thought she was dead. When Tiana closed her eyes, Stacey screamed.

"Noooooooooo! Please Tiana! Don't go!" She shook Tiana's limp body, trying to get her to regain consciousness.

"Move!" a voice yelled, and Stacey felt firm hands push her away. Detective Santana laid Tiana on the ground, wiped the blood from her mouth and started administering CPR.

"Call her secretary!" he said to Stacey. "Bennet!"

Tiana coughed.

"Oh my God!" Stacey exclaimed, just as the phone began to ring.

"Brantz and Brantz. How may I direct your call?"

"Somebody picked up," she told Santana. He took the phone from Stacey.

"Ms. Bennet?" he asked.

"This is Kemya Bennet."

"Kemya, this is Santana."

"Oh, hey."

"Look, Tiana's been shot!"

"Oh my God! What? Where?"

"Do you know where Victoria Maldonado lives?"

"Yes."

"I need you here right now! Bring someone with you who can drive a Lambo and who you can trust."

"I'm on the way."

"Hurry."

By the time Kemya arrived with Anthony Crawford, Tiana was breathing, but barely.

"Oh my God! Ms. Brantz!" Kemya cried.

"I need to get her to a hospital," Santana said.

"No. She has a private doctor. Very discrete," said Kemya.

"I'll follow you," said Santana.

Santana and Stacey staged an elaborate scene at the Maldonado house. The scene told a shaky story, with a few holes, but it was workable. The way it would look on first glance was that Victoria Maldonado walked into the house, killed Manuel Maldonado, then went into her father's office and unloaded the two Desert Eagles into Victor Maldonado, who was able to get off one shot. The shot that killed Victoria. There were many unexplained elements to that story, but by the time the forensic techs sorted it all out and did tests on all the blood in the house, Santana would have Tiana far away.

Anthony drove Tiana's Lamborghini to his house and put it in his garage. Stacey gave Kemya the memory stick that Tiana gave her and went to her house to shower and change. Kemya promised to call and let her know what's going on with Tiana. Santana followed Kemya to a doctor and longtime friend of Tiana's

His name was Dr. Jeff Proudfoot. Kemya called and let him know they were on the way, that Tiana was barely alive, and that she had lost a lot of blood. Dr. Proudfoot said that he would be ready when they got there.

Dr. Proudfoot had been treating Tiana's people for years, but he had never treated Tiana herself. His office was connected to his home and he treated gunshot wounds discreetly for Tiana.

When Kemya pulled in front of Dr. Proudfoot's, he ran out and waved Santana towards the side of the house, and directed him into the garage. Once Santana was inside, the garage door shut behind him.

Dr. Proudfoot helped him carry Tiana inside.

She had lost consciousness again.

But she was still alive.

Tiana's body was placed on an operating table.

"You two go have a seat in the living room. Let me do my work here. There are soft drinks and water in the kitchen. Help yourselves."

Kemya and Santana left the room so that Proudfoot could work on Tiana.

"What the hell happened to her?" Kemya asked Santana.

"I got there too late," he said. "Minutes too late. She was at my house, and I told her who killed her husband. She took off. I knew she was gonna do something real stupid so I activated the GPS tracking device on her car and followed her from a distance. By the time I got here, Stacey Aller was holding her in her arms."

"Oh my God."

"According to Aller, she followed Tiana from her house. Tiana went into the Maldonado house, evidently killing one man at the door. Then Victoria Maldonado showed up. But she was a little late. Tiana killed her father. Victoria shot Tiana. Then Stacey killed Victoria. I got there a minute later."

Kemya took out the 'T' shaped memory stick.

"Tiana gave this to Stacey," she said, handing it to Santana. He looked at it, then put it in his pocket.

"I'll give it to her when she's awake."

"You think she'll be ok?" Kemya asked.

"She better, or I'll kill her my damn self."

Kemya called Anthony Crawford, then she called Stacey just to give them an update, which was really nothing yet. But she promised to call them both when anything changed.

After over five hours, Dr. Proudfoot came from the back looking very somber. Kemya and Santana stood up when he walked into the living room. They both noticed the look on his face.

"What is it doc?" asked Santana. "How is she?"

"She's not good. I honestly don't know why she is still alive. She lost a lot of blood. One of the bullets entered her from behind, just barely missing her spine by mere centimeters. It punctured her stomach, releasing deadly stomach acids and fluids into her body. Infection had already set in. The other bullet ripped a hole in one of her lungs, but by some miracle of God I was able to repair the hole and save her lung. I was able to remove both bullets, but right now she is hanging on by the thinnest of threads. She is in extremely critical condition, and she seems to be slipping in and out of a coma. I've got her on an IV full of antibiotics for the infection and I'm monitoring all of her vitals. If she lives through the night I would be surprised. I'm sorry."

"Can we see her please?" Kemya asked.

"Of course. Follow me."

They followed Dr. Proudfoot to the back and into the room where Tiana was laying almost on her side to avoid pressure on her back. She had three IV lines coming out of her body and sensors everywhere.

Santana grabbed Tiana's hand.

"What the fuck are you really into Brantz?" he said. "Who are you, for real?"

Kemya looked on in tears.

Beeeeeeeeeeeeeeeeep!

Tiana flat lined all of a sudden.

She died.

"Oh hell no!" Santana screamed at her. "You're not getting away from me that easy bitch!" Santana pulled his hand from Tiana's. "You get back here goddammit!" he yelled at Tiana. Then Santana did the strangest thing Dr. Proudfoot had ever seen. Before he could rush to Tiana's side, Santana smacked Tiana in her face as hard as he could.

"You come back here!" Santana screamed with tears in his eyes.

Beeeeeeeeeeeeeeeeeeep...beep...beep...beep...beep...

18

Two weeks later a small private funeral service was held for Tiana Brantz. It was attended by the staff of Brantz and Brantz, Stacey Aller and her daughter Sierra, Dawit Burroughs who was Tiana's accountant, a few members of the Atlanta Police showed up—probably to gloat, the last remaining members of Tiana's drug organization were there also. Santana was there too, but he did not sit with the other officers.

It was a closed casket service, but there was a large picture of Tiana in front of the casket. A few people spoke at the service, including Kemya, Stacey and Anthony Crawford, but it was Smurf who stole the show.

"What the fuck is y'all crying for?!" he exclaimed when he stood up to speak. "Y'all act like you know Tiana like that, but if you really knew her, you'd know she wouldn't have wanted all this bitch ass crying up in here. Tiana was a ride or die bitch! But she was the classiest I ever knew, and it was an honor and a pleasure to ride with her. I would have died with her, or for her if I had that chance. But she knows one thing for sure, and that's black ass Smurf loves her and I will be with her soon—probably sooner than later. If there wasn't so many punk ass police up in this bitch, I'd put a blunt up in the air. But it's all good. I'm gonna miss the shit out of you Lady Scarface."

After the service, Tiana's body was cremated. Kemya agreed to take the urn. Santana returned to Dr. Proudfoot's office.

"How is she today?" he asked when he walked into the office.

"She's awake, she's hungry, and she's grouchy."

"She'll be ok," Santana said. "Can I head on back."

"Go ahead."

Santana spent most of his days by Tiana's side. She stayed unconscious for most of the past 2 weeks, only just waking up 3 days ago and being able to communicate.

Santana was the first person she saw when she opened her eyes.

"Did...di...did you," she was straining to speak. "Did you sma...snack me...did you smack me in the face...and call me a bitch?" she asked Santana.

"Yes I did Brantz."

"What, are we fuckin' married or something?"

"You died. I was trying to bring you back."

"By beating the shit out of me?"

"It worked. Let me go get the doc."

Tiana was still weak, but at least she was alive. For the three days that she'd been awake, her and Santana talked and made some plans.

Starting with Tiana's funeral.

Santana felt that a funeral would be needed to put a stop to any manhunt that might get started. Atlanta homicide still had a lot of questions about what happened at the Maldonado home. With Tiana dead, they wouldn't be looking for her. Only 3 people besides Santana knew that Tiana wasn't dead: Dr. Proudfoot, Dawit Burroughs and Kemya. It was Kemya who arranged the mock funeral.

"So, how was it?"

"Great. I've got the DVD for you."

"Does it come with a Big Mac or a slice of pizza or something?"

"If I knew you were up I'd have brought something with me. I hear you're in a grouchy mood."

"I'm hungry," replied Tiana. "When I get hungry I get cranky."

"I'll see what doc's got that you can eat."

"Ok. Thank you."

He came back a few minutes later with half of a sandwich and handed it to Tiana.

"What the hell happened to the other half?" she asked.

"I ate it. Doc says eat that, and if it stays down you can have something else."

"What are you doing Santana?" she asked before shoving half the sandwich into her mouth.

"What are you talking about?"

"You are aiding and abetting a fugitive and a murderer. Your life is over, you know that right?"

"Actually, you are not a fugitive. Dead people can't run from the law. You are dead Brantz. I know, I was just at your funeral. I've got the DVD to prove it. And I don't think my life is over. Shit, it might just be beginning."

"What do you want from me Santana?"

"I want to know who you really are."

"Is that right?"

"Yeah, that and I wanna know why they call you Lady Scarface."

"Wow, I haven't heard that in a while. It's a long story."

"I've got plenty of time and I'm not going anywhere."

Over the course of the next few weeks Tiana instructed Santana on a few things that she needed done. Santana and Kemya handled everything for her. Santana gave the file on Sabastian Gustavo, the man who killed Divine, to Kemya and instructed her to get the information to Smurf. He in turn arranged for Sabastian to receive a very special visit from an inmate at the Federal Detention Center in Manhattan.

Tiana was getting restless.

She hadn't left Dr. Proudfoot's since she arrived, and she was ready to go.

"Can you call Kemya for me? Tell her to come here as soon as possible please," she said to Santana.

"I'll do that right now."

An hour and ten minutes later, Kemya walked into the room.

"Hi Ms. Brantz!" She beamed, giving Tiana a soft hug. "You look like your old self."

"You don't have to lie to me Kemya. I know I look like shit."

Tiana pulled out an envelope. It was sealed and addressed to Dawit Burroughs.

"Could you please make sure that this is delivered to Dawit Burroughs immediately Kemya?"

"I'll take it to him myself personally. As soon as I leave here."

"Thank you Kemya. How are things with you?"

"Oh, they're good Ms. Brantz. We all miss you around the office. Sometimes it's funny to think about it cause I've got an urn with your name on it full of sand."

"Well, thank you Kemya. I'm instructing Dawit to do something for you, on one condition."

"What's that Ms. Brantz?"

"That you please stop calling me Ms. Brantz. I'm your friend, not your boss, ok."

"Ok Ms.—I mean, Tiana."

They both laughed.

****

Tiana wanted paperwork. She needed a passport, birth certificate, social security card, and everything else to give her a new identity. She was leaving the country.

And she was taking Santana with her.

There didn't appear to be any romantic interest on either of their parts, but she appreciated how he stood by her side and helped her through this time, so when she made up her mind to leave she asked him what his plans were.

"I'm going with you. Plain and simple."

"We can never come back," she pointed out.

"So, there's really nothing left for me here anyway."

"We'll have to change your identity."

"So."

"Are you sure you want to do this?"

"Somebody has to be with you to keep you out of trouble."

"And you think you can do that?"

"I'm doing a good job so far."

****

Once they arrived, Tiana was able to exhale. The Cape Verdean Islands off the coast of West Africa were in non-extraditable waters. They were safe.

It took Dawit no more than two weeks to get a new set of papers for her and Santana. Two weeks later they were in Mexico, where they hired a private jet to Africa. They stayed in Sierra Leone for a week before chartering a boat to take them to the Cape Verdean Islands.

Tiana's money was transferred first into her new name, then it was transferred to a bank on the Grand Isle. Before she left, Tiana made sure that Dawit took care of all of her instructions to the letter, including changing the name on the deed to her Buckhead home out of Mecca and Divinity's name and into Kemya Bennet's name. She also placed 20 million dollars into an account for Kemya and her son. The only stipulation was that her son had to attend college and Kemya must remain working at Brantz and Brantz.

The first thing she did when they arrived was find a home. Tiana purchased a 40 acre piece of land with a 7,000 square foot home on it. Being a cautious and security-minded woman, she had a privacy fence put up around her property and cameras with motion detectors everywhere. It took five weeks before the home was ready to be moved into.

It was a seven bedroom, 6 bathroom, 2 story home with an outdoor and indoor pool, gym, shooting range and state of the art home theater system.

Tiana just wanted to relax and enjoy the rest of her life. She felt that she'd been through enough, put in enough work, and had lost more than enough to last ten lifetimes. She was lucky enough to escape, and now she just wanted to live her life in peace. To be able to breathe easy.

"Why did he call you Lady Scarface?" Santana asked. They were watching the DVD of Tiana's mock funeral, and Smurf had just finished his speech.

"My brother gave me that name," she replied, touching the scar on her face. "When I was young."

"I didn't know you have a brother."

"Had. He was killed in New York a few years ago."

"Sorry to hear that," he said.

"It was my fault he got killed. He wasn't my blood brother, but I loved him like he was."

"How was it your fault?"

"You really want to know?"

"I asked didn't I?"

And so for the next couple of months Tiana opened her heart and soul to Edwin Santana. She told him everything there was to know about herself, from what she remembered about her childhood in the South Bronx, her parents, and their murders when she was just 8 years old. That, she explained, was how she got the distinguishing scar on her face.

She told him about her first meeting with Anthony Crawford at her parents' funeral, and about how she came into money in the first place. She even told him about the nurse who cared for her while she was in the hospital recovering from the gunshot wound and the loss of her parents.

Then she detailed her life in Baychester Diagnostic Center. How Shabazz took her under his wing and schooled her to the streets until he turned 18 and had to leave Baychester.

"I was so sad when he left," she confessed. "But he promised me that when I got out he would be there."

"Was he?"

"Yes. He always kept his word to me. He gave me his word the day he left that when I got out he would be there. Four years later, he kept his word. He was there."

Each day she told him more and more about herself. How she killed the man who murdered her parents, and gave money to her brother Shabazz to finance their drug empire in New York. She went into details about how she came to meet Victor Maldonado, who later became her organization's cocaine supplier and remained her supplier until the day he died. She told Santana about every time she went to

New York and all the people she killed there, including Cashmere Adebsi.

"What about Trey Clark?"

"I killed him the night I got him acquitted," she replied. "I killed him, emptied his safe, and took 40 kilos of pure heroin from him. I had Darnell Gray killed too."

"The witness, Beverly Roman?"

"No, actually that was Victor's doing," she answered. "He did it for me, but I didn't know about it."

"What about Clarkston?"

"Who's that?"

"My old partner."

"Oh, that bastard. That was Divine. I wanted him killed because he called me a bitch."

"Three times," added Santana.

"Yes. Three times."

"You had a lot of power Tiana. In and out of the courtroom."

"Had. I am done with that life. That's why I'm here. I just want to relax and live in peace."

"Do you ever miss it? The excitement? The gunfire?"

"Not really. But when I do, I head down to the range and squeeze off a few shots."

19

Tiana and Santana were having lunch in a small oceanside café on the main island's market square when their table was approached by two men.

"Excuse me Madame, Monsieur. Please pardon the intrusion, but our commissioner would respectfully request a few moment of your time. It is of great importance."

"What commissioner?" asked Santana cautiously.

"Commissioner Unidas. He is the Commissioner of our security forces here. He says he will not take up any more of your time than is absolutely necessary. He asks that you please follow us. We humbly apologize for the inconvenience, and your meal is of no charge."

Tiana looked at Santana, then shrugged her shoulders and stood up.

"After you," she said.

The men were in a Jeep Wrangler. Tiana and Santana followed in a convertible 1963 Corvette Stingray. Ten minutes later the Jeep parked in a reserved parking space in front of the Grand Isle Municipal building.

"Follow us please," the driver said as he led the way into the building. Tiana and Santana followed them up a flight of stairs to the second floor, and into a large office.

"Go right in," a desk clerk said to them. "He's expecting you."

The two escorts stopped at the door and stepped aside to allow Tiana and Santana to enter.

"It is a pleasure to finally meet you," said the man who stood from behind his desk to greet them. "Ms. Brantz, Mr. Santana," he finished as he shook their hands. Tiana and Santana looked at each other. They didn't' know what to think.

"Please, do not be shocked or alarmed. It is my job to know who comes to live on these islands. Especially when someone comes with hundreds of millions of US dollars in our bank, puts millions into our local economy, and in no way seems to be exploiting our community."

"What do you want Commissioner?" Santana asked, annoyed.

"Actually, it's Inspector. Some people can't seem to grasp the concept of progress."

"Ok Inspector, what can we do for you?" questioned Tiana.

"First of all, I wish to extend a very warm and official welcome to the both of you. You are welcomed to stay here on Grand Isle for as long as you wish. As you must likely already know, the United States has no extradition treaty with these territories so you are safe from US law enforcement here. 100% safe."

"So why are we here in your office? You could have had the Chamber of Commerce send us a welcome packet in the mail," said Santana.

"It has come to my attention that there may be some civil unrest on certain parts of the islands over the recent political changes. As a result of the rumors, some of the more prominent members of our community have decided to employ our security forces for their own personal security. I have called you here to offer you those same services."

"For a small fee of course," smirked Santana.

"Of course."

"I'll take ten men," ordered Tiana. "I don't care what it cost," she added.

****

The next day, ten armed men arrived on Tiana's property to oversee the construction of a large security building to be placed at the entrance to the property. After two and a half weeks, the building was in place and there were 10 permanent and heavily armed guards stationed there.

Though it was Santana who dealt with the guards on a regular basis, Tiana made it her business to get to know each and every one of them. The inspector said that their fees were 250 dollars a day per man.

Tiana paid them 500. Once a week she had a delivery truck bring them all the food they wanted, and on the weekends she allowed them to use her outdoor pool if they wanted to.

Whether or not the threat of civil unrest was real or not didn't even matter anymore to Tiana. She felt comfortable and safe with the guards around. So when she received the phone call from Kemya, she knew what she had to do.

She summoned all the guards to a meeting at her house.

"I received a phone call today from a dear friend in the United States. It seems that an old and personal friend of mine may be in some trouble, and I feel compelled to go to his aid. You ten men have proven to be loyal and trustworthy to me. I would like for 8 of you to accompany me to the United States to assist my friend in his time of need. It will most likely be dangerous, and there will be gunfire. If you choose to come, you will be very highly compensated. I will pay you 1,000 dollars a day in addition to your pay. As an added bonus, when we make it back safely, I will pay each of you one million dollars."

The ten men began to speak amongst themselves in their native language of Portuguese for a few minutes. Then one of the men stood tall. He was the head of security.

"Madame," he began. "You have been most generous to us since we have come to work for you here. We would be honored if you will allow us to stand beside you and your friend in battle. We only have one question."

"And what is that?"

"You speak of 8 men. But here you have 10 men ready to assist you in any way we can."

"I'll need 2 men to stay behind and watch the house."

Sensing their concern, Tiana added, "but the two men who stay behind will be paid the same amount as the 8 who go with me. I will let you choose who will remain behind."

"Good enough Madame. When do we leave?"

"Three days."

****

"What the fuck do you mean I'm not going with you?!" yelled Santana.

"You can't go with me Edwin. I don't know what I'm heading into, but it's not gonna be good .I don't want you to get hurt."

"And what about you?"

"What about me?"

"What about you getting hurt?"

"Those men out there are trained in guerilla warfare. They'll have my back."

"What about me?! I haven't had your back?"

"Yes you have. I know that. But I want you here, safe. Waiting for me when I get back." She hesitated for a moment, then she looked into his eyes. "I'm falling in love with you Edwin."

****

For the past six months Edwin Santana had been by Tiana's side almost 24 hours a day. He saved her life in Atlanta when her best friend Victoria shot her in the back two times. He helped her to plan her own funeral and sneak out of the country when the world thought she was dead, and he had become a permanent fixture in her new life. Tiana had confided in him about every aspect of her past. The killings, the drugs, her childhood and her adult life. He had become her soulmate.

But they had yet to make any sort of sexual connection. It wasn't that either of them hadn't thought of it. It's just that no one had made the first move.

The day after Tiana revealed her feelings to him, he couldn't get the words out of his head.

"I'm falling in love with you Edwin."

He was sitting in the pool thinking about what he should do when Tiana appeared at the opposite end of the pool in a crimson red two-piece bikini.

"Stay right there," she said, and dived into the water. She swam the length of the pool underwater until she broke the surface directly in front of him.

"Hi there," she said. Then she grabbed his hands and pulled him into the pool. He was standing directly in front of her. She put her arms around his neck and pulled him down to her.

She kissed him on his lips.

Both of their lips parted, and as their tongues touched, Santana wrapped his arms around Tiana. She lifred one of her legs and wrapped it around his waist, pulling him to her. She pushed herself against the bulge that was growing in Santana's shorts.

"Wait," he said as he pushed Tiana away from him.

"Wait for what?" Tiana pouted.

"When we get back."

20

"How did you know where I was?"

"Kemya called me. She was worried about her cousin Chris."

Tiana and Smurf were at a hotel in downtown Charlotte.

"Who dem niggas you got ridin' wit you?" he asked.

"They work for me. At my home. They are trained soldiers, and they came with me to help you."

"And how you hook up with ole clown ass Santana?"

"Clown ass Santana saved my life, and hasn't left my side since. He's ok."

"You say that like you feelin' him. Are you?" he questioned.

"My business. Now, let's get down to yours. What's really going on here?"

Smurf brought Tiana up to speed. From the time he left Atlanta with all of the cocaine they had stashed, arriving in Charlotte and killing Supreme, and all the spots him and his new crew had taken over. He told her about his Jamaican connection, Dookie, and about the hits on his spots by unknowns.

Knock...knock...knock.

Smurf pulled his gun when he heard the knock at the door.

Tiana laughed.

"Would you chill out. I've got men all over this floor. No one can get next to this room who isn't supposed to."

She stood up and went to the door. She looked through the peephole, then smiled as she opened the door.

"Hey there stranger," she said.

"Tiana!" Kemya squealed as she hugged her friend.

"How have you been Kemya?"

"I've been great. How have you been? You look fabulous."

"Death has agreed with me," Tiana joked. "No but seriously, I couldn't be better. I love it there. You need to come see me. Take a vacation."

"I might just do that." Then to Smurf Kemya said, "Where is Chris?"

"You talking about C.B.?"

"Whatever. Where is Chris?"

"In the next room with the police."

"Oh yeah," she said, looking back at Tiana now. "And how is Detective Santana treating you Miss Tiana?"

"Good I guess. He won't give me any dingaling, but I'm gonna see about changing that when we get back."

While they talked, Smurf's phone rang. He listened intently to the person on the other end of the line for a couple of minutes, then he hung up.

"I guess your timing couldn't have been better because it's 'bout to be on T," he said as he punched in a number.

"Yeah, y'all niggas get in here! We bout to ride!" he snapped, then hung up again.

"What's up?" Tiana asked as someone knocked on the door. Smurf opened it, and in walked an army.

Smurf's men, Tiana's people and Santana all crowded into the room. Once everyone was inside and the door was shut, Smurf disclosed what he had just learned.

"Motha fucka say it's Bloods been hittin' us. I don't know no Blood around this bitch wit balls big enough to step to us 'cept that fat ass nigga Big Mike."

"I told you that nigga wasn't right yo!" exclaimed Young God. "We shoulda been got that fat bastard!"

"Yo, fuck all that I told you so shit. Niggas just hit another one of our spots. We bout to roll on that nigga Big Mike! It's about time we show them North Valley niggas what's really up! T, you and your people strapped or y'all need fire?"

"You're joking right?" she said, opening her trench coat to reveal two shoulder holsters. She crossed her arms and reached into the holsters, pulling out two pearl-handled, nickel-plated .9mm Desert eagles with whistle silencers and laser scopes. Both handles were widened to hold extra wide clips. Each clip held 21 shells.

"Now that's some Lara Croft Tomb Raider shit right there," whistled Young God.

"What about your folks?" Smurf asked. "They straight?"

"AKs, Uzis, Techs, and Macs," replied Tiana. "Oh, and 2 rocket launchers. Trust me, we came ready." Then to Kemya, "you go home. And take Chris with you."

"I ain't goin' no mafuckin' where! I'm ridin' wit the homies!" he declared.

Smurf jumped up and grabbed Chris by his neck, pulling the .40 caliber Glock from Chris's back and putting it into Chris's cheek.

"Don't you never disrespect that woman right there. She been puttin' in work since before you been on your mama's tit nigga! Now apologize to her, and take yo ass home to yo family."

Kemya watched the exchange, but she said nothing. She knew better than to interfere. Not out of fear, but because she understood street respect. And she knew that Tiana deserved it. She commanded it.

"I'm sorry Miss Brantz," Chris mumbled in a childlike voice.

"That's better," Smurf said as he let him go and gave him a slight nudge towards Kemya. He kept Chris's gun.

During the commotion with Chris and Smurf, no one noticed that Sizzle slipped into the bathroom.

"Yo Blood," he said when Big Mike picked up. "Heads up. That nigga Smurf on his way to North Valley. Guns blazing."

"Soo woo!" replied Big Mike.

"Soo woo," Sizzle whispered back.

****

At that very moment, a blue Nissan Pathfinder pulled into the South side of Hidden Valley. Two blocks into the neighborhood, there was a small group of brothers, dressed all in red, standing in the yard of what appeared to be an abandoned house. The driver pulled the SUV over in front of the group.

Both windows on the passenger side of the Pathfinder went down. Before the group of Bloods could react, an AK-47 and a Mac10 were stuck out of the windows.

Tatatatatatatatatatatata!

Both machine guns screamed death til they could scream no more and not a Blood was left standing.

"Yeah, tell 'em the Goons is in town motha fuckas!" yelled Lungee as he pulled his AK-47 back into the vehicle and Five pulled away.

21

To enter the Hidden Valley from the North side, you had 6 entrances to choose from. Smurf and his teams entered through all 6 of them.

At the same time.

They were in a fleet of black Suburbans and Hummers. Smurf rode in a Hummer H3. 2 fully automatic M16s at his feet. An Intratec Tec 9 in his hands. Behind him, two Bloods with Uzis sat ready. The driver was armed with a .40 caliber Glock.

Young God rode in one of the Suburbans. Two Mac 11s with super extended clips ready. Sizzle and one other Blood sat behind him.

Santana drove a Hummer H2 with Tiana in the passenger side. They were following Smurf's H3. In the back seats were 2 of Tiana's Portuguese security force. One had an AK-47 on his lap, the other cradled a rocket launcher. 3 extra missiles on the seat next to him.

In all 18 vehicles entered North Valley.

15 seconds after the first vehicle entered, Hidden Valley erupted. Turning into an apocalyptic-like warzone. Gunfire could be heard everywhere, but Big Mike was waiting.

Waiting, but definitely not ready for the type of force that Smurf came with. Big Mike underestimated Smurf's power. His men were getting slaughtered in the streets.

Suburbans and Hummers were pulling onto the grass in front of certain houses, and the house would be swarmed by no less than 3 men with automatic weapons. Some of the houses had grenades thrown into them. Big Mike had 2 main stash houses in North Valley. Smurf hit one of these houses, killing everyone in the house, then Tiana's man with the rocket launcher destroyed the house and all the drugs that were in it, leaving it in an inferno of flames.

The assault lasted no more than 5 minutes before the vehicles scattered and made their way to the South Valley. As Smurf crossed Lewiston Blvd into the South Valley, a blue Nissan Pathfinder was coming in their direction. He made eye contact with the driver of the

Pathfinder as they passed each other. Smurf waved his Tec 9 at the driver, who sped up really quickly.

Smurf just laughed.

Behind him though, as Santana drove past the same SUV, Tiana looked into the eye of a woman in the back seat.

One killer always knew another killer.

Tiana felt that she would see that woman again.

****

One Suburban didn't make it out of North Valley. The Suburban carrying Young God, Sizzle and one other Blood pulled up to a house and the three of them jumped out, spraying the house with gunfire. Sizzle ran around to the side of the house, then just as quickly turned around. He headed back to the front of the house.

It only took a few seconds for Young God to empty the clips in both Mac 11s. The other Blood emptied his clip and then threw a grenade into one of the windows. Him and Young God were just getting into the vehicle when Sizzle came running from the side of the house, an Uzi in his hand. When he got to the Suburban, he lifted the Uzi and released the entire clip into Young God and the other Blood.

"Soo woo nigga," he said and ran down the street.

****

Five and his team had hit two separate groups in South Valley before making their way into the North side.

"Where you at?" asked Sizzle when Five answered his phone.

"I'm just coming into the North Valley. Where you at?"

"Make a right on Bodine. Hurry up, it's hot as fuck out here."

"I'm making a right now."

Five picked Sizzle up, introduced him to the other 4 members of his squad, and got a rundown on what was going down. He told Sizzle about the 2 hits that his crew just did in the South Valley.

"I need to meet you up wit Big Mike yo," Sizzle said.

"Man, fuck a Big Mike. You need to show us where this nigga Smurf lay his head so we can bag his ass, get that loot, and get the fuck back to the 'Ville."

"You got to hold up cause shit done changed a little."

"What the fuck you mean shit done changed?!" growled Five.

"What I mean is that he brought in some bad ass bitch with a fuckin monster crew. Some big Spanish looking nigga and a bunch of Africans. Bitch showed up in 3 helicopters wit her team. Motha fuckas got rocket launchers, M16s, AKs, and some shit I ain't never seen before."

"Did this bitch have on white?" Honey asked.

"Yeah! Oh shit! How you know that?"

"The black H2," Honey said to Five. "We passed it when we crossed over."

"Oh shit. I remember. They were behind anotha nigga in a H3. Bitch nigga flashed a Tec at me when we passed."

"That was Smurf!" exclaimed Sizzle.

"Oh yeah. I gots to eat that nigga's food," declared Five.

"I want her," announced Honey.

"Oh oh, Honey on that Nicki Minaj shit!" joked Lungee.

"Shut the fuck up, ole fat nasty ass nigga!" snapped Honey.

"You can have her," said Five. "Take me to Big Mike," he said to Sizzle.

22

"Yo my nigga, you got some bad info. But you know what, it don't even matter no more. You wanna set trip, you got the right set to trip with. You did some damage. Yeah, you did a little damage. But now we comin'. So don't sleep." Click.

Smurf looked at the phone in his hands. He had just heard that Young God didn't make it out of the North Valley. He was pissed off and hurt over the loss of his friend. But when he called Big Mike, Big Mike still maintained that he was not behind the hits on Smurf's spots. And to make matters worse, while Smurf and his teams were taking it to the streets of the North side, two of his smaller South side spots were taken out. And of all the houses they destroyed on the North side, they missed Big Mike's house.

"That nigga say it wasn't him. Say we got the wrong man."

"What do you think?" asked Tiana.

"I don't know what to think anymore T. That nigga didn't have no reason to start hittin' us. All he wanted was the North. As long as we stayed out of North Valley, he wasn't trippin'."

"Then who would benefit the most by hitting you?"

"Man, a whole lot o' motha fuckas want the South Valley. A whole lot o' niggas ain't feelin how we straight jacked half the city. But won't nobody step to us like that. Niggas around here is pussy."

"Well, somebody hit you. And you need to give it some real hard thought, because if it wasn't this Big Mike character, then that's real bad, because it's hard to fight a war when you don't know who your enemy is. We already did that."

"For real Tiana, right now, all them niggas is my enemy. And even if Big Mike didn't start this shit, it don't matter, cause it's on now. Fuck that. And my lil nigga Young God laid out somewhere in North Valley. Fuck that shit."

"Wasn't Sizzle with Young God?" asked one of the others.

"Yeah, but fuck that nigga. I never did like his bitch ass. I think he was feelin' some kinda way cause I blew his man's face all over him."

Tiana and Santana looked at Smurf.

"You been real busy haven't you?" commented Santana.

****

"So, you the niggas been fuckin' wit Smurf huh," Big Mike asked after all the introductions were made.

"Nah Blood," responded Five. "We don't go around hittin niggas for free. If it ain't got about 6 figures attached to it, we ain't fuckin' wit it. We don't need no practice. We wet up a few niggas earlier just on the strength that we was bored. That shit don't happen often. Imma keep it real with you. While you runnin' around warring with this nigga, I'm tryna hit his pocket and be outta this bitch."

Honey noticed Sizzle staring at her one time too many.

"Is this your people," she asked Big Mike, pointing at Sizzle.

"Not really," he responded, stunning Sizzle a bit. "He's really one of Smurf's people. But he was feeding me info here and there. Why?"

"Smurf's people?" she responded. "I'm tired of catchin his clown ass checkin out my pussy print." Then she pulled out a Glock 10 and shot Sizzle twice in his chest. "Plus, I hate a two-faced ass nigga. Same as a snitch."

Five watched Big Mike's reaction to Honey killing Sizzle, and he was ready for action if he moved wrong.

"Fuck it," Big Mike said. "You saved me the trouble of having to do it myself later."

"Yeah, but he knew where that nigga Smurf lives at," said Five.

"I know exactly where Smurf stays. He stay on the outs."

"On the outs?"

"Yeah, on the outskirts of Charlotte. Got a big ass spot out there. When you wanna hit it?"

"He keep his loot there?"

"I think so."

"Tomorrow then."

"Tomorrow."

****

"How many men you got out here?" Tiana asked as her, Smurf, Santana and four of Tiana's men walked around Smurf's property.

"Usually I won't have nobody up here. It was just Young God and me. But I think there's 40 something up here right now. 50 something with you and your people. What's up?"

"Who knows about this place?"

"Everybody now."

"You know they're coming right?" she pointed out.

"You think so?"

"I know so. Can I make a suggestion?"

"Come on T. You know this is your shit. What..."

"Stop right there Smurf. This is yours. All of it. I gave it all up when I decided to leave. It all belongs to you now. I'm only here to help. When it's over, I'm leaving, and I'll most likely never come back."

"Why did you come T?"

"Because I wanted to. I heard you were going through a little something, and there's nothing in this world that could have kept me away. I saw the video of my funeral. I really liked what you said."

"I just kept it real."

"You're a good friend Smurf," she said.

"The realest nigga on the planet."

"We're the last, you know that."

"Yeah, it's me and you Lady Scarface."

"Til the end."

They held each other in a tight hug for a couple of seconds til Santana interrupted.

"Um, excuse me. I hate to break up this Hallmark moment, but don't you think we should be getting ready, in case we get a gang banger invasion?"

"What was your suggestion T?"

"Let my people set up a perimeter. They got all kinds of toys with them, and they live for this shit."

"Ok, listen up!" Smurf yelled into the crowds around the house. Everyone began to gather around him.

"Yall see these African brothers right here?" He pointed to Tiana's men. "They about to lay out some Iraqi warfare shit! They trained for this shit so listen to them! Do what the fuck they tell you to do, and make sure all of you get your weapons ready cause we don't know when these niggas gon show up."

Tiana's men began to unload weapons and all sorts of artillery. They split up and began setting up for the attack that everyone knew was coming.

Smurf's house wasn't a large one. But the land that surrounded it was. On one side of his house was a 4-mile deep stretch of woods. The front of the house was far enough back from the road that you could barely see it. His driveway was almost ¾ of a mile long. To his left and right were just open fields as far as the eye could see. There wasn't another house for miles. It was real farm country.

It was gonna be hard to get to without being seen, that much was for sure.

23

The first explosion came from about a hundred yards into the woods at the back of the house. That was where Tiana's men placed the first set of explosive traps. The woods behind the house were turned into a mine field of sorts. Grenade traps and land mines were scattered over a hundred yard deep, hundred and fifty yard wide stretch of the woods.

The only ways to get to the house were through the woods or an all-out frontal assault. They chose both. Not only were men coming in through the woods, but there were two convoys of vehicles coming up the road. One from the left, and the other from the right. In all there were over two hundred and fifty men about to attack Smurf's fortress.

Tiana and Santana came running out of the house when they heard the first explosions roar through the night. It was a little after 4:00 in the morning. She had changed into an all-black tactical suit with a pair of black Timberland boots. In her shoulder holsters were the two Desert Eagles, and on her hip were 6 extra clips full of armor-piercing, Teflon coated, Talon shells. Santana too was dressed in all black and in his hand he held a .44 Colt Commander.

They looked like a couple of death dealers.

Tiana's Portuguese team was ready, and when they heard the first explosion they jumped into action. They began barking orders at the young Bloods. The first explosion turned into a series of explosions. One of the Portuguese soldiers stood at the back of the house, rocket launcher on his shoulder, and ready. Another stood at the front of the house, watching the roads, the other rocket launcher at the ready. As soon as the first vehicle came into view he let loose with a heat-seeking missile of death.

But the vehicles never seemed to stop coming.

Men were coming out of the woods now, those who had made it past the traps, and they were exchanging gunfire with Smurf's men. Most of Smurf's men had automatic machine guns and they were holding their own.

But the vehicles just kept coming.

Men were running all over the place, tossing grenades and shooting at the vehicles.

"Yo, this shit is retarded!" yelled Lungee. "We ain't come here for no fuckin war!"

"Yo, he's right Five. This ain't even our beef," said Mook.

They came in the Pathfinder and were trying to figure out a way to get at Smurf's stash in the midst of all the chaos.

Bullets were flying all around them, and a grenade had just missed the rear bumper of the Nissan.

"Y'all just keep shooting! We getting' to that fuckin' house!" was Five's reply.

The gunfire had turned into a free-for-all. Men were shooting at anything that moved, without even knowing for sure if they were friend or foe. There were overturned SUVs and bodies everywhere. One of Smurf's men went to throw a grenade at an oncoming Jeep Cherokee when he got shot in the legs and chest. He never had the chance to throw the grenade. He dropped it and then fell on top of it. Right after he pulled the pin.

Tiana and Santana were side by side, running and shooting. Santana's .44 Magnum sounded like a cannon, even among all the other guns that were barking in the night.

"You ok?!" he yelled at Tiana.

"Yeah! But they won't stop coming! They're everywhere!"

"Just keep your eyes open! I got your back!"

"Fuck this shit!" yelled Five as he hit the gas. He had been riding around in circles trying to figure out the best way that his team could capitalize on the situation. He finally grew impatient. He spun the Pathfinder around and headed straight for the house.

Tiana was about 40 yards away from the house when out of the corner of her eye she saw the blue Nissan Pathfinder crash into the back corner of the house.

Smurf saw it too.

"Shit!" he yelled as he ran towards the house, bullets flying by him.

Big Mike saw the Pathfinder hit the house, then he heard Smurf yell and saw him running towards the house.

"There go that nigga right there!" he exclaimed as he jumped out of an Excursion and ran after Smurf.

Tiana and Santana started running towards the house too. Tiana was slamming a new clip into each of her guns as she ran.

Big Mike thought Smurf was gonna run into the house, but at the last second Smurf turned around and started shooting. When Tiana saw who Smurf was shooting at, she lifted both Desert Eagles.

Thpt...thpt...

Thpt...thpt...

Two shots each.

Big Mike's head exploded when the Talons made impact. Smurf looked over at Tiana and nodded his approval with a smile. He was about to run into the house when he saw a familiar sight.

A yellow Hummer H2 was coming up the driveway, followed by about 7 more vehicles.

"That's my nigga right there!" declared Smurf when he saw Dookie's unmistakable yellow H2 heading in his direction.

When Tiana saw the new convoy of vehicles approaching, she took aim, but just before she squeezed off the first shot, Smurf stopped her.

"No T!" he screamed and ran in her direction. "That's my people right there!"

The vehicles behind the yellow Hummer broke away and men jumped out of them to join the gunfight. Dookie saw Smurf waving his hands and pulled up right in front of the three of them.

"Wha ya deal wit?" said Dookie as he climbed down from the passenger side.

"What's good Dookie? You here for the party, cause we all outta chips and dip my nigga," joked Smurf.

"In time fo da fireworks though," replied Dookie.

"Yeah, plenty of that."

There was something about Dookie that Tiana didn't like. Something that just didn't sit right with her. There was a falseness about him.

Her instincts told her to be ready.

So she was.

When Dookie made his move, she made hers.

But she wasn't quite fast enough.

Dookie was able to pull his gun and hit Smurf in the chest and stomach at least 3 times before Tiana lifted one of her Desert Eagles and put two pullets into his head.

"Nooo!" she yelled as Smurf went down.

"It was him…" Smurf said as he died.

Smurf was right. He just realized it too late.

****

It was Dookie the whole time who wanted to see a war erupt between Smurf and Big Mike. He had originally tried to get Supreme to step up to the plate, but Supreme was always content with the South Valley. He didn't want to stir up a beef with Big Mike. Supreme knew, deep down, that he was no match for Big Mike.

But then Smurf came along.

Smurf had big balls, and even bigger ambitions. Dookie saw that when Smurf immediately started to take over any spot he could. And people followed Smurf. So his numbers grew. But Dookie felt that to get Smurf to move on Big Mike, he would have to be provoked. So he started hitting Smurf's spots. Then he put out the word that it was the Bloods under Big Mike who did it. That set it off once and for all.

Dookie planned to take over all of Charlotte after Smurf and Big Mike's people killed each other. But he also wanted one other thing.

He wanted Smurf's stash.

When Smurf hit town, he let Dookie know that he had his own work—meaning cocaine. Dookie figured that he must have had a lot because he said he wouldn't need any from Dookie for a while. Well, Dookie wanted whatever it was that Smurf had.

Too bad he would never get that chance.

****

Inside of the house, Five and his team were looking for Smurf's stash. They were so busy tearing up every room in the house that they didn't see or hear when Tiana stepped into the house.

Dreads was the first to see her.

But he didn't get a chance to warn anyone.

Thpt...thpt...thpt...

His dreads flew everywhere as the three bullets caught him in the neck and head.

Tiana heard noises coming from one of the rooms. Santana followed closely behind her as she crept through the house towards the back rooms.

When she looked in the first room, there was a short fat man coming out of a closet.

"Who the fuck..."

Thpt...thpt...thpt...thpt...

Tiana cut Mook down with four Teflon-coated Talons to the heart, blowing him back into the closet.

Some of the gunfire outside of the house was dying down as the body count rose or some of the men decided that today was not a good day to die and made a run for it. You could hear the occasional grenade or mine go off in the woods as they tried to make their escape that way. And with all of the explosions and gunfire, not a single police or any sort of law enforcement showed up.

****

The Portuguese were not going to quit until no one was left standing or until Tiana told them it was over. They worked for her and were loyal to her only. They had formed a perimeter around the house when they saw her go inside, and from there they took their stand. They no longer could distinguish between who was with Smurf and who was against him. And since Smurf was dead, it no longer mattered to them.

Tiana and Santana were their only concern.

From the outside of the house they cut down everyone that moved. But there were more bodies laying on the ground than there were running around. A lot of men died in the woods and never even made it to the fight. Most of the vehicles were taken out by missiles from the rocket launchers or by grenades thrown at and under them.

The fight was basically over.

At least outside it was.

****

Lungee could hear something in the next room. It sounded like someone falling down, but he didn't hear anything after that. No scream. No cursing. Nothing.

He walked out of the room at the same time Tiana did.

But she saw him first.

She sent two bullets his way, and one hit him in the side as he squeezed the trigger of the Mac 11 in his hand, sending a wild burst into the hallway. He fell back into the room, but the burst from the Mac alerted Five and Honey.

Five came running from the back, M16 in front of him, sending shells down the hallway in Tiana's direction. She jumped back and Santana shot twice in Five's direction but missed.

Five kept coming.

Click...click...click...

That was not a sound he wanted to hear.

But it was what Tiana was waiting for.

Five's clip was empty.

Tiana jumped back into the hallway and shot Five 6 times in the chest and head.

Her and Santana walked up the hall towards where Five lay on the ground.

Bloc ow! Bloc ow! Bloc ow!

Honey shot three times from the back doorway.

One shot hit Santana in his shoulder. His gun flew from his hand and he dropped to the ground.

The other two shots hit Tiana square the chest. She fell to the ground on her back. Honey walked up and stood over her.

"You ain't all that bitch," she said as she lifted her .9mm H&K to shoot Tiana in the head.

"Yeah, but you'll never tell," said Tiana, quickly pointing a Desert Eagle at Honey.

Thpt...thpt...thpt...thpt...thpt...

"Won't never let that shit happen again," she said as she stood up and lifted her shirt to reveal the bulletproof vest she wore.

Santana smiled.

24

"You gonna miss it?" Santana asked. His arm was in a sling, but the bullet from Honey's gun went straight through the fleshy part of his shoulder.

Tiana had on a full length white leather Armani trench coat on top of a white Prada pants suit with large Prada glasses. They were walking through the airport headed to the international terminal. Behind them, 6 black Portuguese walked closely. Two of their team didn't make it.

Tiana promised to take care of their families.

They were about to board their flight. Tiana turned to Santana. She put her arms around him.

"You know we have unfinished business right?" she said.

"Yes, I know," he replied. Then he dropped his bag on the floor. When he did that, the terminal erupted in screaming and chaos.

People disguised as regular passengers jumped out of their seats carrying guns of all sorts.

"Freeze! Everybody on the fuckin' ground! FBI! Down! Down! Down!"

There were agents everywhere, and they all had their guns trained on Tiana, Santana and the Portuguese. The Portuguese began putting their hands on their heads and laying on the ground.

Tiana looked at Santana.

"Oh, I've got a whole bunch of bad news for you Brantz," he said as he reached into his pocket and pulled out his wallet. He opened it and showed it to Tiana.

It was an FBI badge and ID.

"You fuckin' bastard," she hissed and smacked him across his face.

Two agents grabbed her arms and handcuffed her behind her back.

"Tiana Brantz," Santana began, "you have the right to remain silent. You have the..."

What happened next Tiana watched unfold in what seemed like slow motion.

One of the Portuguese men spun around as an agent was putting cuffs on him. He grabbed the agent's gun and opened fire on the other agents.

Santana threw Tiana on the ground and covered her with his body.

The Portuguese killed two agents and wounded 3 others before he was gunned downed.

"Get the fuck off of me," Tiana hissed. "How could you?"

"It's my job Brantz," was his reply.

****

When Santana was suspended as a result of his involvement with Tiana's rescue from Chen, he was crushed. Law enforcement was what he lived for. But when Tiana was shot and at Dr. Proudfoot's he came up with a solution. A plan to not only get his job back, but to also get Tiana Brantz once and for all.

He took his plan to the Feds.

He said that he could deliver Tiana Brantz to them on a silver platter. He would get close to her, get her to confide in him and hopefully get confessions out of her.

When she said she wanted to leave the country, at first the Feds thought it would be a problem, but Santana assured them that he would not leave her side and that he would bring her back. He wanted his involvement at Chen's erased and he wanted on the team.

He wanted to be an FBI agent.

They agreed and gave him his space to do his thing. Oh, there was one other thing, they said.

He could never, under any circumstances, sleep with her or shoot anyone by her side.

That was why Santana never made any advances towards Tiana or allowed her advances towards him to blossom. And the .44

Magnum Colt Commander he had during the gunfight at Smurf's—it was full of blanks. That's why it seemed like he always missed.

25

At Tiana's trial, the first thing her attorney, Anthony Crawford did was try to get the case thrown out. He had a list of grounds as long as his arm. He cited misconduct, entrapment, breach of protocol, tampering, coercion, tainted evidence, inadmissible confessions. He said that agent Santana was compromised since he stood with his client during a gunfight and allowed citizens to be killed in front of him without attempting to save them.

Nothing he tried worked though. The judge wasn't interested in technicalities, only justice.

The jury saw through his ploy also.

They took 1 hour and 15 minutes to bring back a verdict.

Guilty on all counts.

Tiana Brantz was found guilty of 19 murders.

Tiana Brantz was found guilty of operating a continuing criminal enterprise.

Tiana Brantz was found guilty of being the leader of a racketeering influenced criminal organization.

Tiana Brantz was found guilty of possession and trafficking with the intent to distribute over 1 million kilos of cocaine.

Tiana Brantz was found guilty of possessing and trafficking with the intent to distribute 40 kilos of heroin.

Tiana Brantz was found guilty of federal witness tampering.

Tiana Brantz was found guilty of money laundering.

Tiana Brantz was found guilty of tax evasion.

Tiana Brantz was found guilty of 64 other felony charges from aiding and abetting to federal weapons violations.

Tiana Brantz was sentenced to 26 consecutive life sentences plus an additional 440 years in the Federal Bureau of Prisons.

She was escorted out of the courtroom with her head held up high and a smile on her face.

The End

ZITRO PUBLICATIONS
Presents

Only The Best In Urban Lit!

ZitrO Publications

PO Box 25594

Fayetteville, NC 28314

910-475-7919

zitropublications@yahoo.com

ORDER FORM

TITLE OF BOOK	# OF BOOKS	Cost each	Total
Lady Scarface******by Divine Ortiz		$15.00	
Lady Scarface 2**** by Divine Ortiz		$15.00	
Lady Scarface 3.4** by Divine Ortiz		$15.00	
Killa Karma******* by Divine Ortiz		$15.00	
Treacherous Times**by Divine Ortiz		$15.00	

The Billionaire's Captive Mistress by Jessica Simmons		$15.00
Urban Love Story*** by Divine Ortiz		$15.00
Chatrooms & Chatlines by Divine Ortiz		$15.00
SeXXXy Sunday****by Divine Ortiz		$8.00
Lady Vendetta by Divine Six		$15.00
Confessions of a Scorned Baby Mama By Marina J		$15.00
The Heart of Justice by Jerrona Campbell		$15.00
Pieces of Me by Rachel Rae		$15.00
No Bitch in My Blood by Divine Six		$15.00

Please note the following:

All books are $15.00 each. 2 for $25.00. 3 for $35.00 Please add $4.95 for general shipping and handling fees. ******

FREE SHIPPING TO ALL INCARCERATED

WE ACCEPT STAMPS (2 new books of stamps per book)

(Please let us know of any special mailing instructions.)

Books are mailed off within 7 days of payment unless otherwise noted.

Cash payments are strongly discouraged.

Payments for books can be made by PayPal, Green Dot, certified bank check or money order (please note that books paid for by personal checks must be cleared before shipment).

Thank you for keeping ZitrO Publications in your thoughts and letting us fulfill you reading needs

Sincerely,

Divine Ortiz

CEO ZitrO Publications

CPSIA information can be obtained at www.ICGtesting.com
Printed in the USA
LVOW12s0849100515

437936LV00022B/602/P